D0626962

Previously published Worldwide Suspense titles by MARY KELIIKOA

DERAILED

DENIED

MARY KELIIKOA

TORONTO • NEW YORK • LONDON
AMSTERDAM • PARIS • SYDNEY • HAMBURG
STOCKHOLM • ATHENS • TOKYO • MILAN
MADRID • WARSAW • BUDAPEST • AUCKLAND

For Robb

Recycling programs for this product may not exist in your area.

ISBN-13: 978-1-335-45443-0

Denied

First published in 2021 by Camel Press, an imprint of Epicenter Press, Inc. This edition published in 2022.

For questions and comments about the quality of this book, please contact us at CustomerService@Harlequin.com.

Harlequin Enterprises ULC
22 Adelaide St. West, 41st Floor
Toronto, Ontario M5H 4E3, Canada
www.ReaderService.com

Printed in U.S.A.

DENIED

ACKNOWLEDGMENTS

To say it takes a village to get a book into the world would be a bit of an understatement. There are many who have encouraged and enlightened me along the way. Here are just a few of those people I want to thank. To my editor, Jennifer McCord, for pushing me to make sure Kelly remains relatable and on point. Agent Michelle Richter, whose feedback and insight are always appreciated. Kate Pickford, whose encouragement and tough love help me to be a better writer. My critique partners Dianne Freeman and Heather Redmond. Both gifted with eagle eyes and kind words, they help me see what's working and not. My beta readers Jessica Jett and Bonnie Mattheny, who make me feel like I know how to tell a story. Detective James Lawrence, who answers my crazy questions regularly. I'm still sure he thinks I'm about to commit a crime but is always so generous with his insight. If anything on the procedural side is inaccurate, that's all on me for not asking the right questions.

To you, my readers. My first year as a debut author has been an incredible ride. To know so many have been asking for the second book in this series is humbling. I hope you enjoy. This one is for you.

And of course, to my husband, who every day makes me feel loved and safe and capable of living this creative life. Forever and always my love. Mahalo.

ONE

AFTER NEARLY GETTING killed during my first murder investigation, I'd spent a good portion of the last months holed up on the couch, nursing my arm where the bullet of a Ruger LC9 claimed a chunk. The experience left me with two options: sell my dad's agency, R&K Investigations, and take a desk job—a choice my ex and his mother championed—or continue to be a PI.

The fact that my basset hound and cohort Floyd and I were parked in front of Vince Burnotas' house in Riverview, Washington, on a Monday afternoon looking for signs that he was home indicated which way I went.

Earlier in the day, a soon to be client had shown up as Floyd and I'd sprinted home after conducting a surveillance on a cheating husband for his suspicious wife. My eight-year-old daughter Mitz, who stayed with me Friday through Monday, was back with her dad for the week and attending Washington School for the Deaf. Dressed in black running tights and an over-sized sweatshirt to fend off the early May chill, I was bent over in front of my house kneading the knot in my bad arm and trying to catch my breath. Athletics had never been my forte, but too much couch surfing had cost me any stamina I had possessed.

"Kelly Pruett," a female voice pierced the air behind me.

I'd gotten upright and found a young woman with

upswept strawberry blonde hair approaching. Her long cardigan hung over a T-shirt, both too small to cover her baby bump. I knew most of my neighbors. Hell, I'd just been through half of their yards dodging swing sets and patio furniture. She wasn't one of them. "Morning. Do I know you?" I'd glanced at my Fitbit, a gift from Mitz, funded by my ex-husband, Jeff. It read eight o'clock.

She'd cocked her head to the side. "You should. Damn girl, you look as pretty as ever."

Sweat trickled down my back, and my thick shoulder-length hair pulled into a ponytail had frizzed under my own humidity. I managed a *thank you,* but I didn't recognize her and I hated *guess who* games. Floyd sniffed her shoes and gazed up at me. He was also at a loss. "Sorry. I give up."

"It's me. Stephanie Burnotas. Well, Jacoby now."

The only Stephanie Burnotas I had known was a large mousey girl from homeroom at Parkrose High. Even though this girl was pregnant, if this was that Stephanie, she'd shrunk in half since then. Unlike me who'd added an extra layer after having Mitz.

"Stephanie as in 'PBJ every day,' Stephanie?" The reference wasn't to her weight. She really did eat PBJ's every day.

She chuckled. "Like you should talk." I laughed too.

Our peanut butter obsession had been something we had in common. I'd missed out on my ten-year reunion using *my daughter Mitz had the flu* as an excuse and hadn't run into any of my old high school classmates in a long time. Fifteen was next summer. I wouldn't be at that one either. "My gosh, Stephanie. You look great. You live here in the neighborhood?"

"Not exactly. I'm glad to find you home. I heard you

inherited your dad's business. I was sad to hear you lost him."

I bounced in place; my leg muscles tight. The business. My childhood home. My dad had left me everything. Including a few of his messes. "I've been taking up where he left off."

She wrapped her arms around herself. "Does that include missing persons?"

"I handle it all." A half-truth. Willing to handle and being hired to handle were different. My PI license with the state of Oregon was current. But after my arm had healed, I'd gone back to my role before my dad died: serving legal papers and a few stakeouts that only sent me running from pissed off cheaters on rare occasions. Her timing was good though. I'd been itching for something different. "Who's missing?"

"My dad."

A breath caught in my throat. Mr. Burnotas, or Vince as he insisted we call him even as kids, had often picked Stephanie up in front of the school and attended events. I had even hung out at her house a few times after classes. Her dad was a quiet man, with a warm askew smile and an easy laugh. She had to be panicked. I invited her upstairs for coffee.

Once we were settled, she launched right in. "At first, I thought he might be busy, but I started getting worried a few weeks ago when he didn't return my calls. I spoke with a Detective Kuni at the Sheriff's office. He took my statement and did a welfare check. My dad's place is locked down and the neighbors said they never saw him around much, even when he was home. Since no one else reported him missing, they aren't willing to do much else."

"Do they think he's just ignoring you?"

"I'm sure." She pulled a picture from her purse and handed it to me. "This was taken a couple of years ago."

Vince held a red pullover sweater up to his chest he'd removed from a Christmas box on his lap. He had gray combed-back hair, with black sideburns—the only signs of his youthful color. His crooked smile and thin lips framed a good-size gap in his front teeth. The deep-set lines around his eyes reflected a rougher life than most. "Have you checked with his work?"

"I tried. He'd been working at a bowling alley at one point, but when I called, they said he wasn't there anymore."

"When was his last day?"

She frowned. "I didn't think to ask."

I drummed my fingers on the dining table. "Is it possible he went away on vacation or has another home?"

She shook her head. "He doesn't have that kind of money. And if he took a vacation, he'd be back by now."

"His money situation could've changed."

"I guess. The last time we spoke was Thanksgiving."

A lot could happen in six months. Like me, for instance. For once, I had a little money tucked away in my account. Even if it had taken me being stalked, beat up, nearly run down and shot to get it. "What happened in November that you're only now trying to reach him?"

"Nothing." Stephanie shifted to get comfortable. "I mean, family stuff. He drank too much that night and I was annoyed with him." She shifted again. "It's not like we talked every day. Time got away. Now we haven't spoken since right after that night." Her eyes misted.

I recognized the guilt of not having done enough. Of

thinking she should have reached out sooner. "I'm happy to check out what's going on with him."

She patted her stomach and sniffed. "Thank you. I'm due in a couple of months with a baby girl. I want to make things right between us. He doesn't even know I'm pregnant and I don't want to deny my daughter knowing her grandfather."

My chest tightened. Mitz talked about my dad, her Papa, often. Regardless of my feelings about my father, or the fact that he was gone, the grandparent and child relationship was an important one. I'd give anything to bring my dad back so Mitz wouldn't have to miss out.

Leaning back in my chair, I explained my hourly rate plus expenses and had her sign a contract. "I'll need five hundred to get started." It felt weird to ask an old friend to pay for services, but I was running a business.

She frowned, small lines creasing her forehead. "I have a few hundred right now, but I can get more."

Her expression was hard to read. "I'm sorry I have to ask at all, but I have Mitz and..."

She raised a hand to her chest. "I didn't expect you'd be free. It's just that..." She hesitated. "Brandon doesn't know I'm here."

"Brandon's your husband?"

Her chin dipped. "Yeah. My pregnancy has him worried about money. I don't want to stress him anymore than he already is." She dug into her purse and brought out three one hundred dollar bills, setting them on the table. "Will this be enough to get you started?"

"It will." I didn't hesitate and tucked the money in the side pocket of my purse on the counter and returned with a notepad and pen.

She gave me the information for the detective who'd

done the welfare check, along with Vince's address and birth date. She handed me the keys. "Unless he's changed the locks, these should work to get you in his house."

I pulled the notepad back. Riverview, Washington, was thirty miles north on the Interstate. "Getting into your dad's house will be where I start. Why haven't you done that yet?"

Her gaze fell onto the wall behind me. "I have a weird feeling about this, Kelly. I have high blood pressure and the doctor says I'm at risk of preeclampsia. If I don't minimize stress, I'll end up in the hospital to avoid premature labor. The police aren't taking me seriously, but I don't know if I'm well enough to find him myself right now."

When we'd finished, I added her into my phone contacts and walked her to the front door, giving her a hug. "Don't worry. I'll bet he came into some money and he's sipping a margarita in Mexico, oblivious that you're worried about him."

Many missing cases were that simple. I wanted to ease her mind, even if I didn't entirely buy my own words. Families often didn't stay in touch and six months wasn't that long. Except Stephanie was an only child. A father not returning his only daughter's call didn't feel right—even if they were annoyed with each other. Having grown up an only child, I didn't want to believe it.

Her brown eyes were moist with tears. "Hope you're right. I hated him sometimes, but loved him. Know what I mean?"

During my last case, I'd learned some things about my dad that had shaken me to the core. Everything I thought he represented—honor, loyalty, steadfastness—had disintegrated in an instant.

"I do," I said.

Before heading north, I flipped through the pictures I'd taken earlier during my surveillance of the roaming eye husband in the act of saying goodbye to his lover. His wife of twenty years suspected he was doing some version of Downward-facing Dog with her yoga instructor. She was partially right. Except it was with the yoga teacher's boyfriend. I'd forwarded the heartbreaking pictures confirming her worst fears.

Much of my work involved information and paperwork that destroyed families. Finding Vince might put a family back together. It would be a welcome change.

However, finding people wasn't always easy. I turned off my car's engine and ruffled Floyd on the head. For whatever reason, Vince Burnotas had gone off someplace. What if he didn't want to be found? I got out and approached his house. Time to find out.

TWO

VINCE LIVED IN a part of town where cars were hopped up on cinder blocks, and rusted mufflers, exhausts, and pieces of engines littered the front yards. Not a place I'd be wandering alone at night. His house, a green one-story box with chipped siding and no garage, was located along the railroad tracks. Random wires sprung like weeds from the roofline, including an aluminum antenna large enough to summon space aliens.

The blinds were drawn. The overgrown grass in the yard gave the impression it hadn't been mowed for over a month, using my own lawn as a measuring stick. Three narrow concrete steps led to a faded front door, framed by dying shrubs that even the incessant rain of April hadn't been able to save. A few knocks didn't result in anyone answering.

I pulled out the key Stephanie had given me and opened the door. "Hello. Mr. Burnotas? Are you home?" I said, pushing it ajar.

The smell of stale cigarette smoke drifted out. "I'm Kelly. Remember me? I'm a friend of your daughter's from school."

Silence.

"Hello? Vince?" I willed a response. None came. Entering someone's home wasn't as easy as I used to think. The last time I'd done it, I'd stumbled upon a bad situation. Taking another whiff, I stepped inside. No foul smells, unless musty counted. I'd count that as a positive.

Shutting the door behind me, I flicked on a light and found myself standing in the living room. Heavy curtains covered the windows making the space feel like a cave. The light of the overhead bulb absorbed into the paneled walls. A worn striped sofa ran perpendicular to a flat screen TV on an oak console. A matching armchair anchored the corner. Goose flesh covered my arms. It might have been the coolness of the house, or just that it felt so lifeless. I zipped my warmup jacket up under my chin.

To the right was the dining room; a card table in the center had lottery tickets and bills piled on top. I started there. Vince might have hit the jackpot and then the road. Upon inspection, the perforated tabs on each of the tickets had been flipped open. More accustomed to Scratch Offs, the game didn't look familiar, but the concept was similar. None had winning combinations. If he'd won big, these weren't the source. So why keep them and not throw them in the trash?

My focus turned to a stack of opened bills. Riverview Electric, garbage service, a subscription to *Popular Mechanics*, and a few others, were all addressed to a PO Box. That accounted for the empty mail receptacle at the street. A letter dated over a month ago from Vince's landlord, L.K. DeWitt, had no postmark and gave him fifteen days to get current on rent. There'd been no red tag taped outside. He'd either paid or they hadn't started the eviction process. The delinquency didn't automatically indicate a problem. Vince could be a regular slow pay. If he was on vacation and returning soon, he could catch up in no time.

He also could have split town because he didn't have

the money. It was about the same time Stephanie had started calling him and he didn't respond. I snapped a picture with my cell of the landlord's information. It might come in handy if it came to checking on whether he'd received payment.

In the living room, I scanned Vince's belongings. Besides the clutter on the table, a thick layer of dust covered every flat surface. Domestic Goddess would never describe me either, but it had been far more than a month since he'd used Pledge and a rag. A remote inhabited the only end table drawer; a few *Us* magazines dated last year littered the top. Two VHS tapes were tucked next to the VCR. Very old school—my dad had a drawer of his own too. Otherwise, nothing stood out that would tell me where Vince had gone.

In the spare bedroom, a small desk had been shoved in the corner with boxes piled around it filled with pots and pans, and linens. They gave the impression that he'd recently moved in. Or he was moving out. The state of the rest of the house might answer that question.

Nothing seemed out of place in the bathroom. The drawers contained necessities like Q-tips, toenail cutters, oral hygiene stuff, and an electric razor.

The medicine cabinet often told a lot about a person, including their mental state. A cabinet full of remedies could reflect a hypochondriac. Whereas an empty cabinet could mean someone healthy, or even unconcerned with their health. Inside Vince's cabinet: a bottle of Tylenol, Imodium, Mylanta, and two rolls of Tums. Something had Vince's stomach in knots.

Behind the Tums was a prescription for Capecitabine and Leucovorin with a few pills in each bottle. Neither indicated what they were for. Zebeta, I recognized as high blood pressure medicine since my dad had taken that one. A generic for Lipitor used for high cholesterol rounded out the mix. In a nutshell, wherever Vince had gone, he hadn't taken his medicine with him and that meant he could be a walking time bomb.

Inside the shower stall, a dry Irish Spring bar stuck to the acrylic said it hadn't been used in a while. Same for the mildew ring forming around the toilet's water line.

In the master bedroom, a crumpled comforter lay in the middle of mint-colored sheets on Vince's queen size bed. An indented single pillow rested where a head would lay. Making my bed had been ingrained in me since the time I could practically walk. Either Vince didn't care or he'd been in a hurry to roll out of bed and get going for the day.

Daily racing sheets from Portland Meadows, a horseracing track about ten miles from my home and office, were fanned out on the nightstand. Another collection of racing sheets had been stuffed into the nightstand.

If Vince had a thing for lottery tickets, a love for the horses wasn't a far stretch. And the man didn't only dabble. A visit to the Meadows was now on my list. With any luck, they'd tell me he'd hit the trifecta and took off with his winnings, making my margaritas in Mexico theory viable. More than anything, I wanted that to be true for Stephanie's sake.

The galley kitchen was my last stop. On the far end of the counter, an answering machine blinked red with pending messages. The old school phone had no Caller ID. No surprise since there'd been no computer or signs of Vince having a cell phone or other technological advancements in the place. I hit the *Play* button and immediately heard Stephanie's plea asking her dad to call.

Ten times to be exact. There was no date or time stamp, but each time more panic seeped into the messages. The last one pierced through my heart.

"I'm sorry, Daddy. Please call me. Please."

If Vince had heard these, he would have called. I couldn't imagine listening to that level of fear and sadness from my own daughter Mitz and not sprinting to her side.

Where did he go that he hadn't heard these messages? I shook my arms to dispel the tension and reset each message to new in case the police needed to rehear them.

Next, I opened the drawers below the machine hoping to find the answer in the form of an itinerary or brochure of a sunny beach. Instead, it was filled with knives and forks, bottle openers, and wooden spoons. Where was the junk drawer? I couldn't be the only person that had one. Someplace to stuff bills, receipts, rubber bands, pens, and unused gift cards.

A few drawers in, I found it. Vince's collection was far neater than my own. A lint roller and sets of keys, along with a lighter, pack of Camels, and reading glasses. A notepad with names, numbers, and random words was also tucked in the drawer with *if you feel the earth move* jotted near the bottom. He had the notepad tucked into a crossword puzzle book. My dad had enjoyed acrostic puzzles, sitting down to the *NY Times* each Sunday. I'd suggested we get him a smart phone and download the app, giving him daily access. That didn't go over well. Dad didn't like technology any more than Vince and enjoyed the process of keeping a scratch pad with potential answers to the puzzles. Vince obviously enjoyed the same approach.

I flipped through the rest of the contents. Nothing

jumped out to give me a clear direction of Vince's whereabouts. No travel agency information. Only more losing tickets and a credit card statement dated last month. I scanned the purchases for major buys, but gas stations and restaurants were the bulk, including a place called the Turf Club in Portland. Sounded swanky and by the amount, expensive. The card was maxed at its two-thousand-dollar limit and current. As of last month anyway, Vince had been making his minimum payment on the balance.

I laid the statement out on the counter and took a photograph, capturing the card number and the other charges for quick reference, before stuffing it back into its envelope and returning it to the drawer.

Slipping the phone into my jacket, I headed to the fridge. The contents might hold a clue as to when he was last home. Until now, I hadn't noticed the smell of something sweet and rotting in the air. Holding my breath, I opened the refrigerator door to a six-pack of Pabst Blue Ribbon beer on the top shelf, a half-gallon of recently expired milk in the door, and a picked-over chicken carcass sealed in a plastic bag on the second shelf. A typical sparse bachelor's fridge. I stuck my nose closer, steeling myself, and sniffed. Whatever the odor, the fridge wasn't the source.

A pile of dirty dishes teetered in the sink, but that didn't seem to be the origin either. The garbage. It had to be. I opened the cupboard underneath the sink and jumped back. Maggots swarmed around the edges of the lined can. My stomach flipped in protest. The stench assaulted my nose making my eyes water. The skin crawled on my arms and back. I forced myself to lean in and inspect the wiggling worms. They were centered around a sausage-size piece of decaying meat in the can. Or I thought that until I looked closer. It was meat, but not the grocery store kind.

It was a finger.

Slamming the cupboard door closed, I ran back into the living room, gulping down air. Bile churned in my gut and crept into my throat at the realization that finger could belong to Vince.

The living room offered little escape now that I'd released the odor into the house, but it wasn't as strong as in the kitchen. I shoved my hands into my gray Nike jacket and paced for a full minute. Thinking. I took a few swallows to quell the nausea and a few breaths to calm down. My head started to clear. I had to call the police. There was no dead body, thank God, but with Vince missing and someone shy a finger, I didn't have a choice. It might be his. Or it might not. Which alone would raise even more questions.

The finger hadn't been discarded recently. While healing from my gunshot, I had time on my hands and had gotten curious about gangrene, infections, and necrosis, which of course led to lividity, body temperatures and rigor mortis. Who doesn't research that in their free time? Anyway, blowflies could find their way to a corpse within 24 hours and lay eggs, which then took 8 to 10 days to mature. By day 14 they hatched, and the process started again. Since the finger was in an enclosed space, it would have taken longer. A month? Not sure.

My hand trembling with adrenalin, I punched in 9-1-1 but waited to hit send. Had I missed something? Blood, bandages, anything indicating Vince had hurt himself. I walked into the bathroom when a large bang shook the house. The front door had crashed open.

THREE

FEAR SNAKED THROUGH my body at the sound, my fright or flight mode kicking in.

A woman's voice screamed, "Goddamn it, Vince. It's about time you showed up. Where have you been, you son-of-a-bitch?"

If this woman was looking for Vince, she couldn't be the one who removed the finger. At least I'd go with that theory for the moment. I dislodged my stomach from my throat. "Hello. I'm not Vince."

I heard no response.

Stepping out of the bathroom, a sixty-something lady stood in the middle of the living room. Her box-dyed copper hair was piled on her head and she wore cream capris and a tight black rayon V-neck that left nothing to the imagination.

Her face twisted and turned the shade of her hair when she saw me. "What are you doing in Vince's house? You that slut he's been sleeping with?"

"I'm not. I'm Kelly Pruett," I said, keeping my voice even. "I was hired by Vince's daughter, Stephanie, to find him. She's not been able to reach him. And you are?"

"Someone looking for him, obviously, which makes two of us."

"Have you seen him recently?"

"If you call being left at the bar a few weeks ago

seeing him." She huffed as an exclamation point to her statement.

I crossed to the living room and perched on the farthest corner of the sofa, motioning her over. This woman knew Vince and she might be able to help me—if I could calm her down. "Let's sit."

She held fast, then relented, plopping down on the corner cushion at the other end.

"Why don't you tell me what bar you were at with Vince and when he left you there, Ms…?" I started.

"The Tip Top and this coming Friday will have been a month since the asshole disappeared." Her face flushed at the recollection. "When I get a hold of him…"

Vince had last been seen over three weeks ago although Stephanie had been calling him prior to that with no response. For some reason, this lady didn't want to give me her name. At least a timeline was taking shape. "When did you begin your search?"

She pushed herself off the couch and paced. "A while ago. I've been by here a dozen times, at least. The jerk's been avoiding me."

Her rage might have had me doing the same. "You never saw any signs of him when you came by?"

"Your car is the first I've seen. Thought you were him finally deciding to show up."

"Did something happen at the bar that made him leave?"

She folded her arms over her chest.

"Were you arguing?"

She huffed again. "What's new? The man's a mule."

"How long were you two dating?"

Her face scrunched. "I'm not dishing details about

my love life with you. If you know where he is, tell me." Her eye twitched.

The twitch said she might care about Vince's whereabouts more than she wanted to let on—and not only to wring his neck. "I'm just getting started myself so any information you can provide would be helpful." She dropped down onto the sofa again, her posture rigid. "Was it commonplace for him to leave you at the bar and go missing?"

"Him leaving me stranded was normal. The man gets a hair and takes off. Or he gets a tip and I might not see him for days. But he always comes back."

"A tip?"

"For the ponies."

That made sense with the daily sheets in his bedroom. "He gambled a lot then?"

"More than any person should."

"What was it about that particular night that set him off?"

"He was talking stupid about his job and I told him so."

"Where did he work?"

The woman's mouth set in a hardline. "Which day? He went through jobs like water."

"But you said he was talking about his job."

"Complaining, in general. Upset about something and going to make it big somehow. Honestly, I tuned him out. Told him to behave because he didn't need to be costing himself a paycheck."

"What did he want to do that was stupid?"

She jumped up again. This time she walked over to the card table, gave it a glance then strode back into the living room. "Look, I already told you, I don't know. The man needs to work. Which I could care less about until he starts having me buy the beer and hitting me up for cash. I'm not a damn ATM."

Time with her made my stomach hurt. "Had he asked you for rent money lately?"

"Rent money, gambling money. The guy had a problem. Like I said, he couldn't afford to lose his job."

I nodded. "When you came in, you accused me of being the slut he was sleeping with. I take it there were others?"

She wrung hands. "No idea. He'd been flighty the past few months. Got me thinking there must be someone else."

Vince was turning out to be far more complex. Wanting to get us back on track, I said, "Tell me more about the night he left you stranded, a few weeks ago you said?"

"Yeah. He picked me up and we went to the Tip Top, like usual. He was more agitated though and started drinking early. Said he was meeting someone later that night."

"There, at the bar?"

"He didn't say, but he was supposed to take me home first. Except he got mad and left."

My mind went to the finger in the garbage can. "Had Vince injured himself?"

"He has a bad back. Is that what you mean?"

I didn't plan to get this lady anymore upset. "More like do you know of any accidents he may have had with his hands?"

Her eyes widened and then narrowed. "He was fine when he left me. Do you know something? Is he hurt? In the hospital?" Her face wrinkled. "Is that why he hasn't been around?"

Oh geez. "Not at all. I'm trying to find him like you. I'm asking questions to point me in the right direction."

Her shoulders drooped. "Wish I could help you. I'm in the dark, too."

We were at the end of our sharing and it was past time that I call the police. I reached for a card in my purse. "I'm going to keep looking. If you want to give me your name and number, I'll let you know when I find him."

Her chin quivered, reminding me of my grandmother. My dad's mother had always kept her softer side clamped down. She didn't want anyone thinking she cared too much about any one thing. I'd inherited that emotional fortitude. Deep down, like me, they were all mushy. Any inkling of caring would simply crack the façade, making it impossible to keep it all in. Better to show almost nothing instead.

"Fine." She returned to Vince's card table, grabbed an old ticket, and jotted the information on the back. Her eyes rested on the stack of them.

I scanned the multitude of paper. "He did like his lottery games."

She nodded, her gaze never leaving the table.

"Where do you suppose he got all these?" I asked.

"Bowling alley, I imagine. He worked there at one time." That's what Stephanie had mentioned. "He thought buying them was his path to millions." Her eyes sprung a leak. "But the jackass there stiffed him." She sniffed hard and thrust the ticket with her information on it to me.

"What jackass?"

She waved me off and headed for the door. It might not matter. When people didn't win they often blamed someone else. It also might be worth checking out.

I glanced at the card. Marilyn Corder. "If you hear from him before I do, Marilyn, please call."

She walked out without another word. I closed the door, hit send on my phone, and returned to the makeshift dining table where Marilyn seemed focused on the tickets. They looked like losers to me. I could be reading something into her behavior that wasn't there.

When the 9-1-1 operator came on the line I asked for Detective Kuni and was transferred to the general office who sent me to the detective. Since Stephanie had contacted him originally, it seemed like the place to start.

"The family hired a PI?" he asked after I identified myself.

"Yes, and I've found something you'll want to see."

"Such as?"

"A detached finger."

"Be there in five."

I waited for him in my car, caressing Floyd's floppy ears. I'd know soon whether the finger belonged to Vince or not. Then Stephanie would be due an update. If it belonged to Vince, that was not a call I'd enjoy making. There wasn't long to contemplate when a tan sedan pulled in the drive next to me.

FOUR

Before Detective Kuni had opened his car door and stretched out his six-foot frame, I was in front of my Triumph. He had short black hair with gray threads and bangs combed to the right. Rectangular metal-rimmed glasses framed tired eyes with bags that had taken residence and rested on his broad nose reflecting his island heritage. He looked hip to me in his khakis, long sleeve button shirt and black vest. I put him in his late fifties, slightly older than my dad would have been if he were alive.

We swapped business cards and he inspected mine with some interest. "Pruett. Any relation to an old timer PI in Portland?"

I tucked his business card in my back pocket. "That would be my father."

"Roger Pruett?"

I nodded.

He smiled, one of those smiles that deepened the already existing lines and enveloped his whole face. "There is a resemblance."

I returned his smile; glad I'd passed the sniff test. Dad had been a larger than life Welshman, and quite handsome. The extra weight he carried most of my life did nothing to diminish his strong chin, knowing blue eyes, and thick chestnut hair, traits I shared with him except for my rounded chin, compliments of my mom. My smile faded. "I lost him last year."

His face scrunched, the skin below his softened eyes wrinkling. "Sorry. I hadn't heard. We'd worked a case together years ago."

His name hadn't sounded familiar. "I don't remember him mentioning you. Who was the client?"

"Another time. He was one hell of an investigator." The implication was that I had big shoes to fill, which I already knew. "What's this about a detached finger?"

I shuddered. "Severed, and it's under the kitchen sink."

The detective's thick brows drew together. "Recent?"

"Based on the decomposition, not more than a few weeks. That's about the time Vince was last seen, although nothing I saw indicates whether the finger is his or not."

He nodded. "Let me grab my collection kit." He went back to his sedan and popped the trunk.

My phone buzzed with a text. Kyle wanted to know if I had dinner plans.

Kyle Jaeger and I'd met at the courthouse over two years ago. Coffee had progressed into seeing each other last October during my first case. After being shot, he'd been more than supportive. Between him and my ex-mother-in-law Arlene, I didn't starve to death. He'd even helped fold laundry and change the sheets, which had seen some action. Between his crazy work schedule and my arm, not as much as one would expect after several months of dating. Always afraid Mitz might drop by without warning, I pumped the brakes a time—or two. They'd met, and we'd even had a few dinners and gone to the zoo together. But I didn't want to confuse her by playing house too soon. At least that's what I told myself.

I texted him back: I'm on a case but should be back in time.

I got a can't wait to hear about it in response.

Detective Kuni reappeared with a caddy filled with gloves, brushes, tapes, and evidence bags and we made our way into the house. He went straight for the kitchen sink, rolled up his sleeves and yanked two latex gloves from the box, shoving his stout hands into them.

"I understand you did the welfare check on Vince," I said. "Take it you didn't come into the house then?"

He crooked his index finger in the handle to not disturb any prints and eased the cabinet door open. Because I hadn't been as careful earlier, mine would be in the mix. At the time, I didn't expect to find body parts and maggots in the enclosed space. It was a newbie mistake. One of these days I'd stop making those.

"I inspected the property and interviewed the neighbors. Nothing looked suspicious enough to justify seeking a search warrant to gain entry. In fact, the opposite. Neighbors reported they rarely saw him. No weird smells emanated from the house. No old newspapers at the door. No mail overflowing his mailbox."

"He has a PO box," I offered.

He shrugged and crouched in front of the wastebasket. "Again, nothing amiss that would prompt us to do a more thorough search. Ms. Jacoby, while concerned, hadn't been in touch with her father for quite some time."

I lifted my chin toward the answering machine. "She left him several messages that don't appear to have been received. Unfortunately, they don't identify when they came in."

"That's speculative. He could have heard them and chose not to respond. It doesn't mean much anyway.

We're aware his daughter has been trying to reach him. The reality is we have a small department, and we're understaffed. Can't tell you how many requests for welfare checks we handle around here. A neighbor's house cat gets out and we get a call convinced the owner has had a heart attack. Someone doesn't show for church and we get asked to conduct a drive-by. If we opened a case for every call, half our caseload would be these."

The world overflowed with busy bodies. Zuckerberg banked on that when he launched Facebook. However, in Vince's case, only Stephanie had felt concerned enough to call. For all of Marilyn's bluster, why hadn't she contacted the police by now? "I bet not many involve potential body parts though."

He eyed the contents. "True statement." The detective must have dealt with dead bodies over the years, but even he held his breath when he saw the maggots.

I stepped back to give him space. "It is a finger, right?"

He pushed away the garbage around the extremity and left the door open. "Looks like."

"You'll be making this an active missing persons case now, I suppose?"

"A missing part is not a missing person, Ms. Pruett. But it definitely falls into attempted assault."

Where'd the attempted come from? The attempt of removing a finger had worked. The maggot-covered proof sat in the garbage can.

"I am interested in having a conversation with Mr. Burnotas, however, to find out what he knows about this," he continued.

Viewing someone as a suspect in an assault wouldn't get the same attention as a missing person's case. Especially if they were that understaffed. "If you can't find him in your initial search, then you'll move him to missing person?"

He didn't answer.

Most cops weren't keen on sharing information with non-law enforcement. But he'd known my dad. "What about his landlord?" I pressed.

He looked up from the garbage. "What about him?"

"There's a delinquent notice over there. He may be a place to start." I pointed at the card table.

The detective walked to the stack of papers and found the letter. He drew out a notebook from his coat pocket and jotted down information. He inspected the losing tickets.

"One of his lady friends came by earlier," I said. "Appears Vince has been MIA for around three weeks and she's been looking everywhere for him. Her timeline matches with Stephanie calling you."

He jotted more in his notepad. "I appreciate the assist. I'll get the report filed, start our investigation and get some tests run. The next step depends on who that finger belongs to. If not Mr. Burnotas, then we'll need to find out whose and why it's in his garbage."

I couldn't see Vince removing someone's finger. But I hadn't expected to find piles of gambling tickets or meet his jilted girlfriend either. Helping Stephanie was supposed to be a quick and simple case to ease me back into investigating. It wasn't turning out that way. "If it's his?"

"Still would like that chat with him. And these tickets here could hold a clue."

We at least agreed on that. "There's daily sheets from the racetracks in his bedroom, too."

His eyes narrowed. "Anything else you've found you want to share?"

I crossed my arms over my chest at his tone. "His high blood pressure and other meds are in the bathroom cabinet. That's about it."

"Sounds like Mr. Burnotas may have gotten in too deep with gambling. Severed body part messages aren't as uncommon as you'd think. If he owed money, that person or persons may have wanted to put the frighteners into him."

"The frighteners?"

"Scare him to death so there's no question they mean business. It's a popular form of communication amongst organized criminals, who are often involved in gambling."

My stomach tightened at the idea. Whether it was Vince's finger or not, it seemed a strong motivation to skip out in my book. Was that what Vince had done? "Should we check with hospitals to make sure Vince or someone hasn't been in recently missing a finger?"

He raised his eyebrows in response.

I put my hands on my hips. "I'm not trying to tell you how to do your job. Vince's daughter is worried about him and with her high-risk pregnancy, the quicker I get answers to her, the better."

He drew in a breath, went back into the kitchen, and removed the finger from the garbage, securing it in a small evidence bag. He didn't respond while he jotted more notes. Detective Kuni definitely moved at his own pace. Finally, he said, "While I understand your reasons, this is now a police matter."

I'd expected to lose some control over what happened once the police arrived. I wasn't sure how much more I'd be able to do, if anything, if the detective took a more aggressive stance in the case. But I had looked Stephanie in the eye and promised to find her dad. Heard her pleas to her father on the answering machine. It wouldn't hurt to inquire a little more. Especially if Vince had gotten himself into a situation with some shady characters.

My Fitbit read eleven-thirty. Enough time to squeeze in some investigating before heading home. The detective had admitted they were short on cops. I'd be doing him a favor. If I found anything juicy, I'd loop him in; if not, no skin off his nose as Dad would say. "Since you've got this, is there any reason for me to stay?"

Detective Kuni looked up from his notebook. "I have your number. What's the name of that girlfriend you mentioned?"

"Marilyn Corder." I wrote the info on the back of another business card and handed it to him. "She said Vince had worked for the bowling alley in town for a while, but she doesn't know where he's working now, and I didn't see any paystubs."

He sighed. "You didn't mess around with anything else in here, did you?"

"No." My taking pictures of Vince's credit card statement didn't count as messing with anything. "She also mentioned that Vince and the guy at the bowling alley may have had issues."

"Like most everyone in town when it comes to Chuck. If I need any more of your help, I'll call." He turned back to the kitchen without another word.

I'd been dismissed. Back in my car, I gave Floyd a nose scratch and contemplated my next move. The pop-up lottery tickets and the town grouch had me curious. While the police were deciding what kind of an assault case they had, if any, I could build a picture of Vince's life before he disappeared—which might lead to a clue of where he'd gone. Since gambling could be a major part, hitting the bowling alley made sense.

I'd hold off calling Stephanie until I had something solid. Besides, I didn't want to reveal my initial thoughts that Vince had indeed taken off, but not voluntarily or his medicines would have been with him. The finger could have something to do with that; or not. But finding a body part was never a good sign when the person it might belong to hadn't been seen in the past few weeks.

FIVE

After leaving Vince's place, I made a stop at Mini Mart to refill my travel mug with fresh brew, grabbed a small jar of peanut butter for later, and did a quick Google search for local bowling alleys. Riverview had only one.

I punched in Tiger Bowl's address into my phone's GPS and it wound me over the Interstate and onto a stretch of Highway 402 where billowing white smoke filled the already cloud filled sky to the north from the nearby fiber mills. The plants were in heavy production mode without enough wind to move the smoke out of the city. Many Riverview and neighboring city residents depended on industry for their livelihood. Pulp mills, industrial plants, and factory farms lined various portions of the river. The fish literally had crap seeping into their homes on a regular basis.

Close off the exit was Gearhart Garden Park. "Time for a break?" I asked Floyd, who stood in the seat, tail thumping against my arm. I took that as *past time* and whipped into the parking lot. A golden retriever and its person played in the fenced area.

While waiting for Floyd to finish his business and romp with the golden, I texted Jeff. In a couple of hours I'd be driving past Mitz's school on the way back and I could bring her to his home. I'd only dropped her off at school that morning, but couldn't miss an opportunity to see my girl. I also didn't want to be accused of being too absorbed in a case. Mitz was my heart and soul. It was important to get out ahead and assure her, me and Jeff that my stepping back into investigating didn't mean my leaving her behind. He hadn't responded by the time Floyd and I were back on the road to the bowling alley.

Tiger Bowl was located inside a non-descript single-story gray stucco building with blue awnings. I'd have missed it except I pulled in at the same time a man carrying a blue and white striped ball bag exited through a fading blue door and headed to his Ford F150.

Inside, the lanes shone from high gloss wax and bright lights; advertising with pins exploding in rainbow bursts played on screens above the pin sets. They'd shelled out a boat load of money to spruce the place up, but the smell of old smoke clung to the walls and deep-fried onion ring stench hung in the air. My dad had enjoyed bowling on a few occasions, so I'd spent some time in them. None had ever shaken their dankness, no matter how many layers of new paint were applied.

An armpit-height paneled shoe counter anchored the middle with a cash register at one end, and a bay of cubbies filled with tan and green shoes as the backdrop. A man dressed in baggy polyester pants cinched up by a black belt under a protruding belly, and a red polo shirt with the collar wide and flat around his neck, sprayed Lysol into the shoes. His mottled arms were covered in graying fawn-colored hair.

I approached, not getting too close to get blasted with chemicals. I reserved that for the third Thursday of every month when I beat back the mold in my basement. "Good morning."

"What size?" He had the voice of a pack a day smoker.

"Not bowling today. Are you Chuck?"

His gaze bore into me from below his bushy eyebrows. "Who's askin'?"

I took that as a yes and understood why some people might have an issue with Chuck. "Kelly Pruett, PI." I slid a card out from my pocket and laid it on the counter. "I'm looking for one of your former employees, Vince Burnotas."

He huffed. "What's the jackass done now?"

Vince seemed to rouse strong responses in people. "Does he have a history of getting into trouble?"

He shoved the pair of shoes he'd been spraying back into a slot. "Look, girly. I'm no gossip. That's Lorraine in accounting's thing and she ain't here. Why you lookin' for him?"

"His daughter hasn't been able to reach him and I'm making sure he's okay."

"Last time I saw him, he was peachy."

"And when was that?"

"A while ago."

Were all of Vince's connections crabby like Marilyn and Chuck? "When did he quit?"

"You'd actually have to work to quit."

"So, he didn't work for you?"

"When he felt like it. He was a decent mechanic when he needed cash. The rest of the time, useless."

I shifted from one foot to another. "When was the last time he needed money?"

"It's not like I write this crap on a calendar. Especially if it had to do with him."

Going nowhere fast, I changed tactics. "Any idea where he's working now?"

He shrugged. "Heard someone say he's driving for some outfit. Probably doesn't show for them either."

This merry-go-round was making me dizzy. "Have you seen Vince since he quit?"

"Once and I told him to get the hell out and stay out."

Finally. "What prompted that?"

His cheeks turned rosy. "He thought I ran a scam on him and I don't take kindly to people accusing me of being shady. This here is an upstanding business. Don't need no sore loser costing me customers."

"What did Vince accuse you of doing?" If Chuck held a grudge against Vince, the severed finger could be something Chuck did to get even with him.

"Closing down a game too soon."

"Bowling game?"

"Pull-tabs." He pulled a basket full of tabs out from under the counter. A sign on the front boasted the different values that could be won. Top prize was five thousand.

The tickets were identical to the ones in Vince's house with ten perforated windows lining the back, but these had three cartoon pigs on the front and read *Hamming it Up*. "Are these actual lottery tickets?"

"No. But it's all gambling. You match the symbol on the front with three of them under those tabs in the back to win."

"What's the difference between the two?"

"Lottery proceeds come out of the Washington State Lottery coffer. Because I have a tavern, I can run my own gambling games in-house."

"Meaning you pay out the proceeds directly?"

"You got it. Want to try your luck?"

Washington State regulated gambling. To be accused of wrongdoing would be serious. But with not much luck to spare, I pulled my purse closer. "No thanks. Was the problem that you didn't pay him?"

"Oh, I paid if he won. A rarity, and nothing big. The problem came when I pulled a game. Within my rights by the way. I don't have to ask permission from no one."

"You mean all these people are buying tabs, and you can decide to end the game whether anyone has actually won the big prize?"

He nodded.

"What happens to the money paid in? You keep it?"

He squinted. "You sound like him."

I lifted my hands in surrender. "Trying to understand the premise."

He sniffed. "Well, it happened about like that. In my defense, the game had been running for several weeks at the time. A lifetime in pull-tab world. I don't print these things. I can't help it if the first tickets sold were full of losers. It's the luck of the draw." He picked one up and flung it on the counter. "Problem with Vince is he didn't know when to quit. Instead of moving on, he decided I was bent on screwing him out of a big payday."

Not quite understanding pull-tabs, I glanced at the sign and tickets boasting a $5,000 prize again. "Wouldn't someone have eventually won if the game hadn't been cut off?"

Chuck grabbed the basket of tickets and popped it under the counter without responding.

Vince might have had a right to be pissed, but Chuck was done talking about it. "After you asked him to leave, was that the last time you saw him?"

"Yup. He caused a scene and riled everyone in the place before making a grand exit."

Seemed like a grand exit would stick in Chuck's mind. "You must remember how long ago that was?"

"Guess I do. A month, maybe."

I tapped the counter. While I could understand having a lot of skin in a game and being upset about it not paying off, I didn't remember Vince being quick tempered. Stephanie had never mentioned her dad being a screamer or heavy disciplinarian, traits I'd expect from someone who might cause a spectacle. Of course, that was years ago, and a lot could have changed. "Why do you think he was so upset about losing?"

"No clue. Guy was a deadbeat. You said his daughter hired you?"

"Yes."

"She shouldn't bother finding him. Vince always needed money, but he wanted easy cash. If she's got any, she's best to lose his number and not answer his calls."

"She's pregnant."

His expression was blank. "Opinion doesn't change."

I'd hit a wall. I scanned the lanes. A men's league had come in and were gathered at one end. Everyone appeared to have their fingers attached—which I expected. Detective Kuni could be wrong about his assertion that organized crime could be involved although I didn't envision the bowling alley as a mob hang out. And who said only mafia types removed fingers? How about angry bowling alley clerks? "When do you expect Lorraine back?" Her gift of gossip might give me some direction.

"Not sure. She's on vacation."

I'd have to either come back, or find another way to catch up with her. A group of teenagers had formed a line behind me. "Thanks for the chat."

He grunted and focused on his paying customers. "What size?"

On my way to the door, a dusty blond baby-faced man about my age in gray coveralls caught my attention. He hovered over the return carriage on the lane closest to the front door with a wrench clutched in his hand. Chuck said Vince had been a mechanic. The man might be able to offer an opinion on Vince's whereabouts.

When I approached, he straightened. He was rail thin, but handsome in a grease-monkey kind of way. He stared down the machine, hands on his hips, contemplating his next move.

"Giving you some trouble?" I smiled and lifted my chin towards the motor.

"Always something breaking around here." He scanned me from head to toe, his eyes landing on my chest.

I scanned him back, frowning. Flirting was fine if it gained me information, but Captain Obvious' locked-in gaze made my skin tingle, and not in a good way. I yanked out my card and tilted my head to meet his eyes. "I'm Kelly Pruett. I've been hired to find a former employee. What's your name?"

"Dylan. Doubtful I can help." He dropped my card in his front pocket and returned his focus to the ball return. He adjusted his wrench around a nut bolt and twisted.

Can't or won't? Guess I should have let him stare at my boobs. "Let's give it a try. Ever hear the name Vince Burnotas?"

"Nope."

"You sure? He was a mechanic here."

Dylan grabbed another wrench and fiddled with the bolt some more. "I'm a part-timer and I keep to myself."

"Chuck ever talk about him?"

"Nope. Just said I was more reliable than the last guy."

"Did he mention anything about the blowout they had?"

Dylan's shoulders inched towards his ears. He stared at the ball unit. Either he didn't like my question, or the mechanical issue was getting the better of him. "Chuck's an interesting guy," he said. "From my experience, pretty set in his ways. It doesn't surprise me he'd have an issue with just about anyone. But as I said, I'm a part-timer. I've learned it's best to not ask questions."

"Not asking questions would make my line of work far more difficult."

"But safer." His bottom teeth worked something tucked into his bottom lip.

So was staying home and watching *The View*, which wasn't going to happen either. "Do you know the book-keeper Lorraine?"

"She writes my checks." He grabbed a Coke can that he had on the floor and spit into it.

I had to keep myself from wrinkling my nose. "Heard she was on vacation. Any chance you know where to find her when she's not working?"

He shrugged, setting down the can and slamming the carriage lid closed. He punched the ball return button. "Seen her at the Tip Top a few times. Could start there."

That was the last place Vince had been with Marilyn before he disappeared. Must be the town meeting spot. "I'll check it out."

He glanced at me again. "I could meet you there for a beer when I'm off work."

Dylan's pale blue eyes lacked warmth. Or connection. Something about him didn't feel quite right. "Tempting if I didn't have another appointment. Thanks anyway." I walked away, feeling his gaze on me.

Glad to abandon the cigarette smoke and the fried-onion grease for the great outdoors, my eyes stung from the fresh air and bright sun. If Stephanie hadn't spoken with her dad for six months, she wouldn't have been privy to his recent job issues or the falling out with Chuck. She might however know if he had a history of issues with work and people—and with gambling. I'd check with her on my way home.

My guess, Vince's problems had been long standing but were only now coming to a head. If he was struggling financially from gambling issues, he might not want to be found. With the severed finger, I didn't blame him. But who was he hiding from?

Back in my car, I wondered what kind of man got upset about pull-tabs not paying out. And what kind of man pulled a game when money sat on the table? That couldn't be good for business. Although, none of it would matter if I found Vince. I wasn't hired to dig into pull-tabs and gambling laws. But the tickle in my stomach made me think I'd only scratched the surface of Vince Burnotas' world.

SIX

IF THERE WAS a lunch rush at the Tip Top Tavern and Cardroom, it had gone by the time I pulled into the parking lot. A black sedan and a Ford SUV were stationed in front of the dirt brown-paneled building. The cardroom part of the sign had been unexpected, but not surprising there'd be gambling any spot Vince spent time.

"We'll walk as soon as I'm out of here, buddy." I ruffled Floyd's ears before locking him in and heading to the solid green door.

The bar married the perfect blend of biker and dive. Two pool tables centered the back, long fluorescent lights hung over each illuminating the green felt. Square wood tables filled the space in between the door and the back wall. A mahogany bar fit for an Irish pub spanned the left, an array of every liquor known to man lining the shelves behind it, black vinyl stools with orange flames tucked under.

Booths lined another wall. A construction crew of four wearing reflective vests occupied one. A police baton hung from a gun belt in the farthest spot, the person's back to me. A woman's pointy shoes sat opposite, but she was scooted too far in to see anything else. The place was complete with an ATM in the corner, and a white door at the far end that read "Poker" above it with a bay of slot machines to the right.

A man in his late sixties stood stoic behind the bar

dressed in a light-blue V-neck and khakis, his black apron tied around his trim waist, said he was ready to serve. The last time I'd been in a bar was six months ago when working my last case. I'd learned a bit about interrogation since then. One thing never changes when it comes to warming people up—money always talks.

Sliding onto the stool and resting my forearms on the bar I said, "I'll take a wine spritzer."

He nodded and returned a minute later with a wine glass filled with spritz. "That'll be five bucks."

I placed a ten on the counter.

He palmed it and smiled. "Thank you, miss."

Tipping well didn't hurt either. "You worked here long?"

"Own the joint. Name's Len. Take it you're looking for someone?"

"That obvious?"

He winked. "You're not our usual customer."

There wasn't a lot of evidence of who the "usuals" might be. If Marilyn was an indicator, I'd guess a little long in the tooth and three packs of Camels away from needing an oxygen tank. "How's that?"

"You're not wearing a construction vest, and you've got some life left in you."

Nailed that part right anyway. At least I looked healthy. "Gotcha. Well, I'm looking for Vince Burnotas and heard he might frequent here. You happen to see him recently?" If he had a quick answer to Vince's location, finding Lorraine for her gossip wouldn't be needed.

Len stood with his palms flat against the counter and stared at me. "Guess at this point I should be knowing who's asking."

"Sorry." I handed him my business card. "His daughter's looking for him."

He scanned my card. "I'll be damned. Wouldn't have pegged you for a PI."

What had he *pegged* me for? Airplane pilot? IRS agent? Waitress? "Have you?"

He shook his head. "Last time was a few weeks ago, if memory serves."

"Was he here with Marilyn Corder?"

He nodded. "I was swinging through to retrieve the night deposit and stayed to help the crew restock. Vince and her were doing their usual Rock 'em Sock 'em routine until he stormed out."

Jeff and I'd played that game when we were kids. Once I discovered the secret of the upper cut, he stopped playing with me. Guess he didn't like being decapitated on a regular basis. "Their fights got physical?"

"Nah. Just an expression, but they often argued."

"Was he with anyone when he left the bar that night?" Marilyn might not have noticed if the person Vince was to meet came to him.

Len relaxed his stance. He could be former military with the way he switched in and out of attention. "Not that I saw. In fact, when I took the garbage out, he was walking to his car alone. Mind you, I wasn't watching that close. It was a regular Saturday night with people coming and going. It stuck more because he'd left after one of his tiffs with Marilyn."

"Any idea what they were arguing about?"

"The usual. When you're on a high, Marilyn wants to swing with you. If you're dropping, she'll let you do that all on your own."

"I assume you're talking about his gambling."

Len tapped the tip of his nose with his index finger. Vince didn't hide his addiction, which might have been even harder to do with the slots and cardroom on the premises. "I understand he owes her money."

"Could be. She's made us all aware that she gets a good monthly benefit check. And Vince gambles. A lot. More than he used to. I'd heard him say a few times his luck was running out."

"Can you define more than he used to?"

"Before, he only dabbled. In the past six or seven months, you'd think he was trying to go professional. Playing poker every time he's here. Playing the slots. Even heard he was playing the ponies."

Not to mention the pull-tabs. "Have you seen Marilyn since that night?"

"Yes, ma'am. Quite often. She likes to play the slots and socialize."

Vince's departure hadn't slowed her down. "I met her today. Has she seemed upset about Vince missing?"

He grabbed a rag from the back counter. "Not at all. Until you asked about him, I had no idea. Figured he'd gone out of town for a while is all."

Len's version didn't jibe with Marilyn busting in on me earlier. If she was so hot to find Vince, wouldn't she be asking the bartender and everyone else in town if they'd seen him? Now might be a good time to see what the gossip mill had to say. "I'm looking for Lorraine, the bookkeeper at the bowling alley. I understand she spends time here as well."

Len focused on a spot on the bar and rubbed it like the stain went clear through to China. "She drops in."

"Often?"

He stopped rubbing. "Quite. But it's been a while since I've seen her around too."

She and Vince were both gone? "Were they a couple?"

"They've been here at the same time, but I'm not saying that amounts to anything. But Vince does have a couple of weaknesses—gambling and women."

That was becoming clear. "That last night he argued with Marilyn, was she here then?"

"Not sure."

"Any suggestions where I might find her?"

The bar door opened, and an elderly couple ambled to a booth. "Can't help you." Len grabbed a couple of menus from under the counter.

That was my cue to go. I scooted the stool back. "This is going to sound weird, but anyone around here had their hands in any accidents lately?"

He flung the rag over his shoulder. "Boy last week had his hand crushed at the mill."

"Anyone missing a finger?"

He grimaced. "No. Why? You find one missing its person?"

That was one way to put it. "No. Just curious. This being an industrial town and all." Nice save. Not.

He wrinkled his nose at me, probably glad I wasn't one of his usual customers. "Can't help you with that either."

Leaving my spritzer behind, I headed out. Vince had been gone for over three weeks. Lorraine, who was supposedly on vacation, hadn't been seen for a while either. My thoughts turned to my Margaritas in Mexico theory.

Vince could be fine and avoiding some rough people who liked to leave threats in the form of appendages. If he had scored on some wagers, it wasn't at the Tip Top playing slots or poker. Or with the pull-tabs from the bowling alley. The next best place for big winnings had to be at Portland Meadows. But first Mitz, who would be out of school soon.

The break would give me time to process what I'd learned about Vince, which wasn't much. All I had so far was a cranky bowling alley owner who didn't think much of him, a bartender who confirmed his gambling, a jilted girlfriend who may not have been looking for him after all, Lorraine who hadn't been seen for about the same timeframe as Vince, and a finger that may or may not have belonged to him. The dots were floating all around me. Now to get them to connect.

SEVEN

THE WASHINGTON SCHOOL for the Deaf off Grand Boulevard was a long brick building surrounded with evergreens and Maple trees that were almost completely leafed out. By mid-June they'd be lush and full. One of my favorite aspects of living in the Pacific Northwest was the greenery and this property was a perfect example of everything beautiful about the area.

I pulled into a snaking line of waiting parents and spotted Mitz sprinting out the front door. She saw my Triumph at the same time and aimed for the passenger side, her red curls bouncing behind her and her face beaming like a jack-o-lantern. I reached over and pushed the door open for her.

"Mama," she signed. "You surprised me."

"Thought you and me could grab some ice cream before I take you home, Ladybug. Sound good?" I signed.

She nodded with eyes wide. "Can Daddy come too?" She pointed to his car two spots back.

I glanced in my rearview mirror and sure enough, Jeff was there in his Subaru. My thoughts had been on the severed finger, Vince, and leaving a message for Stephanie to call when she could, so I hadn't noticed him pull behind. With a few cars ahead blocking us in, I got out. "He must not have gotten my message," I signed to Mitz, even though that didn't seem possible. "Get in, and I'll let him know what's going on."

Jeff rolled down his window and combed his fingers through his light brown hair as I approached.

I stuffed my hands in my pockets. "Didn't you get my text?"

He gave me a faint smile. "Came through a minute ago, but I was turning into the school by then. What's your plan?"

"Ice cream. Then I planned on dropping Mitz back with you after, if that's okay. I happened to be in the area."

"Nice. I'm free. I'll treat." His smile broadened through his mustache and dark full beard neatly trimmed to accent his rounded jaw.

"That's not necessary."

"I know. Sorry about butting in. I was going to call you anyway. We need to talk."

"About Mitz?" I asked, keeping my worry and defensiveness tamped down. Successful co-parenting with Jeff was a priority, but with our past, it was easy to expect the worst when Jeff wanted to talk.

"I'll see you at Benny's."

He gave me two thumbs up that he pushed away from his body. The sign for *follow me.* I was on his time by dropping in but my shoulders inched closer to my ears. It must be important if he wanted to talk to me.

In my Triumph, Floyd was greeting Mitz with wet kisses. She squealed and returned his nuzzles. Mitz then turned to signing stories with full animation of playground mishaps and her friend cheating off her test this morning. Between nods and responses, my thoughts turned to Vince and his gambling habits. Jeff had done some betting on the horses in the past. Having him join us might work out for us both if he could give me a better feel for the sport.

We pulled in front of Benny's, a fifties style malt shop, and filed into the small, but hustling space full of other kids with their parents who had the same idea. Mitz ordered her usual double decker rocky road with cherry syrup and sprinkles. I went with double peanut butter fudge and Jeff a scoop of vanilla. Waffle cones in hand, we found a corner booth. Mitz scooted onto the black vinyl seat first, and I joined her. Jeff sat across from us.

Mitz gave us the rest of her day's update. She had been deaf since birth, a result of Waardenburg syndrome that came from my father's side. In the beginning, I believed my faulty genes had ruined my girl's life. Instead, Mitz had learned to sign right away. Deafness wasn't a curse. It even did something that talking to each other didn't always achieve—one had to pay attention to converse. While our little group might have its share of problems, communicating wasn't one of them.

After a bit, Mitz focused on not letting her ice cream drip down her hand and I took advantage of the pause. "Do you remember Stephanie Burnotas?" I asked Jeff.

"Cute red head, of course I do."

We did all go to school together. "That's the one. She's still cute, and very pregnant."

He licked his cone. "Didn't she marry some guy named Brad?"

"Brandon."

"Right." He'd kept up with her more than I had.

"I took on a case this morning to find Vince Burnotas."

"Stephanie's dad?"

I nodded. "What can you tell me about betting on horses?" I asked while he was mid bite.

His elbows rested on the table. "A bit, but what does her dad missing and horse racing have anything to do with each other?"

Good question. I filled him in on the daily sheets in Vince's house. "Whether betting on the horses has anything to do with where he's gone off to, no clue, but he loves gambling. He has piles of opened pull-tabs in his living room and tons of dailies, simulcast and race schedules for the Meadows. He's kept what looks like stacks of what I believe are losing tickets, although I'm not sure how it works."

"That part's pretty straightforward. You bet on a single horse to win, place or show, or on a combination of horses to come in. When our dads went down there, I'd hear them talk about bookies and off book bets. It's very regulated these days. Oh, and you get a ticket, which if it's a loser is usually tossed on site after the race. The fact they're in his house and not stamped with something from the tracks, says to me they're probably all losers."

My stomach flipped. Out of all he'd said, I'd caught one thing. "Our dads gambled?"

Jeff chuckled. "Don't you remember them talking about their winnings?"

Nothing came to mind. "Was this before or after my mom died?"

"Before. After, I think your dad was pretty much all business."

Yes, he was. It bothered me that I didn't recall his gambling or winning. Prior to my mom passing away when I was fourteen, I did live the life of a self-involved teenager and with school, only helped him after class and on weekends. Only recently had I learned that he had his own secrets about his life. This could be another one of them. “Didn’t Arlene complain?” My ex-mother-in-law had an opinion on most things.

“You know she did, but our dads were a lot alike in that they danced to the beats of their own drums and she lived with that.”

Every other day I learned something new about the man whose footsteps I’d never fill and now about Jeff’s dad, Jack, too. It surprised me that Arlene, being so headstrong, would live with anything she didn’t like. It’s possible that’s who she’d become after Jack died. My dad being a maverick went without saying.

Jeff continued, “Well, I hope you find Vince. I don’t know much about him, but Stephanie’s a good girl. That’s a bummer that she’s going through this.”

“Me too.” Mentioning the severed finger wasn’t going to happen with Mitz next to me. Jeff had an overprotective streak. Divorced or not, he hadn’t been able to give up the idea that he was supposed to protect me. “I called the police in. There were some delinquent notices on his table, and I thought they should be involved.”

His eyebrows raised. “The police don’t show for delinquent notices. What aren’t you telling me?”

Having someone who knew me well could be a real bitch. “You’re always saying I’m not cautious enough. I’m following your advice.”

He lowered his chin.

“I learned some lessons during my last case, and I’m trying to be more careful,” I said, shoving the last bite of ice cream in my mouth and smiling.

“Fine, don’t tell me. Whatever it was must have set

you off or you'd never make that call." He wiped his mustache and mouth with a napkin.

Mitz yawned, a sign our conversation was not interesting to her. She finished her cone and left us to wash her hands. When the bathroom door shut behind her I said, "Your turn. What was so important you had to crash our girl time?"

Jeff crumpled the napkin in his hand. "I got a call from Linda yesterday."

My stomach curled. "Linda?"

He nodded, a crease etching the space between his eyes.

"Oh joy. How is her life going?"

He ignored my tone. "She's good."

"That's awesome." After their one-night-stand that ended our marriage, my former friend had taken off to California. "Is that it?"

"She has a son now."

She'd always wanted kids. Four to be exact. Two boys and two girls. "Wow, she got married. Good for her."

"No."

"No what?"

"She's not married."

"Oh. She have it with that boyfriend she was with when you slept with her?"

He didn't answer. His face turned white and he looked away.

My chest tightened at the implication. I signed, "You're the father?" I tapped my thumb on my forehead with enough force to make me wince.

He wouldn't make eye contact. "I don't know."

I couldn't breathe. "That's why she left town, isn't it?"

He plopped his elbows on the table and buried his face

in his hands and rubbed, trying to scour the truth out of his skin. "I guess. She says he's mine, but like you said, she had a boyfriend at the time. I demanded a DNA test and they did the swab last week."

"Smart. Good idea."

"It might turn out to be nothing."

Nothing was that easy in our lives. "How old is her son?"

"Year and a half." His frown said he'd already done the math.

I slunk back in the bench, stunned.

Mitz bounded back into the room. "I have homework, Daddy," she signed.

I forced a smile at our little girl. Jeff and I were divorced. Nearing two years now. This revelation shouldn't bother me, but it did. Time to get back on the case. To get to the Meadows before dark. To get far away from Jeff. Linda's name and the bombshell that her son, who might be Jeff's son, was information that I was going to have to think on. "Thank you for the date, Ladybug. Love you." I signed and ran my fingers through her strawberry curls, adoring the freckles that covered her rounded nose that resembled mine. She had Jeff's and Arlene's brown eyes. My father's strong chin.

"Miss you already," she signed.

"Miss you more."

We parted in the parking lot after I gave Mitz a bear hug. Ten minutes later, I was back on the Interstate and stuck in traffic. The monotony of inching along gave me time to think about Jeff's admission. His choices had consequences, which neither of us saw coming. The possibility that Mitz might have a half-sibling didn't go unnoticed. Were we all destined to live with the aftermaths from the poor decisions of the men and women in our lives?

My phone rang with a Washington area code and an unrecognized number. I punched speaker. "This is Kelly."

"Ms. Pruett, Detective Kuni here."

"Results already? That was fast."

"It doesn't take long to rule things out when the print is intact. Thought I'd let you know the finger we found, while decomposed, did not detach from Vince Burnotas."

An inkling of relief made its way in. "You say that like it was the finger's choice to move on."

"Ha, ha."

"Seriously, Vince had prints in the system?"

"Yes. He was booked for a trespassing charge."

The surprises never stopped. "Could that be relevant?"

"I'll check it out. It could be a day or two. The case was dismissed and has already been sent off-site. It will be nice when we go digital around here."

"Any idea who the finger does belong to?"

"Print didn't come back matching anyone in the system."

That didn't ease my worry. "The question is of course why Vince has a finger in his garbage can."

"Let me remind you again, this is an active investigation, Ms. Pruett. I'll expect you to share anything you find on Mr. Burnotas' whereabouts since I understand you've continued to look."

Bowling alley Chuck was a bit of a gossiper himself it seemed.

"Are we clear?" he asked.

"Absolutely." And with this new information, I felt more driven to find Vince. Whether that finger was being used to intimidate him, or he had an altercation and it ended up in the garbage, Vince might be on the run.

But there was an unsettling alternative to that. The guy missing the finger might have exacted some serious revenge. What if Vince had tried to get away and had been caught?

EIGHT

PORTLAND MEADOWS WAS right off Interstate 5. Several homeless camps made of tarps and grocery carts were within walking distance. Litter lined the main road all the way to the automotive supply store I passed to get there.

It had a parking lot the size of two football stadiums. Sandwiched between grey sky and cracked asphalt, shocks of grass reached for daylight. The spaces were marked with faded paint. The only redeeming feature of the venue was the view of Mt. Hood in its snowy glory which looked like a backdrop on a postcard. Heck of a setting for wasting one's hard-earned money.

In my thirty-two years, I'd never been to the Meadows. Jeff's revelation that our fathers had been was on my mind. It was another layer of things I hadn't known about my dad.

Jeff's situation was a reminder of that fact. Except we'd handle that revelation much different. There'd be no surprises. If he brought another family member into our lives, we'd tell Mitz and work through her reaction. Although I was getting too far ahead. Jeff's paternity test results weren't in and, for the moment, it didn't affect my life—or my case.

Parking near the entrance, I got out. The monstrosity of a dull beige building with a black ribbon painted along the top filled my view. On the face of the building it read *Portland Meadows* in huge red neon letters. Next to it was a galloping neon horse and the declaration that racing there had been alive and well since 1946.

With so many nearby gambling avenues available including cardrooms and casinos, I wouldn't expect horse racing around these parts to be a draw. Little did I know. The partially filled parking lot didn't reflect the true crowd humming with activity on the other side of the four double doors. They must bus these people in from all over town.

A poker room off to the side was clearly designated. In the middle, I had the pick of two bars. The Paddock Pub and Horseman's Circle, both full of people nursing drinks and staring at screens.

At least a hundred television sets were peppered throughout the large, cavernous space anchored by dingy cement floors. A wall of glass lined the track. Little old ladies hunched over racing agendas strewn in front of them filled long white tables. The sheer number of blue hairs suggested half those buses came from retirement homes.

Everyone had tickets in hand. The clientele ranged from pierced and grungy, to preened and tailored. Every TV cluster simulcasted a different race. A line of cashiers stood ready to cash in winning tickets, dressed in their green-polyester suits, vests, white shirts, and bow ties. They took the getting lucky and leprechaun look seriously there.

Despite the sounds of excitement, there was an air of desperation in the room. A string of self-serve bidding machines were parked against a wall. Piles of the same losing tickets I'd seen at Vince's place were stacked on the counters in between. Somehow, there had to be enough winners to give the gambler hope. I'd learned about that when training Floyd. Sporadic reinforcement they called it. Give them enough to believe there's a treat in play, and they'd be more likely to come to you. How many wins had Vince experienced to prompt him to keep buying the tabs piled in his house? To hear Chuck tell it, not many.

I scanned the room for a friendly face and spotted a woman at the lottery counter outside the slot room. This place had something for everyone.

The forty-something woman's tag read "Claire". She wore blue jeans and a teal ribbed tank top. Her boy cut blonde hair with jet black undertones framed an oval face, and flower tattoos wrapped her well-insulated arms. She had finished talking with a black man who towered over me by at least a foot and could bench press me with one arm. "Hi. I'm Kelly Pruett. I'm trying to find a customer who I believe spends time here."

"Oh honey, that would be a lot of these guys. Who ya looking for?"

I pulled the Christmas picture out of my jacket and handed it to her. "Vince Burnotas."

She studied the photo and flashed a quick smile. "That's Vinnie."

Her smile was a good sign. "Have you seen him?"

"Not today, but I've been on vacation for a couple of weeks. Spent some time with my sister in Vegas."

Traveling to the gambling mecca of the world from a day job at the tracks wouldn't have been my first choice. "Did you see him before you left?"

"Imagine I did. He was here most evenings, which is when I work. I do the late shift, three to close—that's eleven or midnight, depending on the day."

I tapped my fingers on the counter. If she'd been gone for two weeks, but remembered seeing him right before she left, then my timeline was off. "Was he ever with a woman? Maybe a Lorraine?"

"Not that I recall."

That didn't mean they weren't dating. He could prefer to bet on the horses alone. "You're sure you saw him right before your vacation?"

The towering black man had reappeared and hovered behind me. Claire caught his eye. "Need something quick, hon?"

"Turning in my Keno sheet."

She tsked at him like he should know better. "Cashiers do that, sweetie."

He nodded and left us to talk again. "Do you remember?" I prompted.

She closed her eyes. "There are so many regulars, sometimes it's hard to keep track."

I skimmed the premises again. "I didn't realize it was so popular."

She brightened. "This is nothing. Wait until the horses start running. End of September through first week of April, it's crazy town."

The fact people were there at all spending hard earned money equaled crazy town in my book. "When you last saw Vince, the horses were running then?"

Her memory was sparked by my question. "They were. In fact, I *didn't* see him the week before I left. I remember now because it was the last live run and he wasn't here. Thought that was odd. He's been a regular for quite a long time and he's always been here for the big races."

"You're positive about that?"

"Yes. It's a big deal. Always held on a weekend. Everyone dresses up. He enjoyed that day. Everyone does." She had a far off look in her eyes, then snapped her attention back to me. "Anyway, I haven't seen him since before then, but can't say exactly when."

Claire had helped me nail down the timeline with some certainty. Over three weeks ago now, Vince fell off the planet. He didn't show for the last racing day, and the night before that live race, he'd been in Riverview where he'd left Marilyn after an argument at the Tip Top bar. Wherever Vince went, it was that night. A retrace of his steps before then might narrow where he'd gone and how that severed finger fit in.

Thanking Claire for her time, I gave her a card and asked her to contact me if she thought of anything else that might help me find Vince. Before leaving the premises, I went into the slot room, curious about what the rest of the venue had to offer. The room was shaped like an upside down horseshoe. Everything I'd ever seen on the subject of horseshoes said if it wasn't nailed upright, it wouldn't hold in the luck. From a business standpoint, the house would count on someone's lack of that for a healthy bottom line.

Passing by a bank of flashing Wheel of Fortune and Lobstermania slots, I came out the other side closest to the track and a set of elevators. The building index reflected what occupied the various floors. My eyes settled on the one located on the top: Turf Club. I'd seen that before. On my phone, I retrieved the picture of Vince's credit card statement. Dated April 1 was a charge at the Turf Club for $532. That was only a month ago, and the week before the final race that Vince had missed. Somebody might remember him there.

The Turf Club occupied the entire sixth floor. Hunter green carpet covered the space, and the floor to ceiling windows provided a perfect view of the dirt track. Red and gold booths lined the walls. The faded fabric looked original from 1946. White linen tablecloths covered the tables. The place probably improved as the night set in, the lack of light and focus hiding the flaws. Booze might help too.

It was nearing evening, and the place was empty of customers, but the wait staff hustled through setting up tables, filling salt and pepper shakers, and lighting oil candles at each of the tables. A weeknight couldn't see a lot of visitors during off season, but they scurried about as if the place would be full soon.

The maître d', a lanky white-haired man, dressed in a black tux approached and looked me over with his assessment ending in a tsk. That was the second head to toe inspection in one day. With the diversity of gamblers downstairs, I wasn't convinced the restaurant had a strict dress code, but his demeanor had me feeling underdressed in my usual jeans and light-gray Nike running jacket.

"Yes, ma'am, may I help you?" he asked.

I pulled Vince's picture out of my purse. "I'm trying to find this man. I understand he had dinner here last month."

He glanced at the photo and then the room. "He doesn't appear to be here this evening."

"Do you recognize him?"

"Vince, yes," he said slowly.

"Can you tell me the last time you saw him?"

"He only came to visit us during celebratory meals." He paused for a few seconds. "He was by no means a regular."

He talked so slow I searched for a speed up button. "As in he didn't have reasons to celebrate often?"

"Correct."

"Was he usually celebrating alone?"

"No."

"Who was he with?"

"Couldn't say."

"You mean you don't know, or won't tell me?"

He didn't answer, but his eyebrow arched.

If it raised any higher, it might freeze there. At least then his highbrow attitude would make sense in this dated place. "Does that mean yes?"

"For the privacy of our guests, I don't believe that is something I can answer."

"Vince is missing. Has been for a few weeks. I'm trying to retrace his footsteps. A credit card statement shows he was here the first of April. By the size of the bill, he must have been celebrating."

"Ah yes, if I remember correctly, that was the day Bodacious Tatas brought it home."

My face warmed. "Who has bodacious tatas?"

"Not who has, but who is, ma'am. A long shot, and a few of our guests had placed bets on her. It was glorious to see the excitement."

A long shot payout had to be good. "How much did people win?"

"Guests don't talk about their winnings. But Vince bought a round for everyone in the restaurant."

"Spendy."

"Quite. But like I said, we didn't see Vince here often." He glanced at his watch. "Must get back to my duties. Anything else I can help you with?"

"Sure you can't tell me who he was with that night?"

He smiled and with a single finger salute, turned and

walked away. The dining room staff had cleared leaving no one else to ask.

My Fitbit read five o'clock. Traffic home would be a mess and I'd be stuck in it if I didn't get moving. I headed to the elevators assessing what I'd learned. Vince had won some money a week before the final race of the season and before he went missing. He didn't pay his rent, but he bought rounds for an entire restaurant. The man had a problem—money management and a severed finger in his garbage the most glaring.

When the elevator opened, the black man from downstairs crowded the opening. I smiled. "You coming out?"

"Taking the scenic route." He stepped back. "Meant to get off on the previous floor."

"Hate when that happens." I got in and hit "G" for the ground floor.

As the doors closed, the car moved down. The man reached around me and slapped the stop button with his massive hand. I flinched and jerked away from him, my blood pressure shooting skyward.

NINE

MY HEART AND the elevator jolted to a stop at the same time. Followed by silence. Where was the alarm sounding a problem? Because there was a definite problem. My eyes flitted to the control panel and the green *call* button below the one labeled *run*. I flung my arm out to smash either of them. The man's hand wrapped around my forearm before it reached. The hairs on the back of my neck prickled at the same time my insides turned to jelly.

Whipping around, I broke his grip, and pressed myself against the wall closest to the panel. Without breaking eye contact, I yanked out the cannister of pepper spray inside my purse and aimed it at him. "Don't touch me again."

"Whoa." He stepped back. "No need to get violent."

The thud of my heartbeat pounded in my ears. Enough heat radiated off my body that I could have fried an egg. The walls closed in. "What do you expect when you trap someone?"

"Just want to talk, that's all," he said.

"Heck of a way to get my attention." I'd felt trapped once before. Panic induced hormones soared through my limbs at the memory of what had happened that night. I reined in the reaction to start hyperventilating and paced my breathing. This time I wasn't completely alone. People were above and below me—perhaps even on the other side of the metal doors. Although that didn't help me now. I pointed the pepper spray at his eyes. "Who are you?"

"Tyrone. Heard you asking about Vince."

"So?"

"What do you want with him?" he asked.

He should have joined my conversation with Claire if he was so interested. Telling him that might not be one of my better ideas. Tyrone didn't make any more moves my direction. That didn't stop my heart from continuing to crash in my chest. "His family hasn't heard from him and they're afraid he's in trouble."

He frowned. "What kind of trouble?"

"The kind where he's not answering the phone."

He folded his thick arms over his barrel chest. His foot planted against the wall, he stood on one leg and leaned back on his shoulder. "What have you found so far?"

"Enough to bring me here and get you asking twenty questions, and not enough to have made actual contact yet. Why do you care anyway?"

He gave me the once over, which sent a shudder through me. "I suggest you stop looking."

My mouth went dry. "Why?"

"Don't want you in my way."

"Are you trying to find him too?" That didn't sound like a good thing.

"I'm not asking. I'm telling. It's my job to make sure you listen."

Had he also been charged with placing a severed finger in Vince's garbage? My stomach flipped at the likelihood I was standing close to someone capable of mutilating another human being. I straightened, trying to stretch another inch out of my 5'5 frame. Trying for bravery. Tyrone didn't know anything about me or what was in my best interest. Or how giving me direct orders only fueled my desire to get to the bottom of things. But

I wasn't that stupid, or that brave, to debate those points in this small space. I shrugged with more nonchalance than I felt. "Whatever."

He cocked his head to the side. "You're one of those."

"One of what?"

He shook his head. "Fine. We'll visit my boss on your way out. Maybe he'll be more persuasive."

I didn't see an army to assist him. "I'm not going anywhere with you." I kept my spray leveled at his face.

"Don't get yourself all worked up. He's downstairs in plain view."

Tyrone was trying to intimidate me to do what he wanted. Obviously, Vince had gotten involved with some bad guys. To what extent, was the question. "If you're looking for Vince, we can help each other. When did you see him last?"

Tyrone didn't answer.

"He owed you money, right?"

He tucked his chin towards his chest.

"I'd heard he won some big race a month ago. Guess he had quite the celebration upstairs."

Tyrone's face grew stern but he made no sudden moves.

My teeth were clenched to keep them from chattering. I cleared my throat. "You don't seem happy about that."

He leaned in. "Blowing someone else's cash is never a good idea."

I forced myself to hold my ground and kept my spray aimed at him. Confirming what Detective Kuni had suggested didn't feel like a victory. Vince owing a loan shark wasn't a good idea on any level.

"Hmm." He lowered his foot. "You spray that shit in here and we're both going to feel it."

I'd hold my breath until I turned blue if I had to. "I'll take my chances." Despite my best effort, my voice shook.

He reached around me and punched the start button. The elevator lurched to life. I willed it to move faster, never taking my eyes off his. When the doors opened, I thought of bee-lining it out to my car.

Tyrone's large hand rested on my arm. "Why don't you put that spray away now. We wouldn't want anyone getting the wrong impression. Would we?" He applied pressure for emphasis.

My pulse quickened before I heard the simulcast races and cheers coming from nearby patrons. Tyrone wouldn't do anything in public. With limited choices, I might as well find out what the boss had to say about Vince Burnotas. I tucked the cannister in my pocket.

Tyrone steered me in the direction of an isolated corner table where an older man had dailies spread in front of him. He wore a tan Members Only style jacket I'd seen in a few retro shops, a tweed flat cap, and an unlit cigar hung from the side of his mouth. A tumbler of amber-colored liquid, with a pick skewering a cherry and orange, sat in front of him. The man liked whiskey sours. My dad enjoyed those on occasion.

He nodded at Tyrone, who stepped away leaving me at the table. "Please sit down," the man said. "My apologies if my associate scared you. That was not my intent."

I didn't believe that for a second. My jaw ached from clenching my teeth so hard.

When I didn't sit, the man stood and pulled out my chair. "Please."

Despite my instincts to run, something about his calm demeanor commanded compliance. Tyrone watching my every move was an influence too. My legs wobbled from the receding adrenalin and I plopped into the chair, clutching my purse in front of me. "Tyrone tells me you don't want me looking for Vince. Why?"

He studied me carefully.

I resisted the urge to fidget, keeping locked on his eyes which reminded me of the game of whoever blinks first loses.

"Who do I have the pleasure to be speaking with?" he finally said, plucking the cigar from his mouth and resting it on top of the glass.

I didn't reach to give him a business card. The less he knew of me, the better. "I'm a PI. I'm assuming from Tyrone's directive not to look for Vince, that you're already doing that. We could help each other." I didn't expect he'd go for it, but I had a better chance at getting more information if he thought we were on the same team.

He cocked his head an inch to one side like I was joking. "I assure you, we don't need your assistance. I'm certain Tyrone communicated you'd only be in the way."

"He has. Only problem is I've been hired to find Vince for his family. I take my obligations seriously."

He leaned back in his chair and his frown said he was deciding on how much he wanted me to know. He was going to have to tell me something other than stay away if he expected any level of cooperation on my part. "Vince owes me money. We had an arrangement. If you're poking around, you might upset the balance."

"The balance of what?"

He smiled again. "I don't have time, or how do you say, the inclination to debate the specifics. My position with regards to your lack of involvement stands."

Tyrone stood at the bar; his eyes had never left me.

Unsure of how much bravado I could fake while my insides agitated like a washing machine, I had to try. If I offered what I knew, the old man might soften. "Here's the deal. I don't know where Vince has gone. Sounds like you don't either?"

His blank expression didn't give anything away.

"I do know that nearly a month ago, he left a bar in Riverview and hasn't been seen since. Is it possible he took off with these big winnings from the previous race?"

Nothing. The man was Fort Knox in terms of trying to get information or reading him.

"You think something else has happened to him?" I asked.

His face hardened. "You're not making it easy to be a good guy here."

While this man went against what I imagined a mobster to be—dressed in black, matching tie, and hair slicked back—a good guy seemed a far stretch. "Why?"

He itched his ear and popped the cigar back in his mouth. His face relaxed. "You're Roger Pruett's kid, aren't you?"

Had Claire given me up? I glanced back at the lottery counter. She was nowhere in sight. How did he know my dad? I forced a smile. "And?"

He rocked his head back and forth. "Your father and I go way back."

Was my dad's connection to organized crime yet another part of his life I'd been oblivious about? How much more was there? My stomach hurt. "How exactly?"

"We had an understanding. Let's say I owed him. Telling you to back off is my repayment of that debt."

"He passed away nearly two years ago."

"I'm aware."

"Who are you?" Why had he been tracking my dad? I had to swallow the lump of fear rising in my throat again.

Tyrone had crossed the room and stood at the old man's side. Had he made a signal I hadn't seen?

"You've been warned," the man said. "Now go." His tone left no room to argue.

I scooched the chair back and got to my feet. In one step, Tyrone was next to me, ready to be my escort. My legs were unsteady, but I wouldn't let them know they'd gotten to me. "I can't promise I won't keep looking. But I will stay out of your way."

He glanced at the table, then back at me. "Your father was a smart man. He learned to work within the system. Not against it. I suggest you do the same."

He did not mean the legal system because nothing about him or Tyrone suggested they worked within the law. Tyrone's hand gripped my elbow. I forced away a shudder as he moved me towards the door.

Outside, Tyrone said, "My boss is serious. Don't get in our way."

The fresh air restored some of my confidence. I wanted to tell him that I didn't take orders from thugs. Antagonizing him wasn't a good idea. Too much anyway. "Like I told him, no promises."

"You're a lot sassier than you should be. This isn't lottery tickets and pull-tabs, we're talking. Horse racing is serious business. You don't screw around with the people here. Got it?"

His lottery ticket and pull-tab comment confirmed my earlier suspicion. I couldn't fight the tremor that rippled through me stripping away any imagined bravery I had with it. Tyrone had been in Vince's house and might have been responsible for that finger. If these men were willing to sever body parts, what else were they willing to do? How did my father work with these kinds of people? The continuing ache in my stomach didn't want the answer to that. "Loud and clear. I'm not trying to screw anyone."

"You're like the rest of them." He turned toward the door.

"Rest of who?"

"The women in Vince's life. None of you know when to quit." He'd turned back around, staring at the parking lot.

I followed his gaze. "Is one of those women here?"

He lifted his chin in the direction of a car backing out of a far-off parking space. "Crazy bitch was here asking about him before you. Better not see her again either."

Who else was looking for Vince—Marilyn, Lorraine, or someone else? When I spun around to ask, Tyrone had gone inside and the glass door had closed behind him. Afraid she'd get away, I sprung down the stairs and towards the late-model green Chevy.

The car had long cleared the stall and was headed out of the parking lot, but I caught the license plate. BCP353. I repeated it over and over in my head while sprinting to my Spitfire.

"Hold on, Floyd," I said, as the engine sputtered. "Come on." It turned over and started. We accelerated to the edge of the lot where it met the main road. No cars in sight. The Chevy had disappeared. "Damn it."

Floyd perked his ears and I ruffled them. "We're okay, buddy." I gave him a cookie from my pocket and he turned and flopped back into the seat. I contemplated which direction she might have gone. I opted for north on the Interstate toward Riverview. When a few miles later there were no signs of the Chevy, I exited and U-turned in the direction for home. I'd run a check on the plate from there and see if I could find out who was looking for Vince that way.

As I settled into my seat, the fear dissipated the further I got away from the tracks. But the words of Len the bartender were stuck in my head. Vince had said his luck was running out. Had Tyrone and his boss made that happen sooner than later?

TEN

Even though I lived alone half the time, coming home rated the best part of my day. This time I came home to my ex-mother-in-law and neighbor, Arlene, standing in the middle of my driveway. She didn't look her sixty plus years. Her pixie cut blonde hair framed her narrow face. Without trying, her style exceeded anything I'd ever manage dressed in her trim boot-cut jeans, a white linen button down, its arms cuffed at her elbows against a chocolate cashmere sweater. The reason for her current visit hung from the crook of her index finger.

"Beautiful," I said, exiting my car with Floyd at my heels. "But you didn't have to bring us flowers."

"It's a fuchsia, dear. It needs plenty of shade and water. Thought you could use something to care for when Mitz isn't with you," she said as a way of greeting me.

Arlene and I had made a lot of progress over the past year in our relationship, but sometimes I sensed she was dropping hints that she didn't approve of my parenting arrangement with her son. I was going to hope that wasn't the case. "I'm not great with flowers; I'm not sure you want to leave that with me." With plenty of things in my world to fail at already, I didn't need one more. My fingers were crossed that honesty would inspire her to take the plant home with her.

"I'll come by and check on it once a week for you. Feed it with fertilizer when needed."

No such luck. I should have been appreciative. She had kept me well-fed and cared for while I healed from my gunshot wound. She'd even offered to help me out in the office at R&K Investigations. But I didn't go there often myself these days, so I wasn't sure how that would work out. And I wouldn't put her in harm's ways, despite her comments often containing small slights or my tendency to push back. Truth was, Mitz bound us. We were family. We even liked each other and on some levels found common ground, but those levels were sometimes buried under layers of mud, and history. "I'll keep it here in front so you can do that."

"Southern exposure?" She raised a hand to her chest. "Oh no. I'll put it on the east side of your house."

"Wherever's fine."

She nodded. "When's your sister coming back? She mentioned she loved gardening. She could help you with it."

"Good question." She'd only hung out in the weeks right after my last case ended. She and Arlene had hit it off, better than Arlene and I did on most days. "No idea. Last I heard she was in Seattle. By the way," I said, aiming for a new subject, "I recently learned my dad and Jack liked to gamble. How'd I miss that bit of info?"

She waved her hand. "They did, here and there. Nothing serious. You and Jeff would have been off gallivanting around together when they were doing that. You two used to be inseparable, you know."

A reminder of our past. "Could be. I was under the impression they spent some time at the Meadows racetracks. That true?"

She nodded. "Roger sometimes took Jack along when

he was on a case. They landed there occasionally after a few of their bets paid off."

Their investigating together was a new twist. The surprises never stopped. I was about to ask if either of them had mentioned an old man at the tracks, when Kyle, driving his 4x4, pulled behind my Spitfire.

Arlene frowned. "I'd wanted to invite you to join the family for dinner. Looks like you have other plans." She set the fuchsia down. "East side. Don't forget."

Before I could respond, she set the plant on the ledge near the stairway to her house, letting the flowers and foliage cascade over the rocks, and climbed the stairs without greeting Kyle. He'd been over many times, but she rarely conversed with him. Acknowledging him might make him too real for her. I only needed to see his wavy blond hair, green eyes, and beach body to remember how real he was.

"Hey, stranger." Kyle climbed out of his truck and retrieved a grocery bag from the seat.

"Dinner?" I asked.

"Ribs and salads from the deli."

I almost said *I love you* as the day's events started to dissolve out of my shoulders. "The way to a woman's heart."

"And self-preservation. After Mitz leaves from the weekend, your cupboards are bare."

"Cute and smart." I rubbed his arm.

He pumped his eyebrows and we both laughed.

On our way into the house, I hung the flower basket near my front door. It was early May. Southern exposure shouldn't be too harsh this time of year. Besides, I'd move it before Arlene checked on it for resuscitation purposes.

Inside, we unpacked dinner. Two cups of kibble in a

bowl for Floyd, a plate full of barbecue smothered pork and salad for me and Kyle, and we were settled at the dining table chatting about his day. When we were almost through, I filled him in about Stephanie coming by and my trip to Riverview. "Are you familiar with a Detective Kuni?"

"He's an old timer if I remember right. We've had a few jurisdictional cases where the crime was committed up north, but the perp used Portland as an escape route."

I nodded. "He knew my dad and even had a case with him at some point, although I don't recall his name coming up. Seems like a good guy."

"I've heard the same. I'm sure your dad worked with a lot of different people you might not be aware of. It's the nature of the business to have connections and associates to help with information."

Is that what Tyrone and his boss were? "With me in school and his tendency to keep things to himself, I'm sure that's true." Whether reasonable or not, at one time I thought my dad had shared everything with me. Cases with detectives in other jurisdictions and potentially a mobster, indicated he clearly hadn't.

"Why'd you run into him? You find out something about Stephanie's dad you haven't shared yet?" His eyebrow arched.

He'd experienced firsthand my downplaying or omitting information. This wasn't one of those times. I gave Kyle the rundown of the daily sheets and losing tickets.

"You found pull-tabs in his house?"

"Yeah, I don't get what they're all about, but he had a bunch of them scattered on the dining table and in drawers. It's weird to me that he didn't just throw the losers away."

His brow furrowed. "Not only that. Pull-tabs are generally played in the bar. They're like Keno. People play while they're eating and collect their winnings right then. It wouldn't be normal to bring them home. Or to collect the duds."

"Huh," I said. Why had he then?

"Is that why you called Detective Kuni?"

I grimaced at the image that popped into my head. "No. I found a severed finger in the garbage can."

Kyle stopped with his mouth on the rib and lowered it to the plate. "Stephanie's dad's?"

"Vince. No. They've already determined that part. They're not sure whose though. Since the prints didn't match anyone in their database, they're running DNA tests, but those could take a while."

"Has the detective officially made it a missing persons case?"

"Possible assault. I get the feeling he's contemplating whether Vince removed that finger off someone, or whether it was planted there as a warning."

He crumpled his napkin and set it next to his plate. "Who would be warning Vince?"

I launched into Marilyn's drop-in that led me to the bowling alley and learning about the falling out between Vince and Chuck. "There might be more to the story I don't know yet, but he's not my first choice."

"Did Kuni have an opinion?"

Kyle wasn't going to like it, but I knew he could handle it. Unlike Jeff. "He thinks it's consistent with organized crime."

His eyes narrowed in concern. "Vince was involved with the mob?"

I didn't look at him. He wouldn't be happy that my

path had crossed with such shady characters, but my ability to be honest with him was one thing I counted on. "It's a possibility. The Meadows was my last stop. That's where I met a couple of men that I'm pretty sure fit that description."

He leaned back in his chair, folded his arms over his chest, and flung one leg over the other. "Busy day."

I nodded.

"I've heard of the mob using body parts to make their point, but why would those particular men be involved with Vince?" he asked.

"He owes them money. And while I didn't come right out and ask, Tyrone's reference to pull-tabs and lottery tickets made me think he'd been in Vince's house."

"Tyrone is one of the men?"

"Yeah. Big black burly guy. I didn't get his last name. The other is an older man, and he's clearly the boss. Any chance you could find out more about who they are for me?"

"Meadows isn't in my patrol area, but I know who does that beat. I'll touch base with him."

"Thank you. Just please be discreet. I get the feeling they wouldn't like me asking questions about them."

Instead of meeting Kyle's concerned stare, I focused on my plate, taking the last bite of salad. The whole thing had me on edge, but I'd been hired to do a job. Even if I'd run through that first three hundred already, it had become more than that to me. I wanted to help Stephanie fix things with her dad. Something I'd never be able to do with my own.

"What I don't get," I said, "is Vince had won big on a race before he disappeared. Why he wouldn't pay them off and keep Tyrone and his boss off his back doesn't make sense to me."

"He could have owed several people money and Tyrone and his friend were at the bottom of that list."

"Those two at the bottom of anyone's list doesn't seem likely." But if Kyle was right, how would I even begin to find who else Vince might owe? My cell phone rang. Stephanie. I wiped my hands on my napkin and answered. "Hey. Thanks for calling me back. How are you feeling?"

"You called me?" she asked.

"Yeah, on my way back from Riverview."

"I didn't hear it. Guess I slept all afternoon. My blood pressure is through the roof and I've been nauseous. But I just got a call from Detective Kuni." Her voice cracked.

"What's wrong?"

"They've found his car submerged off Gee Creek Road."

My heart squeezed. "Your dad's?"

Silence.

I closed my eyes. "I'm so sorry." The day my mom had died in a car accident flooded back. She'd been driving down Marine Drive along the river when she lost control. Her car floated a mile toward the ocean. I breathed through the ache, shoved the emotions deep, and forced my focus back to Stephanie.

She cleared her throat. "They aren't saying that it's him. They want me to identify the body. I told them physically I can't do it." She sniffed. "I asked if they could use fingerprints. They said no." Another sniffle. A long pause. "Kelly, I can't go."

The desperation in her voice clutched my heart. Kyle, who could hear her, nodded before I even asked the question. "I'll do it, Steph. My friend, Kyle, is here and we'll drive up."

"God, thank you. I really appreciate it."

My chest tightened at what we'd find. "It may be that someone stole his vehicle and that's not even him."

"You think that's a possibility?" Her voice raised an octave.

Even after finding the finger and learning about his gambling habits I wanted to believe that. "I do. I'll check it out and let you know where we're at. But Steph, you need to tell Brandon about hiring me."

She sighed. "He's going to be upset."

My hand tightened on the phone. "You tell him you have a right to know where your father is. I'll tell him for you if you need my help with that." I wasn't in the mood for the Brandons of the world who thought they should run everything their wives did.

She must have harnessed some of my strength because she said, "You're right. I'll tell him."

Kyle met my eye as I promised Stephanie I'd call with any updates and clicked off. "You sure you don't mind taking a road trip with me and Floyd?"

He already had our plates in his hands and headed to the kitchen. "Right behind you."

ELEVEN

COWLITZ COUNTY CORONER'S office was a cold, stone-gray building, its visual offering no reprieve from the travesties and heartbreak inside. Even the red and brown bushes planted in the same reddish barkdust surrounding the structure was depressing. Not one spring blossom in sight. Arlene would never approve and I'd agree. If my day job required coming to this place on the regular, I'd find another career. Like coffee barista, a position I would embrace at the moment.

While Kyle, Floyd and I had crammed into the Spitfire and made the drive to Riverview, Stephanie had called Detective Kuni to let him know that we would be viewing the body. Once we'd arrived and got inside the building, I made introductions.

Detective Kuni reached out and shook Kyle's hand. "Always nice to meet a fellow officer. Wish it was under better circumstances. Follow me."

As we navigated the maze of Formica-floored halls, the echo of our footsteps filled the empty space. Until now, I'd never had an opinion about the hollow and ominous sound hard floors like these made. "Stephanie said the body was found submerged in his car," I said as we rounded a corner and traversed another hallway.

"A few miles out of town on Gee Creek Road. A post will be performed after you identify him."

"Post?" I asked.

"That's what we call an autopsy. Postmortem exam."

Kyle said, "Foul play?"

Detective Kuni lifted his palms. "Hard to say at this point. Car has been impounded as evidence and we're making our way through that. The body had begun decomposing, but we lucked out. Mountain run off is feeding the rivers so they haven't started their warmup."

"How long you think he was there?" I asked.

"A few weeks, max."

The timeline was panning out to about the time Vince had left the Tip Top Tavern in his car. Had he headed out to Gee Creek at that point? I was getting too far ahead since I hadn't confirmed it was Vince on the table. "Will he be recognizable?"

"You'll have to tell me. We find it easier to rely on dental records and such, but that can be time consuming and we don't have a place to start. Testing for DNA will take at least a week if there isn't a backlog, which we can use as confirmation. This is our first course of action."

"We're reviewing pictures, correct?" Kyle asked.

"Figured it would be easier to have you identify the actual body," Detective Kuni said.

He meant because we wouldn't fall apart like family members, he wasn't going to waste the time to take photos and shove us in a conference room with a grief counselor. Fine by me. Identifying the body quick and getting out of here worked. "How about fingerprints?"

"Unattainable at this point."

My lip curled. That could mean the skin had come off the bones. I was glad they hadn't explained that to Stephanie when she asked them to use fingerprint identification. "I'm guessing they're all intact. The fingers I mean."

"Yes."

Of course they were. The detective had already determined the severed digit didn't belong to Vince. If this victim had been shy one, I wouldn't even be here. My thoughts rambled. I did not want it to be Stephanie's dad—or anyone's dad.

We approached the exam room. "Okay, let's do this," I said.

Detective Kuni reached into his pocket and handed us face masks. "You'll want these."

I pulled the elastic bands over my ears and gave Kyle a look that said *take me out of here*. He only nodded. Stephanie needed me to do this. Escaping wasn't on the multiple choice.

Holding my breath, I followed the detective into the stark white room, made even brighter with the blinding overhead lights. My skin prickled as the AC blasted from a corner ceiling vent. A stainless-steel circular saw I'd never want used on me or someone I loved, rested on a nearby metal pushcart along with an array of other autopsy tools. While it wouldn't matter with me dead, the entire idea of that saw made me shudder. Except with the organ donor notation on my license, there would be no avoiding it forever.

I blinked a few times, trying to distract my brain which babbled on like a raging brook. A small Asian woman dressed in blue scrubs stood next to a body draped with a white sheet laid out on a hard gurney.

"This is Dr. Chen." Detective Kuni introduced us.

She gave a knowing nod. We didn't shake hands. How many times had she remained calm and professional while conducting an autopsy, or consulting victims' loved ones who'd had their hearts ripped from their chest?

My attention returned to the lump beneath the ghostly

sheet. Dr. Chen pulled it back as far as the man's shoulders. My body tensed, not wanting to see more than necessary. If his bloated face was an indicator of the rest, I'd lose the dinner stirring in my stomach. Gray hair scarcely covered the man's head, with the slightest amount of black on the sideburns. Like Vince—or countless other older men. Only one way to confirm.

"Can I see his teeth?" I asked.

Detective Kuni gave Dr. Chen the go ahead and with gloved hands, she lifted his lips to reveal a set of crooked incisors. They were like those that formed Vince's smile. To be sure, I pulled the Christmas picture Stephanie had given me from my pocket and compared the two. I nodded. "It's him."

"Vince Burnotas?"

I nodded again.

"You sure?" Detective Kuni asked.

"No doubt." My legs wobbled with the full realization that Vince Burnotas was no longer a missing person's case. Had Tyrone and his boss warned me away from trying to find Vince because they already knew? Had I been trapped in an elevator with Vince's killer?

KYLE AND I sat on dingy striped cushioned chairs across from Detective Kuni in the cramped reception area. The city's office staff had long clocked out and we had the lobby to ourselves. My stomach hadn't recovered. Even the thought of my go-to peanut butter made me queasy.

"What is the status of the case at this point?" Kyle asked.

"I'm approaching it as suspicious. At least until Dr. Chen and her team make their full assessment. The higher ups say we don't have the time or resources to dedicate unless something solid comes back. The initial report by the Traffic Division has deemed it an accident, but they're still finishing their part."

Processing what I'd seen, Kyle and the detective's muffled voices faded. The idea of breaking the news to Stephanie that her father was dead looped in my head. She'd be devastated. With her blood pressure already on the rise, the information could send her into premature labor.

"Don't you think?" Kyle nudged my arm.

"Huh?"

Detective Kuni's eyes crinkled and he pursed his lips. He'd had to relay facts like these countless times. It could never get easier. I wasn't blood to Vince and Stephanie, but they'd been a thread in the tapestry of my life. I knew Stephanie at a time when our fathers were heroes in our lives. The men we idolized. Counted on. A frayed and fragile thread, but there, nonetheless.

"That he should call you when the post is complete?" Kyle said.

"Please." I nodded, refocusing on the conversation. "What do you know so far? You mentioned your Traffic Division, and that he was found in Gee Creek?"

"Right. It's a smaller creek that feeds into the Cowlitz River watershed. Gee Creek Road runs above it and parallel. There's a portion where a steep embankment drops off. There's no guardrail due to an earlier accident last winter and the repair order hadn't been completed. That's where Mr. Burnotas left the road. The creek is often deep in that section in early April. His vehicle would have submerged immediately."

My nerves twanged at the idea of Vince careening toward the water. Thinking of him alive, panicked, banging on the window, had me shifting in my seat.

"He fell asleep at the wheel?" Kyle asked.

"Quite possibly. Traffic hasn't found any skid marks from Mr. Burnotas' vehicle or any others. Also possible that alcohol was involved since he was last seen at the bar, which would have made nodding off at the wheel more likely."

Not being able to find Vince for the past weeks appeared to be answered by the car accident. But the accident didn't answer his whereabouts before that when Stephanie couldn't get a hold of him and was leaving messages on his phone. "How did you find him?"

"It's in the area where a casino and waterpark are slated to go in. One of the dump truck drivers headed to the construction site saw a glimmer of metal when the sun hit the water as he drove by. Upon inspection, he realized it was a car."

"Vince supposedly drove for a company after he'd left his bowling alley job. Did the guy who found him recognize him? Was it the same company that Vince worked for?"

Detective Kuni shook his head. "The man who discovered him, Dylan Schaefer, works for Enterprise. He said he'd never seen him before. He was pretty shaken up. So much that the poor guy found a tree and lost his lunch."

What I'd seen of Vince was a cleaned-up version. "I bet." My mind went to the mechanic named Dylan at the bowling alley. A bowling alley maintenance man wouldn't be driving a dump truck. There had to be more than one Dylan in Riverview. "What's next? I assume you'll notify Stephanie?"

He swiped his thumb on the side of his nose. "You're right on protocol. Normally we would do a personal notification. In this case, she lives out of our jurisdiction.

If I can't get someone at the local precinct to assist, I'll go tonight."

"I could do it," I offered, the memory of my own father lying dead in his office hitting me. An orange-sized lump lodged in my throat. "I want to do it." Not really. What was I thinking? Why would I offer to deliver bad news?

He looked at Kyle. "You accompany her?"

"Sure."

He thought about it for a second. "That'll work. It might be easier coming from you anyway."

Too late to back out now. It wouldn't be easier to hear about it from me or anyone else. "I'll do my best."

"Good. Just be prepared. Grief can take many forms." He stood, stuffing his hands in his pockets. "I'll keep you apprised of any developments. While it looks like the poor guy ran off the road, if the coroner says different, I'll need to interview her. In the meantime, we'll wait for the post results and I'll start my investigation locally."

Kyle and I stood. "You don't expect the tests to tell you much in the way of blood alcohol, correct?" Kyle asked, showing his knowledge of forensics and the time limits of how long things lasted in the blood. An area I didn't know much about. I reached for his hand to steady myself.

"No. The window is forty-eight hours to get a decent blood alcohol reading, a week if we're lucky with the cool water conditions. We're looking more for time of death, and of course any indicators that Mr. Burnotas met up with foul play."

"The severed finger doesn't concern you?" I said.

"It does. But as mentioned before, it's not an uncommon tactic if Vince was involved in gambling, either illegally or legally, which the tickets and daily sheets suggest. However, unless the autopsy surprises us, Vince Burnotas died in a car accident."

"I spent some time at the racetracks this afternoon and ran into a couple of guys that he owed money to. I'm pretty sure one of them could have planted that finger to scare Vince, but I don't have any proof of that."

Detective Kuni frowned. "Thought you were going to keep me updated."

While the detective was slightly older, something about him reminded me of my dad. His look of disappointment rattled me. "I ran out of time before the call came from Stephanie."

He nodded. "Did you see anyone the finger might have belonged to while you were there?"

Would have been nice if it had been that easy. "No stubbies to be found."

Kyle gave me a side-ways glance.

My comment was inappropriate, a sad attempt to dispel the shock I felt. "I mean, I didn't make the rounds and shake everyone's hands to confirm, but I looked. Believe me."

The detective's eyes brightened. He got my humor. Those eyes grew serious. "Everything points to this being an accidental death, even if Vince was in deep. It might be time to close your file on this one."

I didn't respond and followed Kyle out. The facts of Vince's crash did suggest an accident, which presented me with a choice. I had been hired by Stephanie to find her father, and he'd been found. Case over. Except despite the detective's and his team's thoughts, Vince's death didn't sit right with me. Besides not calling his only daughter back, why had he been out on a backroad that led to nowhere? Stephanie would want to know the answer to that question.

We stopped at a Mini Mart and grabbed two black coffees before heading back to Portland. On the drive, I caressed Floyd's ears. Kyle and I rode in silence, lost in our own thoughts, until we crossed into Oregon and Kyle said, "You want to head straight to Stephanie's place?"

"Don't you have to work graveyard?"

"I'm on at midnight. I've got time."

I gave him a small smile, his presence grounding me. "I'm sure she's going crazy inside about now, so let's go. But if you don't mind, would you wait in the car?"

He reached over and put his hand on my leg. "If you want."

The warmth of his hand would have stirred my desire for him if I weren't about to deliver such horrible news. "I know her grief all too well and I'd rather deliver it alone. Because she doesn't know you..."

"Understandable," he said as I stared out the window. "You okay?"

I was many things in this moment. Okay wasn't one of them. I took a long drink of coffee. "I'm not as certain as Detective Kuni that it was an accident."

"Because of the guys at the track?"

"That and the circumstances. He's at the bar with his girlfriend, Marilyn. He tells her at some point before their blow out he's meeting someone later. After he storms out, he doesn't go home. At least not for long. While I don't know how Vince lived every day, at first glance, nothing seemed out of place—except for the finger in the garbage. His clothes are untouched, his bills are on the table, his medicines are in the cabinet."

"Meeting someone could have been an excuse to get away from Marilyn."

"Why say anything about it then ahead of time to her? That doesn't make sense."

"Agreed."

"It feels more likely he went home to meet whoever he said he was going to and saw the severed finger. That could have sent him running." I ran my hand through my hair. "Except if he had fled at that point, he would have taken things with him and headed north or south towards one of the borders. Instead, he's on a backroad out of town where he falls asleep at the wheel. There's a missing piece." I pressed my face to the glass. "Or I could be reaching, and falling asleep isn't that far off from what happened."

"It happens more than you can imagine."

I shrugged. "It just doesn't answer why he's out there. Another thing bothers me. When Marilyn showed at Vince's house today, she acted all frantic to find him. Yet when I visited the tavern, the bartender Len said she hadn't said a thing about him since he walked out of that bar that night. Why isn't she asking everyone in town? Unless she knows he's not coming back."

"Why corner you at the house?"

"Good question." And what about Lorraine? Clearly, she and Vince had not run off together. Where was she and did she fit into any of this? I didn't have time to contemplate. Stephanie's duplex came into view and my throat went dry. Time to tell my client—my friend—her father was dead.

TWELVE

KYLE AND FLOYD stayed in the Spitfire. Standing at Stephanie's door, my shoulders ached, and not only from the weight of the news I had to deliver. If she hadn't taken my advice to tell Brandon about hiring me, this conversation could go south fast. A text to confirm might have been in order if I wasn't afraid she'd have demanded answers right then.

Despite the fact this information was best delivered in person, I hit the buzzer willing them not to be home. But the silver Nissan Sentra we'd pulled next to in the drive said otherwise. The doorbell chimed the happy song of *Take Me Out to the Ballgame*, oblivious to the fact that nothing about this night would be.

Brandon answered. He looked familiar, though I wasn't sure why. By the set line of his mouth, Stephanie had brought him up to speed. At well over six feet, he had a shaved head and defined biceps. A young Mr. Clean. If his dark brown eyebrows were an indicator, he'd sacrificed some thick brown hair to perfect the look—a trend that a lot of men my age did that I couldn't get behind.

"I'm Kelly Pruett." I handed him my card. "And an old friend of Stephanie's."

"Oh, I'm aware of who you are." He didn't step aside.

Clearly, he didn't like the idea that I was involved. Then it came to me. "Didn't you play for Crescent Valley?"

He nodded, his mouth in a straight line. "I did. Go Raiders."

Attending sports events had not been a common Friday night occurrence, but even I couldn't help but get caught in the excitement when my school competed at the basketball state championship. We took the Raiders down 81 to 79. "Go Broncos."

He grimaced.

Okay, not the best way to endear myself as he hadn't forgotten that loss any more than I'd remembered the win even fifteen years later. "Is Stephanie here?"

"She's in the living room." He stepped aside, and I followed him into their home where Stephanie lay on the couch. She wore the same T-shirt and cardigan from this morning. Her strawberry blonde hair cascaded around her thin shoulders. Her eyelids drooped. She must have been napping. Her feet were propped on a flowered pillow and her hand rested on her baby bump. The pink tinge to her cheeks made her look frailer than when I'd seen her twelve hours ago.

Stephanie pushed herself upright, her face scrunching at the effort, her legs remaining stretched out. The circles around her pale eyes reflected her fatigue and apprehension. "Was it him?"

I chose the chair across from her and waited until Brandon removed the pillow and flopped down on the couch next to her and lifted her feet onto his lap.

A swallow caught in my throat as I glanced at her face. I should have left this to the professionals, but like walking the plank with a pistol fixed on my back, the only way out was to jump. "Yes."

Stephanie's eyes brimmed. She clasped her hand over her mouth and cried, tears spilling down her cheeks faster than my heartbeat. Brandon sniffed and rubbed her shin. I sat motionless in solidarity of their grief, the rawness of my own dad's death bubbling to the surface, until I couldn't sit any more.

Escaping into the kitchen, I turned on the water and let it run until ice cold before filling a glass. A frog scrubby had been left to dry in a lemon shaped bowl near the faucet. On the counter, red canisters labeled flour, sugar and tea were lined against the black and white subway tiles. A coffee maker was set to brew at 6:45 a.m., a rack of mugs next to it. I imagined Stephanie's new baby arriving, bottles being prepared and eventually a little girl sitting in a highchair for her first meal. My heart squeezed at the list of moments Vince would miss—and Stephanie would forever long to share.

I left the couple to grieve in private for as long as possible without being obvious I was avoiding their gut-wrenching pain. Even if I wanted to, I couldn't stay in the kitchen forever. Grabbing a box of Kleenex on my way back into the room, I handed it to her along with the glass of water.

She wiped her eyes with a tissue and took a long drink. "What happened?" she whispered.

I gave her the rundown of what Detective Kuni had said. "They believe it was an accident."

"How can they be so certain?" she asked.

"There were no skid marks near the scene and he'd left the bar right before."

She lowered her head. "He was drinking and driving?"

"Potentially, although any tests would be inconclusive at this point. Regardless, they suspect he fell asleep at the wheel and realized it too late. If alcohol was involved, delayed response would have factored into that."

She shook her head slowly, trying to understand. "So like that, it's over?"

"They don't have much else to go on."

She swung her legs over the edge of the couch. "But they can't close the case yet," her voiced strained.

Brandon caressed her back. "It was an accident, honey."

She bristled at his touch. "You never liked him, anyway."

He lifted his hands. "Steph."

"Don't Steph me. If you two hadn't been fighting at Thanksgiving, none of this would have happened."

Stephanie hadn't mentioned any conflicts between Vince and Brandon before. I turned to Brandon. "What were you two fighting about?"

"Nothing important," he said.

"Important enough that my dad called a week later and wanted me to divorce you." My look of surprise must have been apparent because she added, "Of course, I wouldn't, but it was crazy their fighting." She glared at Brandon.

"Your dad and I always had disagreements."

"You could have been the bigger man."

"I'd like to hear more about those arguments," I said.

Stephanie waved me off. "They were stupid men being stupid. But it is what started the rift between us. I was upset with my dad's call, and I stopped talking to him." She placed the palms of her hands on her face, trying to keep control. "I have to know what happened to my dad. Despite what the police say. If they were any good, they would've taken my original call seriously. Instead, they acted like I was bothering them. What if he was fighting for his life out there? What if they had found him sooner?"

The carnival ride of *what ifs* was a horrible place to spend time. She needed the truth. "It wouldn't have done any good, Steph. According to the detective, it's a long drop."

Stephanie squeezed her eyes closed. "Okay, well, I'd been trying to call him at least a week before that night you say he left the bar. Why didn't he call me back?"

"Ten of your messages were on his answering machine. Unheard." The fact he didn't hear them might help her reconcile this tragedy.

She grimaced. "I called more than that. He must have heard some."

"We might never know." My heart ached at my lack of answers. "But the detective isn't closing the case until the Traffic Division finalizes their report and the autopsy is in."

She leaned back into the couch, drawing in deep breaths. Fresh tears spilled over her cheeks. "I want to understand what led to that night. I need to understand. Based on the police's performance so far, I don't trust them to be thorough."

"The whys don't matter at this point," Brandon said.

If Stephanie's eyes had been bullets, Brandon would have dropped to the ground.

"Look," I interjected, not wanting to play referee, "Detective Kuni is a good guy. They're just understaffed and he answers to people who rank higher. I did find out some weird things, and I'm happy to keep filling in the blanks if that's what you want."

"What weird things?" Her voice shook.

"How much is that going to cost?" Brandon asked.

How did Stephanie end up with this piece of work? His wife was wrecked and he wanted to balk at my fees. "We can figure that out later. I had history with Vince too and I want answers as much as Stephanie. As for the weird things—your dad might have been engaging with some shady characters. It's an angle that needs exploring."

Her face crumpled again. "Thank you."

Brandon's face turned red; he didn't like losing.

I pulled out my notepad. "Are you up for a few questions to help direct me?"

She nodded.

"What did you know about your dad's gambling?" I asked.

"Gambling?"

"Honey, this is ridiculous." Brandon came back to life. "You don't want to talk about this right now."

Her eyes narrowed, and she ignored him.

Brandon should be worried about spending the night on the couch, or outside in a tent, if he kept at it. "I found pull-tabs all over his house. There was also plenty of proof he'd been spending time at the Meadows betting on races," I said.

Brandon huffed, stood and left the room. Interesting response with his wife in anguish, despite whether we ignored his wishes or not. Vince may have seen through Brandon more than Stephanie wanted to admit. Something had prompted his phone call encouraging a divorce.

"I didn't know anything about that," she said. "What are pull-tabs?"

"They're essentially lottery tickets that private entities can sell. Do you know much about his health?"

"He always told me he felt fine. Was he sick?"

"There were cholesterol and high blood pressure meds

in the bathroom. A couple of other bottles were nearly empty, but I can't recall the names. You didn't know about any of those?"

"Other than high cholesterol, which he'd had since I was a kid, no."

I thought about the Tums and antacids. "How about stomach issues?"

She shook her head.

In the past six months, Vince had developed some health problems. Or developed them prior and didn't tell Steph. Either way, gambling and being in debt to a couple of thugs might have caused or exacerbated them.

"Why did your parents get divorced?" I asked.

She stared at a spot on the wall across the room. "They never talked about it. One morning we were having breakfast, and all seemed fine. Then Mom burned the toast, and Dad said she couldn't even get that right. It escalated from there and by the evening, my mom and I drove to my grandma's house." Her face crumpled in a new wave of grief. "We never went back. Although I did later during my high school years."

"Do you think he had a gambling problem then?"

She shook her head, struggling to regain her composure. "I remember stacks of scratch off lottery tickets and he never missed Powerball. I don't recall him ever going anywhere to place bets when I was younger or later when I stayed with him. Although it's possible I didn't pay close enough attention."

"Did he have a hard time keeping a job?"

Fresh tears streamed down her face. "Always."

We talked for another twenty minutes. She didn't offer any more information on his gambling and I learned that Vince's trail of random jobs had been long. The marriage may have weathered through much of it, and one day caved from the pressures. An argument over burnt toast wouldn't have caused the destruction of a strong relationship. Stephanie's mother had had enough and clung to it like a spider on a web.

Like my marriage to Jeff. While having an affair was a bigger issue than a charred breakfast, we'd been on the way down for a while. His sleeping with my friend Linda had clinched it for me, and despite pleas of forgiveness, I had used it as the catalyst. Amazing what a couple of years of reflection and Googling psychology could get you—far cheaper than a therapist.

As I rose to leave, Brandon returned.

With a big hug and a pat on Stephanie's tummy I said, "I'll be in touch." She managed a small smile as thank you and I met Brandon's eyes. "How about you walk me out?"

THIRTEEN

OUTSIDE, I FLASHED Kyle the peace sign indicating two more minutes. The earthy smell of rain on its way filled the air and I wrapped my Nike jacket around me as I leaned against the garage and waited for Brandon, who had wanted to get Stephanie settled first.

Brandon approached, running a hand over his bald head. “You’re not seriously going to keep looking into Vince’s death, are you?”

“Stephanie asked me to, so yes.” What was with the bad attitude? “I’d like to hear your side of what you two were arguing about.”

He rolled his eyes. “Vince loved being dramatic. We were having, what do they call it, a gentleman’s disagreement.”

“Must have been a doozy because fathers don’t usually warn their daughters off their husbands without good cause.”

He shifted feet. “Doesn’t matter. He’s gone. My wife and our baby is what’s important and this stress isn’t good for either of them. Which is why you should drop it. The faster Steph can bury her dad and move on, the better.”

Everyone grieved different, but I hadn’t seen any real signs of Brandon upset that his father-in-law was dead. Even though Arlene and I had our differences, I would mourn her loss if for no other reason than Mitz’s and Jeff’s devastation. “I’m aware there may be things that could be upsetting and I won't share every detail, but learning what happened will help her find peace. The quickest way to get me out of your hair, excuse the pun, is to tell me what you know, including what you and Vince were discussing that created the rift in the first place."

He ran his hand over his head again. In the chilled air, he might miss having that hair. I would. "That was months ago. It has no bearing on why he was drinking and driving."

"That's only a theory at this point."

"Look. Vince was a driven man. He liked to control what Steph did and how she did it. Always had an opinion on me and her life. I was never good enough."

"If he was truly a control freak, he wouldn't drop out of your lives."

"He didn't drop out. She told him to stay out. Only recently has she changed her mind."

"Then answer why he disliked you so much?"

He shifted his stance again. "I've had issues keeping a job."

"That doesn't sound like enough to get Vince making a call post-marriage. There has to be more to it."

He frowned. "I'm sure he thought I was a deadbeat."

Vince might have seen himself and wanted more for his own daughter. "What do you know about Vince's gambling at the racetracks?"

"Only that he had a problem. The horses started a year ago. Vince would often tell me about some horse that had come in and paid out well. Or some race that he was sure he'd hit a trifecta on. I protected Stephanie from all that and never told her about it."

"Did he ever borrow money from you?"

His jaw muscle twitched. "No."

Addictions were hard on the entire family. How much had Brandon shouldered on his own? "Any chance he went around you and asked Stephanie for money?"

"No way. Steph would've told me." He blinked, like something was in his eye.

Like she'd told him about hiring me? "Did Vince ever mention a guy by the name of Tyrone?"

Brandon folded his arms over his chest. "Never heard of him. Who is he?"

"A guy at the tracks that I ran into, along with an older man that's his boss. Vince owed them money and they warned me off trying to find him yesterday."

"Anybody who lends money at a racetrack is probably not a good dude. You should heed their advice."

"Except now that Vince has been found, I don't see the problem."

He shrugged a couple of times, trying to loosen his shoulders.

Brandon didn't like my questions, but why so intense? "You're sure Vince never mentioned them when he talked about the tracks?"

He glanced at the ground. "Not them specifically. He had talked about a big pay day he'd expected to score on, but no details."

"A bet? Because he apparently did win some money before he went missing."

"No idea about that. He just kept saying he had information someone would pay for. That was it." His phone chimed, and he drew it from his back pocket. "It's Steph. Got to go."

"And this was all happening the last time you spoke to him?"

"Yeah, yeah. But I've told you all I know. Please wrap

this up as soon as possible. It's only going to be hard on her."

His demeanor bothered me. I couldn't put my finger on why, but Stephanie needed him. "If you think of anything else, call me." I handed him another card.

He stuffed it in his jeans. "Sure thing." He turned to go back in the house.

"By the way," I said before he'd gotten far, "when exactly did you speak to Vince last?"

He paused; calculating? "Whatever Stephanie told you."

"February?"

"Sounds about right."

He trotted back into the house and slammed the door. Stephanie had said the week after Thanksgiving. Could I have misunderstood, and she'd meant the last time she saw Vince was Thanksgiving and there'd been subsequent phone conversations? I didn't think so. Using Stephanie as the excuse sounded more like he wanted to keep his story straight. I'd ask her another time to get that timeline nailed down.

I slunk into the passenger seat and tilted my head back, taking a beat to decompress.

"How'd it go?" Kyle asked.

"As well as one could expect. Brandon wasn't that upset about it. Doesn't sound like Vince held a high opinion of him."

"That could grate on a person."

Indeed, it could. "I also think there's more to the story about Vince's life." I reached behind and scratched Floyd's nose, gave him a treat for his patience, and relayed to Kyle what Brandon had said about Vince possessing some information that someone might pay for. "He could have had insider information on a racehorse."

"He could also be holding information over someone's head," Kyle said.

"I suppose. Hard to know at this point. Only other thing I couldn't quite determine was the timing because Brandon didn't seem to remember when he'd spoken to Vince last. Which sounds bogus to me. Yet if it was five or six months ago, does it even matter?"

"One thing is certain, if he was peddling information, most people don't like to be shaken down for money," Kyle said.

"True. But does it have any relevance to Vince being out on Gee Creek or driving off the embankment?" Or to the finger in his garbage can?

"We may never know the answer to that," he said, but finding the answer was exactly what I intended to do.

A HALF HOUR later we pulled into my driveway. I'd forgotten to leave an outside light on. A hole in the clouds allowed the full moon's rays to bounce off the street. I got out, Floyd right behind, and Kyle headed to his truck. We followed him; the chill in the air making me shiver. I reached for his hand. Despite my bravado, seeing Vince and then consoling Stephanie had thrown me, bringing back the grief of my own dad's death. Of all nights, I needed Kyle. Even if he had to be to work soon.

Leaning into him, I kissed him hard on the lips. He wrapped his arms around my waist and pulled me in. The scent of his cologne and the warmth of his body sent a tingle down to my toes. He nibbled on my lower lip and played with the end of my hair with his fingers.

Eyes closed, I said, "If you've got time, we could..."

"Hey, Kelly. Sorry to interrupt."

My eyes flew open. Jeff stood in the shadows at the top of the stairs between my property and Arlene's. Kyle loosened his clasp. "Hey?" I said stepping back, smoothing my hair and straightening my jacket after shooting Kyle an *I'm so sorry* glance.

"Hoping you had time to chat before me and Mitz head out."

Kyle grabbed my hand and squeezed. "I'll catch you tomorrow?"

I nodded but didn't let him go.

"Call if you need me." He winked.

My hand dropped away from his. "I will." Wrangling my emotions back in check, I watched him drive away.

Jeff trotted down the stairs. "Sorry about that."

"Shouldn't Mitz be home and in bed by now?"

"We were playing dominoes with Mom and lost track of time."

I nodded. "Did you get results already?"

Before he could answer, Mitz leapt down the steps and ran straight into my legs, pressing her head against my stomach. I hugged her close. I'd only seen her a few hours ago. Something was up. When she backed away I signed, "How was dinner?"

She signed good and said, "Jaycee wants me to go with her to get her ears pierced and her mom said she'd even pay to have mine done too." Her face was serious. "If it's okay with you. It's okay, right, Mom?"

I looked at Jeff who looked away. "Well, Ladybug," I signed, "we were going to wait until your birthday, remember? I'd really like to be there with you."

"But Mom," she signed. "C'mon. I really want them."

After having just come from Stephanie's home, and

seeing Vince, my desire to not miss out on moments with my daughter was at the surface. But Jeff wasn't jumping in to assist me on this one. I pushed down my annoyance and focused on Mitz. "You can go with her of course, but no piercings. Can we agree on that? Jeff, you agree, don't you?"

Before he answered, Mitz said, "Daddy says it's all up to you." She emphasized that index finger point right at me.

Why was I not surprised he'd let me be the bad guy? I ran a hand over her curls. "Okay, then you have my decision. Your birthday is just a couple of months away."

She stomped her foot. "But Jaycee's mom said…"

I glanced at Jeff for help. He looked away again. He really was okay with me disappointing Mitz all on my own. I shook my head, not wanting to fight. "Let's talk about it later," I said. "Do you guys want to come upstairs for cookies?" I'm sure I could find some in my cupboards.

Her lower lip protruded, and with a huff, she darted back up the stairs.

I turned to Jeff. "Well, thank you for that."

He shrugged. "Jaycee called her while we were having dinner and Mitz was like a freight train coming at us. Even my mom couldn't get her off the subject. Let's face it, she's growing up. We can't control everything she does forever. And why do you look so down? She's always going to want to do something her friends are doing."

"She's only eight, Jeff. I think we have a few more years that we can control things. But it isn't that, I just told Stephanie that her father was dead."

"Oh wow, I'm sorry. How?"

"Car accident, but I don't want to talk about it. And

before you ask, I'm still investigating." I folded my arms over my chest.

"Of course you are," he said. I shot him a *please don't go there* look. "Okay. I get it. But as for Mitz, whether you want to admit it or not, she's like you. Determined to do it her way. This won't be the last of her requests."

I understood that and she was like me in many respects. The teenage years might be a bit rough on both Jeff and I if this was a precursor. "By the way, since you didn't answer my original question, I assume you haven't heard back from Linda. Did you tell your mother that you might have fathered another child yet?"

"Later," he said.

M-hmm. I bet. "She's not going to take it well, I'm sure. She's no fan of Linda's either." What Arlene would do with the information was an unknown and I wasn't in the mood to allay any of his concerns.

He headed to the stairwell. "Don't forget Friday night. Six o'clock."

I racked my brain as he turned to me for confirmation. "What are you talking about?"

"The talent contest at the school. Remember? Mitz, jump rope, pogo stick. Sound familiar?"

"Yes. Of course." Mitz had mentioned it to me, but I hadn't seen the actual notice that provided the date. No matter. "I'll be there."

"Good. You are taking her this weekend too, right? No blowing her off because of your working?"

Any chance to go there, he took it. Some things would never change. "Yes, Jeff. I always take her Friday night."

"Well, last time you had a case…."

"I'll see you Friday night."

By the time Jeff and Mitz left, I was exhausted. Between identifying Vince, breaking the news to Stephanie, dealing with Brandon, and now disappointing my only daughter, I craved a tall glass of wine, a few of those cookies, and bed. Better yet, a spoonful of peanut butter.

An hour later and half a jar demolished, my body found the bedsheets while my brain kept churning. Brandon had been hiding something. Why hadn't he been sad that Vince was gone? Why not come clean about why they'd been arguing? He knew more about Vince's horseracing than he'd let on. How much more and did it matter? At some point, I fell asleep with Floyd nestled next to me.

It was three a.m. when my eyes flew open. BCP353. Who had been driving that car and searching for Vince at the Meadows?

FOURTEEN

Floyd snored in the seat next to me, his nose twitching and back legs jerking. The rotten egg stench of Riverview's industrial plants in full swing seeped into my car as I passed through. He must have thought he'd caught the scent of something awesome and was on the chase.

When I'd flown out of bed to do my search on the license plate, the owner came back as Lorraine DeWitt residing at 3344 Montgomery Street, Apartment 302. Searching my phone's photo gallery confirmed why that address had sounded familiar. It was the address on the letter from Vince's landlord that had been signed "L.R. DeWitt." No wonder Lorraine was on the hunt for him if he owed her rent. Although trips to the Meadows seemed a bit overzealous, unless they were more than landlord and tenant.

Lorraine answered the door in black slacks, a flowing red sheath top, and perfectly French manicured toes in black strappy sandals. She had a model's height, her salon blonde hair whipped in a swirl on her head. She smelled like roses, my grandmother's favorite scent. In her seventies, her blush and mascara were too heavy for her flawless skin, but her nails had a light shade of pink and overall, she had the look of someone well-to-do. The Chevy she drove, which turned out to be a Monte Carlo from the late 1990s, hinted at a practical side. That would explain her bookkeeping job at the bowling alley and being a landlord. Elegant and smart.

I introduced myself and handed her my card. "Do you have a minute to talk about Vince Burnotas? His daughter hired me to look for him."

Her polite smile dropped into relief. Or curiosity. I couldn't tell as she took my hand and pulled me into her apartment. "I'm glad you're here. Sit. I'll make coffee." She directed me to a mauve crushed velvet sofa with crocheted doilies laid perfectly on the arms in the living room while she plugged in a silver percolator with water and grinds at the ready on a buffet. Silver spoons were laid out with meticulous precision on the silver tray next to it. Lorraine disappeared into the kitchen. Her hospitality was a welcome change from the usual people who avoided my questions.

When I'd first seen the address, I wondered why Lorraine would be living in an apartment when she had rental property. However, the view of the lush green park out her back-patio French doors, the landscape artwork on the walls, and the dainty English cottage china cups we would sip coffee from, said it all. She lived a good, and maintenance-free, life here.

"I didn't realize he has kids," she hollered from the kitchen around the corner. "He's never mentioned them." She paused. "I'm privy to most things about my tenants."

That surprised me that Vince hadn't spoken about his only daughter. "There's just the one. Stephanie. And a grandbaby on the way," I hollered back.

"Oh dear. That's exciting. I have ten grandbabies myself. Love every one of them."

"They live close?" Small talk was a good distraction. Vince's death had not reached Lorraine. Polyester Chuck's assessment that Lorraine knew everything about everyone was off, which meant I'd be the conveyor of bad news. Again.

"I wish. Arizona. They don't get here often enough, and I'm so busy."

She seemed eager to chat, understandable with her family so far away. "That has to be hard."

"You have no idea." Her voice caught.

"Actually, I do. I'm divorced and don't see my own little girl near enough either."

"I'm sorry," she said. "Same thing happened with one of my other tenants, Gertie Max. She was a divorcee, and her ex and his new wife got custody. Rarely saw her son, and now he only calls on Mother's Day out of obligation. Joe in 105, gets the occasional Christmas card from his daughter who lives across the country. And there's Len, the owner of Tip Top. He's had nothing but women trouble since the dawn of time. His twin daughters won't have anything to do with him."

Lorraine did know plenty of tidbits about people, but the list of single parents not connecting with their children and the terrible outcomes was more than I needed to hear after Mitz stormed off last night. "That's a shame."

"It is and I wish I had better results in my search to share about Vince for his daughter's sake," she said. "I've had no luck."

I didn't respond. Too restless to sit, I sprang off the couch and wandered the room. I picked up a blown glass frog displayed on an antique hutch.

"He owes me money, you know," she said.

"How much?"

"Couple thousand. I mean he's not the only one. I have another tenant, Mr. Pilsman, who's in hot water with the

IRS. In Vince's case, he had a bet he wanted to make, and I couldn't tell him no."

She could take lessons from me if she needed help with that in the future. "Why not? Especially if he was having a hard time paying the rent. I saw your notice of delinquency on his table."

She peeked out of the kitchen, looking flush. "Cream and sugar?"

"No thanks. I'm a purist. Do you need help?"

"I got it." She smiled, a smudge of burgundy lipstick on her front teeth.

I grinned back and motioned my index finger in front of my teeth.

She frowned and ran her tongue along her pearly whites. "Thanks, sweetie." She disappeared back into the kitchen.

I sat the frog down. "You didn't answer. Why lend him the money?"

"Honey, I'm an optimist. Nothing goes on in this town that I don't know about and if I can help, I do. Like the widow upstairs. She's another one with financial problems. At least her Social Security covers her rent. But I can afford it. I've been dealt a blessed hand. I own property. Keep busy doing books around town."

"That's right. You work for the bowling alley. What can you tell me about Vince and Chuck having an issue over a pull-tab game?"

"What's there to tell? Chuck ended the game, and Vince wasn't happy about it."

"I'd heard that story direct from Chuck," I hollered. "Sounded shady."

"It's legal."

That's what Chuck had said too. "But legal and ethical aren't always the same."

She didn't answer. If he was her boss, or at least a client, she might not want to disparage him. But I couldn't afford to let any angle go untouched, like I'd done in my last case. "You think there was enough animosity that he'd go after Vince?"

"What do you mean 'go after?' Has Vince been hurt?"

Shoot. Not ready to answer that question, I shrugged, even if she couldn't see me. "I meant, was Vince threatening Chuck for not letting the game continue? Chuck sounded very upset."

She rounded the kitchen corner carrying a tray of tea biscuits, sugar cubes, and a small pitcher of cream. "Ah, I see. Well, that's Chuck. Anyway, it all stemmed from Vince needing money, which I helped him with, so done deal."

"You two dating?"

She laughed. "Dear no. He's just my tenant." She stopped in front of the buffet and placed the silver urn on the tray before setting it on the coffee table and motioning me to sit. Filling two cups to the brim, she handed one to me and set hers down.

My pinky straight, I enjoyed one of the best brews I'd ever had as she grabbed a napkin and walked over to the antique hutch and swooped up the glass frog. Self-conscious, I tucked my pinky back in and took another drink as she polished the trinket, wiping away my finger smudges. I appreciated the extra time. I didn't want to break the bad news about Vince.

She set the frog down and scooted it until it was in its original spot. She liked things in their place and her home was beautiful for it. My own décor, with no rhyme or reason, and a bit of dust, might drive her nuts.

She sat down and took a long drink of coffee. Her eyes were on me when she said, "Where are you at in finding him?"

Clearing my throat, I said, "The thing is, I already did." I placed my hand on her arm, not sure whose benefit that was for—mine or hers. "Vince was involved in a car accident on Gee Creek Road."

She pressed her fingertips to her chest. "I haven't heard of any accidents. When?"

"The wreck happened a few weeks ago. He was found yesterday."

She huffed, shook her head and sniffled. No tears. "That's terrible. Just terrible. His poor daughter."

I cupped my coffee tight between my hands. Stephanie's messages on the answering machine asking, then begging her dad to call her back, played in my head. "If he was only a tenant, why were you searching for him these past weeks? Seems like you cared about him too."

She bit into a biscuit, her moment of sadness dissolving like the cube of sugar she'd popped into her coffee. "I care for all my renters. That's how I make sure they pay their bills and keep me in the lifestyle I've grown accustomed. However, I am a businesswoman. If he was going to skip out on me, knowing sooner than later was better so I could get his things out and someone new in."

Lorraine's sweet smell and good treats belied a little coolness. It could be reflective of her era, or her all-business side. Neither of which jibed with her lending him money. "I'd seen the delinquency notice you sent Vince, as I mentioned. What got me here was seeing you leave the Meadows. I heard you met Tyrone."

She took a long sip. "Were you following me?"

"No. I followed the trail of the daily sheets found in Vince's house. When I was leaving, Tyrone pointed you out in the parking lot. Said you'd been looking for Vince as well."

She thrust her chin out and nose up. "That Tyrone character thinks he can tell me what I can and cannot do."

He was consistent at least. "Did you meet his boss?"

"No."

"He's a character himself." Perhaps my dad's connection was what had caused that private audience. "Do you know where Vince worked?"

"Enterprise Trucking."

Lorraine might not be as tuned in to her tenants as she implied since the Enterprise driver who'd found Vince's body said he hadn't recognized him. Unless they were a large outfit. "Did you go by there and confirm whether they'd seen him when you were looking?"

"Only drove by. When I didn't see his car, I kept going."

The goodies on the plate called my name. I took one. "Do you happen to know a Marilyn Corder? I believe she was Vince's girlfriend."

Lorraine's face wrinkled. "That woman is a disgrace."

"How so?"

She waved her hand in the air. "She follows the money. When Vince had some, she paid attention. When he didn't, she moved on. The only thing she ever helps is herself."

Len had said the same thing. "I'd heard Vince owed her as well."

"Not surprising. He wanted out of debt, and it's likely

he borrowed from a few people to achieve that. Which is why I lent him the money I did."

"I'm not understanding the why on that."

She frowned. "He was sick, honey. When he came to me and asked for a little cash to settle his affairs, I had no choice."

"Sick?"

"Very. I don't know with what, but he'd started to lose weight in the last couple of months."

What were the medicines in that cabinet in his bathroom? "Not high blood pressure then?"

She shrugged. "It could have been. He didn't say. But he seemed upset and I could help him, so I did. He promised when he hit it big, he'd pay me with interest."

For being business savvy, that wasn't a sound investment. "Had he been late with his rent in the past?"

"Never."

"He ever talk about his financial concerns specifically?"

She shook her head and dabbed her nose with her napkin. "No. Although he did say once the medicines he had to buy were killing him."

"The medicines themselves, or the expense of them?"

"Exactly."

Even with Mitz's great coverage through Jeff, there were always deductibles and co-pays. If Vince had a hard time keeping a job, his best option could be state insurance which meant some items might not be covered. That's if he even had it.

I hadn't stopped to question why Vince was borrowing from Tyrone and his boss and making bets in the first place. Was buying medicine the motivation? The bottles only had a few pills. He was running out. He may have been getting desperate to refill them and didn't have the funds. I needed to find out what those medicines were for. "Do you think it's possible the gambling and the need to, as you say, settle his affairs had something to do with his illness?"

"Possibly. In the last couple of months, winning seemed to mean everything to him. I've known a few kinds of gamblers in my time. Hellfire, I married and divorced one of them when I was young and dumb. The full-blown I'll do anything for the adrenalin rush and to keep it coming kind. I assure you, that was not Vince."

"What are the other types?"

"The ones that go for the fun." Her eyes softened. "The lonely who want to be around the buzz of the races or the slots and the people." She stared at her cup. "Then there are the desperate, like Vince. A sensitive soul that thought winning would fix everything. At least recently he did. I'd never known him to gamble much before, and like I said, I'm very tight with my tenants."

If he was desperate for medicine, a big win might have fixed it all. "Unless you lose, and then it makes things worse." What kind of gambler had my dad been? Or had it just been business?

"Indeed."

Except that wasn't necessarily the case for Vince. "Did you know that Vince had actually won recently?"

"No." Her brow furrowed again.

I told her about the charge at the Turf Club restaurant. "He'd won a race and had celebrated upstairs at the tracks. That all happened one week before he had gone missing. He also owed money to other people besides you and Marilyn. Tyrone for one. But even after winning, Vince didn't make good on that debt, or your debt either."

She folded her hands in her lap. "Perhaps he thought he might save the winnings and use them to bet on the next big race for a larger payout. He clearly owed much more money than he let on."

Desperation might cause such a bad decision. Avoiding Tyrone and his boss until he could pay them in full might have seemed like a good idea if Vince had wanted them off his back for good. Celebrating in plain view didn't seem wise though. But he was human. Sometimes wisdom had little to do with actions. Avoiding trouble had never worked out for me, and clearly not for Vince either.

"Well, hon, I'm going to need to scoot," Lorraine said. "Work to do and people to see."

I left with a promise to keep in touch. Getting to Vince's place to check on that medicine cabinet was on my list. His being sick enough to want to rid himself of any debt was new information. Not wanting to worry Stephanie might have been why he hadn't reached out to her when she called. If he was in the middle of trying to fix things, not to burden her. But first, Enterprise Trucking to confirm Lorraine's assertion that he'd worked there since the driver who'd found his body had said otherwise.

FIFTEEN

ENTERPRISE TRUCKING RESIDED at the point where Industrial Way intersected with Hagen Street. The office itself wasn't huge, but the yard was filled with an assortment of gravel haulers, dump trucks, pump trucks, and tankers.

I flicked on my blinker and parked in a spot close to where the rigs pulled in and out for good visibility and prayed no one would shortchange the turn and clip my Spitfire. It was in decent shape for its old age and I intended to keep it that way. Floyd stood in the passenger seat, expecting the dog park, but flopped back down when he didn't see grass nearby.

"A little longer, bud." His droopy eyes said he didn't believe me. There were times I felt bad bringing him along everywhere I went, but it had to beat waiting for me by the door at home. That would come soon enough when the summer heat made it dangerous for him to join me. I kissed his long nose. "Promise."

Inside, the offices consisted of concrete flooring and dingy white walls. Sparse and industrial, it had the chill of the coroner's office. One worn receptionist desk sat center stage. Behind that, four gun-metal gray desks like the kind my elementary school teachers had in their classrooms clustered in the middle. Each were framed-in by short blue dividing walls that didn't hide the correspondence and Bill of Lading forms in triplicate piled high. It must be the lunch hour since the desks were empty.

"Hello?" I listened for a response.

A loud bang sounded. "Damn it. Hold on a second." A woman from one of the middle desks popped up in her chair, rubbing the back of her head and holding the end of an electrical cord. "Stupid lamp's on the fritz."

The woman, easily in her forties, was half my size. She wore a denim shirt over a black tank-top showing far more cleavage than I had even when pregnant. Dark brown hair framed a heart shaped face.

The thud had sounded painful. "You okay?"

"I'll survive." She approached the reception desk. "What can I do for you?"

"Tell me I'm in the right place. I'm Kelly Pruett, a private investigator out of Portland." I gave her my card. "I'm looking to find out if Vince Burnotas worked here."

She waited a beat, thinking. "Who?"

"Vince Burnotas. He may have been a driver." Four offices lined the back wall, all of them empty. A large corner office had the door closed.

"You need to speak with Mr. Wheeler. He's the owner, and the one who hires everyone. I'm new here."

"Perfect. Is he in?"

"Conference." She motioned her head toward the corner office.

"I can wait."

Her eyebrows arched. "Not a good idea. Mr. Wheeler likes appointments."

Her expression said she'd been reprimanded at least once for letting someone pass. "I understand, but..." The corner office door swung open and a tall pretty brunette strode out. The waves of her long thick hair caressed her narrow face. Her aqua-colored eyes could only be achieved by designer contacts and were framed by sculpted brows. She tossed her locks and swished past in her black straight skirt, silk blouse, and a cashmere sweater. Her red high heels clicked on the floor. A cloud of perfume surrounded her.

She stared straight ahead at the exit on her way out. A manila folder she had tucked under her arm slipped, dropping to the floor. Papers flew. She didn't say a word, just stopped and lowered her gaze at me. Her look had me scrambling to gather the papers labeled land surveys.

I handed her the refilled folder. "Here you go."

She tilted her head and gave me an upturned mouth-only grin. It was about as sincere as Jeff being sorry last night for interrupting my kiss with Kyle.

As she turned and strode out the door, I blinked a couple of times to loosen the wide-eye expression that had frozen on my face. What a piece of work. Was she a client? She didn't seem the type that would be doing her own truck transportation scheduling. Her air suggested she ran things, or at least expected to.

Before I could contemplate further, a large statured man filled the corner office doorway. His thick shock of gray hair was combed back away from his forehead and he had a natural indentation like a halo from years of wearing a hat. My money was on the cowboy variety. His flushed face was pinched as he watched Ms. Legs disappear out the front door. He must be Mr. Wheeler.

"Ms. Clark, I'm going to be heading out for the day," he bellowed.

I took a few steps his direction. "Mr. Wheeler?" Ignoring the confusion on Ms. Clark's face, I waved at him.

"Yes?" he said.

"Do you have a few minutes?"

"I'm so sorry," Ms. Clark said. "She's asking about a possible employee."

He flipped his hand at her. "That's fine. I always have time for a pretty woman." He winked at me.

Dressed in my blue jeans, jacket, and donning a ponytail, I was surprised by the compliment. If it bought me five minutes, I'd take it. "Appreciate that. It won't take long."

In his office, I settled on a hard-wooden chair while he closed the door and then rounded his desk and squished down into a comfy leather seat. A man who concerned himself more with his own comfort than his guests. Unless his usual guests were employees, and he didn't want to encourage chit chat. I shifted to get comfortable.

"What can I do for you, little lady?"

Jackson Wheeler—the southern gentleman. "I'm here because a man by the name of Vince Burnotas was found dead yesterday. I was hired by his daughter to track him down, and now to unravel what happened to him."

He pursed his lips together. "You think I can help you with that?"

"I understand he worked here."

He dropped his head, his chin nearly disappearing into his neck. "What was his name again?"

"Vince Burnotas."

"I'm a busy man, as you might expect. I don't always catch the names of people working for me." He leaned back in his chair, puffing his chest out. "There's quite a few."

"I saw your trucks on my way in. Very impressive." He responded with a self-satisfied grin. I continued, "Which is why I was surprised your secretary said you did all of the hiring."

"She did?" He pressed his lips together.

"Yes. Said that you liked to handle things yourself. That's quite impressive as well." Not completely true and I didn't intend to get the young woman in trouble. But I suspected I was pushing up against some HR laws asking him anything related to his employee roster. Keeping him focused on himself might work to my advantage and not get me dismissed before we even started.

He cleared his throat and sat a little straighter. "Wish I could help, but name doesn't sound familiar."

I scanned Mr. Wheeler's office. His desk had more Bills of Lading, claims for damage, and a file labeled "Land Sale." My gaze rested on the tall cabinet that had a personnel sticker on the front. "Perhaps your files would jog your memory? I'm pretty sure he worked for you, at least at some point." Unless Lorraine was just wrong.

He glanced at the cabinet and back at me with a smile. "It's coming to me. If I remember right, he was a smaller fellow, late fifties."

"That's him."

He huffed. "I do remember now. Real loser that one. Never showed for work. When he did, he might as well not have bothered."

Vince had a reputation. "Did he work here full-time?"

"Part-timer. Come to think of it, he's been a no show for a while. Course if he's dead, as you say, that would explain it."

Jackson Wheeler didn't seem troubled by that part. He hadn't even asked how it happened. "What did he do for you exactly?"

Mr. Wheeler checked his watch. "As I said, not much."

"When was the last time he worked here?" I glanced at the cabinet again. If the man needed assistance opening the drawer and pulling out the file, I'd be happy to play secretary.

He looked at his watch again. "I am out of time, miss. Leave your number and when I get a chance, I'll check and give you a shout." He stood.

The hairs on the back of my neck rose to attention at the abrupt end to our conversation. "I appreciate that," I said, not budging. "Again, I'm just retracing his steps. His daughter's pregnant and she's looking for closure. Anything you can tell me might be helpful."

My eyes met his. He blinked first. "The man was a loser. There's nothing to tell. Please send his daughter my deepest condolences."

He'd told me Vince was a loser twice now. A certain statement from a man who didn't remember him five minutes ago. "I will."

Mr. Wheeler rounded his desk and opened his door, his hand on the handle. "Good day."

I took my time standing and extended my card. He took it as I walked by him and tossed it like a frisbee onto his desk, shutting the door behind me.

I'm sure he thought I'd keep walking. Jackson Wheeler's demeanor said when he was done with you, you didn't dally. Only our conversation had felt off and he didn't know how bad I was at taking hints.

In the main office, Ms. Clark was nowhere to be found. Probably gone to lunch. An older woman with graying brown hair now sat at the reception desk. "Did you hear about what happened to Vince? It was just horrible," I said approaching, as if we were old friends.

Her eyes darted from side to side before getting misty. Was she concerned someone was listening? "I have a friend who works in the morgue. I heard this morning that they believed it was him. He was such a sweet man."

I gave her a sad smile. "He was. How long did you know him, Ms...?"

"Gladys. Since he started here last year."

"Had he been working here a month ago?"

"No. At first, he was on the schedule regularly, then Mr. Wheeler put him on call. Then he didn't call. Which was a shame. Vince needed the money."

"You two must have been close."

Her eyes softened. "Just co-workers. I usually gathered the paperwork for his routes when needed. But I'm married. Happily."

"Do you know why Mr. Wheeler would have taken him off schedule?"

"Rumor has it..."

The corner office door flung open and Jackson Wheeler strode out, that cowboy hat I'd suspected square on his head. His eyes narrowed when he saw me. "Good day, Ms. Pruett."

Gladys gave me a hard stare and then glanced back at Mr. Wheeler. She clearly didn't want me to say what we'd been talking about.

Mr. Wheeler's attitude threw me. Or was it that Gladys seemed afraid like Ms. Clark? "On my way. Just thanking your lovely employee for the hospitality."

His nostrils flared as I walked out. When I glanced back, Gladys' tears had disappeared and she pulled paperwork out of a drawer. I sensed she was about to tell me something important. Vince had been reliable in the beginning and yet Jackson Wheeler had removed him from the schedule. Why had he lied and tried to convince me Vince was a loser?

SIXTEEN

FLOYD WAS FAST asleep when I ducked into my car contemplating my options after being stonewalled by Jackson Wheeler. Option A: Wait for Gladys to get off work and press her for more information. Option B: Come back when Wheeler wasn't there. The Dodge Ram parked next to me had "BigWheel" vanity plates so it would be easy to know when it was all clear.

In an effort to keep moving, I went with Option C: Vince's place. He had been sick, and the medications I should have taken pictures of in his medicine cabinet might provide a clue as to why and whether his sickness had served as his motivation for tangling with Tyrone and his boss. My cell hummed before I started the car. Detective Kuni.

"Aloha, Ms. Pruett. How did breaking the news to Ms. Jacoby go?"

My chest tightened at remembering her grief. "She's a wreck."

"It's never easy delivering the news. I do appreciate the assist."

I'd have said any time, except I didn't intend to volunteer again for a task like that. "Has the autopsy come back on her dad yet?"

"Preliminaries, which support drowning as cause of death. Traffic stands by its initial report. It'll be at least another day before we know the full results."

My shoulders tensed at the confirmation. There was only one way to pinpoint that Vince had drowned. "He was alive when he hit the water?"

"He had to be breathing to get the water in the lungs, yes. However, with that drop, undoubtedly unconscious."

I'd told Stephanie that Vince had died on impact. If the detective wanted to tell her otherwise, it was on him. Stealing even the smidge of comfort she found in that fact seemed heartless. "What happens next?"

"We'll be releasing the body to the mortuary of her choice after the results are in. We also found a $5000 pull-tab in Mr. Burnotas' wallet. That might help with expenses."

"The ticket was still intact in the water?"

"He had it tucked in a plastic photo sheath."

"An active game?"

"I assume."

"From what Chuck told me at the bowling alley, that's not a safe assumption. He and Vince had a falling out over a game being closed and my understanding was that big win ticket was never produced."

"No idea then. We'll release it to the family. They can decide what to do with it."

"Sounds good." If Vince had a winning pull-tab and Chuck wouldn't pay, that would have fueled their argument. But what if the ticket was part of an active game and Vince hadn't gotten back to cash it? Marilyn might have known about it and that's why she'd been inspecting Vince's table that day when she'd come to his house. Death brought out the vultures. She did say he owed her money. Redeeming a winning ticket would be one way to get paid. And not only Marilyn fit into that category. "Anything new on the severed finger?"

"The report came back an hour ago. There's no DNA match in the CODIS system, so it doesn't belong to a convicted felon anyway. If the finger belongs to some random Joe with no record, the only way to identify it would be if someone files a report."

"Or arrives at the hospital shy a digit."

"Which hasn't happened," Detective Kuni said.

"Don't you think the thugs at the racetrack are worth investigating at this point?"

"For what? Even if they put that finger in Vince's garbage, a missing finger in and of itself does not mean a crime of assault or worse was committed."

I hadn't thought of it any other way. Did Tyrone have a chum at some research facility where body parts were donated? What was the going price for buying random body parts? "Okay, fine. But I want to understand why Vince left the bar and headed out on Gee Creek Road in the first place. Don't you?"

"People go there for lots of reasons. Kids make out and party near the end. Some have gone there to kill themselves."

My shoulders inched skyward again. "You're not saying Vince committed suicide?"

"I'm not saying anything, It's a pretty drive. People go out there for no other reason than to just go."

"Except according to Marilyn, Vince was planning to meet someone. I'd think you'd want to get their side of what they saw or didn't see that night."

The detective cleared his throat. "The word of an angry ex-girlfriend isn't good enough. There's no proof of a planned meeting. I don't have the time or resources to look further, or justification to do so. My hands are tied. If you're not satisfied with that, which knowing your father like I did, you won't be, then you let me know anything you find out. Otherwise, I'll be closing this down."

For a moment my anger at my dad for being less than honest with me, for having connections like Tyrone and his boss—softened. "You must have known him pretty well."

"Well enough. He was a bulldog."

Yes, he was. "Hey, one last thing. I'm sitting in front of Enterprise Trucking and met the owner, Jackson Wheeler. Vince did work here, but I got mixed information on how often."

"Interesting."

"What is?"

"I finally got that trespass file transferred back. Vince was arrested for breaking into their offices. The call to 9-1-1 was made by Mr. Wheeler himself."

I slunk in my car seat. That could be the rumor Gladys had mentioned and would explain taking Vince off the schedule. "Mr. Wheeler didn't say anything about that. In fact, he did a decent acting job of not remembering Vince until I asked him to check personnel records."

"Not sure why he'd do that, except he didn't press charges and perhaps he often had trouble with employees and has lost track. I only know the DA didn't have a case without his cooperation and the matter was dropped."

Wheeler's low opinion of Vince and his refusal to cooperate in his arrest didn't mesh. After shooing me out of the office, I had the impression Jackson Wheeler didn't lose track of much. "Sounds like I need another conversation with Mr. Wheeler."

"Don't rile him. I don't have time for a phone call to have you removed."

I chuckled. "I won't."

He clicked off. Often when working with the police, information only flowed one direction. Detective Kuni and I seemed to be forging a relationship that felt even more reciprocal than the one I had with my dad. Where my father tended to not share information attempting to protect me, the detective was willing to have it go both ways. He'd given me permission to investigate further. At least I'd take it that way.

I had my hand on the door handle to go back inside when a dump truck approached from the main road. The driver was blond and baby-faced. I did a double take. It was the mechanic from the bowling alley, Dylan. Instead of stopping, he accelerated—the Enterprise Trucking logo sailing past me.

Apparently there wasn't more than one Dylan in town. If he worked for Enterprise, how had he not known about Vince? Unless he'd started after Vince was gone. Seemed odd Dylan was always on Vince's heels in the job department. Then to have been the one to find Vince's car in the creek and call the police.

I looked back at the Enterprise offices. Jackson Wheeler had lied to me once already. Dylan might have too. He also might be a better chance for information. I stepped on the gas and zipped in behind him.

Dylan took a right onto Highway 402.

Slowing down to gain some distance between us, I waited to turn the same direction.

Following had come up a few times while process serving and I'd had the chance to practice some on my last case. Staying far enough away that I didn't get Dylan's attention was key. He may not think anything of a Triumph Spitfire following, but the car did make me conspicuous. If this was going to be a habit, I'd need a more generic model someday.

Dylan headed out of town. We passed the Tip Top Tavern, and a long expansive golf course. We were driving toward the river. A few miles later, he took a left onto Gee Creek Road. Shadowing a good quarter mile behind, I debated whether to follow or go back. I'd be driving by Vince's crash site, which made me uneasy. My desire for answers outweighed my apprehension.

Posted at the turn was the announcement: *Future Home of Riverview's First Waterpark & Lodge.* Winding the narrow and curved roads to nowhere, I was surprised by the sign. Unless they planned to do some major widening, they couldn't bring tourists and locals out this direction.

Why had Vince been out here the night he died? Even if he'd driven dump trucks for Enterprise and knew the area that didn't explain why he'd come back in the middle of the night. First impressions indicated there wasn't anything else worth coming out here for.

As I climbed a hill, orange paint on the ground caught my attention. Four hazard cones had been placed near the edge where a guardrail should have been. Slowing to ten miles an hour, I approached the corner where Vince's car must have gone off.

Dylan's dump truck had disappeared. According to Detective Kuni, the road ended. Dylan couldn't get too far ahead if I made this stop quick. I eased to the shoulder and got out, walking to the other side of my car to peer over the cones and the cliff. My stomach clenched at the distance to the creek. Spring runoff had begun to recede, but it flowed fast toward the river where it had covered Vince's car. Looking back toward the road, I didn't see any skid marks, just as Detective Kuni's Traffic Division had reported.

Had it been raining that night? There were no streetlamps. Nothing to illuminate the road except for two headlights piercing the void. The rubber of his tires leaving solid ground. Sailing. Dropping. Hitting tree limbs on his way down. The jolts waking him. Had he realized in that moment where his car would land? His head slamming against the steering wheel, knocking him unconscious. Water rushing. He wouldn't have stood a chance against what the current must have been a few weeks ago, even if the cold water roused him.

My breath caught, thoughts teetering on my mom's accident and if she'd suffered when her car had left the road. I couldn't let myself go there. Not now. Not ever. I wasn't a practicing Catholic, but God wouldn't hold that against me as I crossed myself and offered a *sorry, Vince.*

Standing there, lamenting Vince's plight and Stephanie's new reality, was depressing. I wished I'd come sooner to the scene. My dad would have been out here first thing. Seeing what the experts saw, drawing his own conclusions. My priority that night had been to get to Stephanie. Had I made another rookie mistake? I gazed at the embankment and again at the water below and shuddered. Not this time. It wouldn't have made a difference.

I'd seen enough and rounded my car to the driver's side to catch up with Dylan. Before I could get my door open, a black Lexus SUV crested the hill followed by a silver Mercedes sedan, and two white news vans, Channels 8 and 12.

They must be out here to report Vince's accident. Though that wouldn't make sense. Accidents happened every day. TV stations didn't send crews out to report on them so long after the fact, did they? Whatever the story was, they were in a hurry to get there. I hopped back into my car and followed.

SEVENTEEN

THE CARAVAN CONTINUED to wind until it reached a turn-around and the official end of Gee Creek Road. Beyond the asphalt, waist-high grasses and bushes filled the land-scape in front of what must be the Cowlitz River. Detec-tive Kuni had said the creek fed into it. The cars parked single file, filling the arc. Choosing a spot away from the group, I eased to the edge of the road and watched.

First out of the Lexus' driver side was a short small-framed man, his black hair combed forward into a peak on his forehead reminding me of Count Dracula. He wore black slacks, too-shiny black shoes for an old country road, and a trench coat, even though there'd been only traces of rain for over a week. He might not be from around here because true Pacific Northwesterners didn't pull out raincoats for springtime drizzle. He opened the back-passenger door and a man in his mid-fifties dressed in brown slacks, blue shirt and a herringbone sports jacket stepped out. With sharp features, his wire rimmed glasses rested high on his beak.

The birdman waited while the Count ran to the Mer-cedes and opened the driver's door. A bright red shoe came out first, followed by leg and the rest of the woman I'd seen at Jackson Wheeler's office. While she hadn't fit in at a trucking office, I wasn't sure how she fit here yet either.

A woman around my age climbed out of the Channel

8 news van. She had the reporter-in-the-field part down with her logoed jacket and gray chinos. Her almond-colored hair framed a youthful but thick foundation-covered face. A dark haired man who gave off a game show host vibe and who I'd seen reporting on Channel 12 ten o'clock news numerous times followed and a cameraman from each van emerged with shoulder cameras and tripods.

TV investigative reporters intrigued me. Aside from my work being in the shadows, our jobs were similar. Digging for truth. Reporting the facts. Taking a few risks to get the story. Mitz had mentioned an interest in TV and being an on-air interpreter. With her smarts, and tenacity, she'd make that happen. She could do anything. Our earlier argument hadn't lost its sting that she thought I'd hold her back unnecessarily.

The Channel 8 duo beat them all to the open space where the foliage was ankle high and the river ran as a backdrop in the distance. Channel 12 hustled in behind and Birdman swooped in beside Ms. Legs and offered his arm.

The power couple took a position in front of the camera, making sure the river would be in the shot. Grabbing Floyd's leash, I got out. The pup needed a break if anyone asked why I was skulking around listening. I wasn't lying. My boy had been more than patient.

As they continued to set up and do checks, we picked an area of grass to explore. A few minutes later it was go-time and we eased closer to hear what all the fuss was about. Ms. Legs had her arm looped in her husband's arm, revealing a large rock on her fourth finger. At one point she looked my direction without registering recognition. People cleaning her messes must be commonplace in her world.

"Mayor Chambers," the woman from Channel 8 said. "Sounds like your plans for expansion are about to become a reality."

"Indeed. The final pieces are coming together and with nothing holding us back, construction will begin in the next month."

"Does that mean that a deal has been reached for the land between you and the casino?"

"We're close."

The man from Channel 12 stepped in. "Can you discuss the details of that agreement or what's holding it up?"

The mayor shifted, but never dropped his smile. "You know I can't, Rex. These concerns must be kept private to protect all parties."

Rex smiled back. "Your constituents would love to know something. Doesn't the entire deal hinge on whether you can get those access rights from Mr. Wheeler?"

He must be referring to Jackson Wheeler. That explained the land sale documents on his desk and the file folder of surveys that Mrs. Chambers had dropped.

The mayor shifted again. "Suffice it to say we're looking for more than rights."

"So the city is purchasing it outright?" Channel 8 pushed.

He flashed a tense smile at the reporter, clearly not intending to answer the question. "It will all be public record once the deal is done."

I understood privacy, but if the mayor was dealing in city owned land, the people should know.

Channel 8 must have agreed as she continued, undaunted. "There were some environmental concerns with the park and lodging being so close to the river, Mayor. Have those agencies given their blessings?"

There were also safety issues since a man had died on the road. Vince might not be big news in the scheme of things; safe roads were everyone's business.

"We wouldn't be standing here if they hadn't," Mayor Chambers said.

"You must be proud of your husband." Rex thrust his microphone toward the tall woman whose beauty didn't quite match her bookish counterpart.

She flashed a toothy smile. "Absolutely. When Charles Chambers decides he wants something, nothing stands in his way. After years of envisioning this waterpark for the benefit of the Riverview community, it is about to come to fruition. The people of this city should be proud of what he's accomplished on their behalf."

An image of a cat swallowing a bird flitted through my mind. Mrs. Chambers was polished and professional, yet not altogether genuine. Even though I couldn't put my finger on exactly why.

"Not everyone feels that way, do they?" Channel 8 said.

"Dora." Mayor Chambers shook his head. "It is obviously impossible to please everyone. Some are willing to keep this town in the dark ages. However, industrial jobs are going overseas. If Riverview is to survive, it must evolve."

Spoken like a true politician. Most of the time that meant ways had to be found to keep the money lining the pockets of those in power. If industry wouldn't suffice, a new way had to be found.

"What's next for you?" Rex from Channel 12 asked.

"After this, you're going to get some state-wide recognition. You tossing your hat into being the next governor?"

Mrs. Chambers beamed. Her husband laughed. "One thing at a time."

Politician speak for you bet your ass.

"That's a wrap," Rex said. His cameraman dropped the camera from his shoulder and collapsed the tripod.

Channel 8 nodded at her cameraman and closed off. "This is Dora O'Reilly for Channel 8 news." She held her smile. "And cut." She wasn't done. "Off the record," Dora said in the mayor's direction, "How'd you do it? Mr. Wheeler was adamant about keeping the land."

The man who'd opened the car doors for the mayor and Mrs. Chambers raced past me and swooped into the conversation. I hadn't realized he'd been at my back the whole time. Had he been watching me or wanting a different perspective of the interview? "That will be all, Ms. O'Reilly." To the mayor he said, "You have another meeting. We must go."

The mayor smiled. "I'm sorry, Dora, another time. My assistant here is a stickler about my schedule."

His assistant was something. Slick hustled the mayor back into the SUV and then Mrs. Chambers back into her Mercedes. I wondered why they hadn't ridden together, but there may not have been time. I'd only left the Enterprise offices twenty minutes before she did. She would have had to push to meet her husband's team, explaining why she'd been in a hurry.

Channel 12 had their gear back in the van and pulled out right behind. Dora O'Reilly stood by while her cameraman took a few more shots of the area.

Curious to hear more about the land deal, I approached. "That was a brief interview."

She flashed me a smile and stuffed papers into her shoulder bag. "There are two kinds of politicians. The kind you can't get away from the camera, and others who would prefer never to see one. Albeit those are few and far between. Mayor Chambers is a combination. When he wants something, he calls us. Even then he doesn't give us much time."

"His wife seemed to enjoy the spotlight," I said.

"Olivia Chambers? Definitely. She's the socialite of the two, and the one with the money."

I could see that. My gaze scanned the area behind her. "It's a beautiful area for a waterpark and resort."

"It is. It should do well."

"What was that about the land Mr. Wheeler owns?"

"That's the land between the casino and the waterpark. They want to cut the road in from the south giving access to the park. You came here via Gee Creek Road, I assume?"

"I did. It's very narrow."

"Right. And they're not going to widen it. Too much environmental impact on the creek itself. The endangered Spotted Owl habitat lines one side, and the creek and main watershed for Riverview lines the other. The only other viable access to that park is through Wheeler's property, and he hadn't been willing to give permission. No access, no park. Things must have changed."

There'd been no signs of the nocturnal creatures when I'd driven down, but I was happy to hear they weren't willing to destroy their home for the thrill of water slides. "I wonder what."

She laughed. "You throw enough money, it eventually sticks."

The cameraman hollered from the news van. "Dora,

we've got to run. There's a wreck on I-5 and they want us to cover it."

"Great," she said. "That'll put us behind schedule. To think I volunteered for this. Although I was vying for an anchor job, not chasing politicians and pile ups."

"Somebody's got to do it, right?"

She gave me a smirk. "Yup. In this industry, like most, there are dues to be paid before you get into the golden chairs."

She was right about dues. I had years to go before I'd be anywhere near as good as my father. I had a better chance of improving my status as a mom in the short term. "You don't happen to give tours down at the station, do you?"

"We don't do them for the public, no."

I frowned. "Bummer." I'd have to think of another way to get Mitz talking to me again.

She smiled. "You interested in chasing politicians too?"

"Not me. My daughter. She's deaf and has some interest in being an interpreter. She'd get a kick out of seeing things in action. But I understand."

Her face softened. "I grew up with my cousin who's also deaf. I'd be glad to conduct a tour for your daughter." She pulled her card out of her jacket. "Call me direct and I'll make it happen. Number's on the bottom."

"Awesome." Operation *get Mitz talking to me* might happen after all. "Thanks." We walked toward her van. "What direction on the Interstate is the accident?" I asked.

"Southbound. Semi overturned in Kalama," the cameraman said.

I wouldn't be getting home for a few hours myself.

"Nice chatting," Dora said as she jumped into the passenger seat. "Give me that call."

The van reversed and sped up Gee Creek Road. My focus returned to the river at the same time my reason for coming this direction in the first place. Dylan. I never did see him or his truck on my way down. With my focus on the news crew, I must have missed a turnoff.

Floyd settled, I climbed behind the wheel and headed out. The clouds had gathered overhead, and it began to drizzle. I turned on the heat to take the chill out of the air. Spring in the Northwest. If you didn't like it, wait five minutes. Guess the Count in his raincoat hadn't been wrong after all.

At the hill's crest, the dirt road I missed came into view, along with a large *No Trespass* sign. That had to be where Dylan went. They didn't want visitors, but I was determined to have my conversation with him. For a beat, I hesitated. Then I made a hard right.

EIGHTEEN

THE ROCK-FILLED DIRT road skirted the future location of the waterpark. The small boulders that I weaved around threatened to beach my car. Each rut bounced me like a paddle ball from my seat. If my Spitfire had any shocks left by the time I got to the end, I'd be amazed. Even Floyd raised his eyes in concern.

After another wind around, the road opened into a massive clearing of green grass. I came to a stop and unclenched my teeth. From this spot, I had a peek-a-boo view of the Cowlitz River, along with piles and piles of fresh soil next to a bulldozer at the farthest end near the tree line. No people.

If this was Dylan's destination, he'd come and gone. If he was removing or bringing dirt, he might be back. I got out. The light rain hit the ground, releasing pleasant earthy smells combined with something more pungent, but unrecognizable. In the distance to the left, a rise of land blocked the visibility beyond it. The casino must be slated to go in over there. On the right, a red flag about a football field away marked what could be the beginning of the waterpark land.

While I couldn't see the entire scope because of the hill, the land where I stood sat square in between the two projects. Assuming Jackson Wheeler owned all of this, it was easy to see the need for this strip of property to blend the venues. At least the waterpark did. The casino owners had full access to their project from the other side. Unless they needed this for overflow parking. But according to Dora, the waterpark couldn't exist without this land for access.

A rumble sounded in the distance, but quickly drew closer. The ground vibrated as a dump truck came into view from the road I'd come up. It could be Dylan returning. The rig bounced up the makeshift street, spewing rock and dust from under the tires, and headed right for the property.

A piercing blast from his horn had my skin nearly jumping off me. The driver wore a baseball hat, his brown hair shooting out from underneath. Not Dylan. His hands flew up in frustration and I followed his glare to my Spitfire, which blocked his path. I waved an *I'm sorry* and hopped in, pulling to the side so he could navigate by. The truck had the logo of a large H and a circle around it on the side doors and the slogan: *If you Feel the Earth Move Under your Feet, it's Us Moving You.* I'd seen that before somewhere.

The driver passed, giving me a hard look that said he was pissed at being slowed down. I shuddered at the hostility. I should get out of there. The sign had said No Trespass. Instead, my eyes were glued on him as he drove to the edge of the property, drove into the roundabout, reversed, and released the load a good distance away from the already existing piles.

The trucker didn't take long before he thundered back my direction. This time, he didn't glance my way. When his taillights disappeared, I got out again. The rain had stopped. Keeping Floyd in the car with the window down, I started to walk toward the area the soil had been dumped but didn't get far. Another hauler roared up the same road towing a trailer and an even larger dozer than the one already on the property. A red-headed guy with at least a day's growth of beard stopped short of my location and swung his body out of his half-opened door.

"This is private property, miss. If you know what's good for ya, get out of here."

I flashed my most innocent smile. "Sorry. Was just looking for a place to give my dog a break."

He eyed my car. As if on cue, Floyd had made his way to my driver's side and his head hung out of the window. "Don't matter. Owners don't like anyone around here. Even been known to call the police and prosecute for trespassing."

I couldn't leave empty handed even if the *no trespass* sign had been too big to feign ignorance. "Okay. But I have a friend who's working out here. Name's Dylan. You know him?"

"No idea."

"You with Enterprise?" I asked.

"You should leave." He ducked back into his cab and slammed the door making my insides jump and ending the conversation. He proceeded to the roundabout the dump truck had gone.

I'd pressed my luck enough. Hopping into my car, I hit the dirt road and grasped the wheel, trying to shake the uneasiness of this place that didn't like visitors. Except I hadn't seen Dylan yet. If I could find a place to park out on Gee Creek, he might return and I could get him to stop without running me over, or without me breaking any more laws. But with the road so narrow, and no indicators of when he'd be back, finding out why he lied might have to wait.

As I struggled to keep my car out of the potholes, I

glanced at the area designated for the waterpark again. The property covered at least four or five city blocks. The place would be massive. Too bad for the buyers and builders that such a big, lucrative project hinged on Wheeler's land to make it all work.

Thinking back to the reporter's conversation, Wheeler might not have been as willing to sell up front, or he was holding out for more money. Was everything as amicable as they'd made it out to be? If not, that could have been why the mayor's wife had been there talking to him before the interview. Although why would she be involved? Whatever the situation, the sale file on his desk said he was on board. Apparently, everyone had a price.

I patted Floyd on his back leg. "Even you. Anything for food."

He gave me his best *don't know what you're talking about* look and resumed his nap.

The land deal wasn't my problem, of course. My problem was finding out what Vince had been doing before his accident. Which led me back to Wheeler denying he knew him at first, and then switching his story to put Vince in a bad light. Why lie about a low-on-the-rung employee? I beat my head about the *wall of why* until I was back at the main road and came up empty.

Including why Vince had been out on this road in the first place. If someone wanted privacy, Gee Creek Road would be the place to go. If Vince had chosen this area for the supposed meeting the night he disappeared, being in the area that didn't welcome visitors could have caused him a problem. The bigger questions were why would Vince want that kind of privacy and who had he planned to meet?

As I made my way down the 402, another Hildebrand

truck passed on its way back out to the waterpark. The slogan caught my attention again right before the realization. *If you feel the earth move….* I had seen those exact words in the kitchen drawer of the man who'd been found dead on the road on which those trucks were travelling.

NINETEEN

For the second time in thirty-six hours, I parked in front of Vince Burnotas' house. Another rusted out car on cinder blocks had been moved out onto the street, adding to the rundown vibe of the neighborhood. Overfilled cans and boxes teetered at the edge of curbs and driveways. At least the homes had some life to them, unlike Vince's place. The front shade pressed against the front window, askew. I hadn't noticed that the first time, and it only added to its gloominess. I'd make this stop quick.

Using the key Stephanie had provided, I inserted it into the lock. Without warning, the door dropped from its hinges with a hard thump and toppled on me. Throwing my arms in front of me to protect my head, I shoved it away. It came back on me fast, heavier than before. My heart pounded. Like the time I'd run through a spider web that covered my face, I couldn't get the thing off me fast enough. Under attack, I thrust it with enough force to make it shift and waited. Nothing. It took a minute to realize no one was on the other side. Waging battle with an inanimate object had me feeling dumb. Wooden door one, Pruett, zero. Except that door had been fine during my last visit.

I leaned the door sideways in the frame so it wouldn't assault another unsuspecting person, all the while listening and watching for movement inside. On closer inspection, the frame had splinters jutting out from around the lock that had clearly been kicked in. My senses tingled as I debated the wisdom of entering. My luck hadn't always been good when going through unlocked doors. It might be smarter to call Detective Kuni. It would also be smart to have a clue what I was calling him about. This part of Riverview wasn't known for its upstanding citizens. For all I knew, kids could have been up to no good.

I stuck my head inside. "Hello. Is anyone here?"

No answer. Retrieving the pepper spray from my purse, I held it out in front of me and stepped across the threshold. My ears perked for any sounds. A couple of old house settling creaks was it.

Scanning the living room, my hand tightened on the cannister. Someone had done more than kick in the door. The couch and chair cushions were strewn on the floor. A blade had been used to rip them open, their guts and foam and white fluff in a pile. The living room blind hung weird because a cushion had come to rest on the sill.

The card table in the makeshift dining room had been flipped to its side, tickets and daily sheets scattered on the floor. If this were the work of kids or vandals, there would be graffiti on the walls. The TV was untouched. Probably not a burglar either. Whoever had broken in, was looking for something. Marilyn Corder's full attention had been on those tickets on the table that day. She could have come back to look for the $5000 ticket found on Vince.

But why bust in now when he'd been gone for weeks? Unless with him just being found dead, there was hope he'd left something behind. Which led me to that ticket and Marilyn. She didn't look strong enough to kick open the front door. However, I'd been wrong before about what people were capable of.

In the kitchen, fingerprint dust remained on the counters and cabinet handle underneath—signs of Detective Kuni's earlier visit. The garbage can had been removed from the premises.

The coolness of the space made the hairs on my arms stand at attention. I'd known this feeling before. When my dad was alive, whether he was there or not, I felt his presence in his home. Surrounded by the items he'd loved and knowing he'd be returning made him real. When the day arrived where he never came back, everything faded to gray and lost its luster. No matter how angry and disappointed I was in him, that moment of loss would never lessen.

With a shiver, I pushed the thoughts aside. Time to get what I'd come for and get out of there. Comfortable that I was the only one in the house, I dropped the spray in my pocket and headed straight for the medicine cabinet in the bathroom. The bottles whose name had evaded me sat on the bottom shelf. I punched in Capecitabine and Leucovorin into Google search and while waiting for the information, went into Vince's bedroom right next door. Another inspection of the bureau drawers, the closet, and under the bed confirmed that nothing else had changed in there since my last visit.

The spare bedroom where stacks of boxes were kept was another story. Everything had been ripped open and dumped out. Like in the living room, someone had been looking for something in here. What? One pile consisted of pots and pans. Old photo albums were tossed in another.

Grabbing one, I flipped through the pictures of Stephanie and Vince. Stephanie smiling on her dad's lap. Stephanie at her sixth birthday, her first Halloween, a Christmas where she got a Barbie Big Wheel. There wasn't any chronological order to how the pictures were laid out, but they showed a well-loved daughter.

I was terrible at taking pictures. If I had enough to fill half an album of Mitz and me, or my life with Jeff, I'd be surprised. My dad had been worse. The only two pictures of my mother, I kept tucked away, afraid oxygen might destroy them.

Seeing Stephanie and Vince's memories made my heart hurt. At least she had something to hold onto even if it wasn't her dad. I needed to get back to capturing moments of my life with Mitz. At some point, it would be all she'd have of me—of our life together. Just as that was all Stephanie had now.

I tucked the albums back into the box and set them in a corner before inspecting the other items on the floor. Old DVDs of mostly Clint Eastwood movies and westerns; a few smaller VHS tapes labeled "A Day." More family stuff. Miscellaneous clothes and toiletries. A camcorder of at least ten years old was in pieces below an indent on the wall. Could be a sign of frustration if whatever the person was looking for hadn't been found. Whatever that was.

Another box had been tossed on its side, its flaps open, filled with writing and mailing supplies. Envelopes, paper, pens, and a sheet of stamps. A half-dozen empty plastic containers, with screw top lids.

I walked out of the room uncertain what anyone would have wanted with any of the items in there. When I'd pressed Brandon, he'd mentioned Vince talking about some big payout for information he might have. Is that what someone was trying to find? If true, I hadn't seen any signs of what that might be. I glanced at my phone.

The connectivity icon continued to swirl. Reception wasn't good in this area and Vince didn't have wi-fi to tap into.

Next, I went into the kitchen, hoping my search wouldn't reveal any more severed digits or maggots. My stomach flipped—that image wasn't going anywhere for a while. In the junk drawer, I checked for the notepad to confirm the slogan I'd dismissed as having to do with the crossword puzzle it was tucked into was the same as on the Hildegard truck.

I grabbed out the pad and flipped through the pages. My confirmation wasn't there. The sheet I'd expected to find had been ripped off. Lifting the pages again, I searched to see if it had been stuffed somewhere else, but it wasn't. The sheet was gone. Detective Kuni might have taken it before his team deemed Vince's death accidental. I could ask when I called, but I might have a way to get the information sooner, if my dad's old trick worked.

Pad in hand, I walked over to the kitchen window. If someone pushed down hard when they were writing, the impression of what they'd written remained on the underlying pages. Tilting the pad into the light, I searched for those impressions. They were there, though hard to make out.

Returning to the drawer, I dug around and found a stubby pencil. Taking the edge, I moved it back and forth, shading the page. Slowly, part of a number appeared, but the pen pressure had been inconsistent. I kept shading. Letters started to form. Random words. An H with a circle, which I hadn't caught before. The beginning part of that slogan: *if the earth moves.* The rest of the line illegible. The rest of the number became clear. At first glance, I thought it had been arbitrary. Now it looked like it could be a phone number. Perhaps Hildegard Construction's office. It would make sense given the logo and slogan Vince had jotted down.

Despite the Google search taking forever, my phone worked. I dialed to confirm who the number belonged to. A few rings later, the voicemail message came on. "This is KGW reporter Dora O'Reilly."

As the message played, I slipped the business card I'd received less than an hour ago from my pocket. The numbers matched.

"I'm not available at this time," Dora continued. "If you have a story idea, feel free to leave it after the tone, or leave your name and number, and I'll return your call within 48 hours."

I waited for the beep. "Dora, this is Kelly Pruett. We met today on Gee Creek Road in Riverview. When you get a moment, please give me a call. It may be important." I left my cell number and clicked off. Why would Vince have Dora's phone number?

My phone dinged. My Google search completed. I flipped the screen to read the results. I had to blink a couple of times and leaned against the counter as I read. Capecitabine and Leucovorin were a combination chemo treatment used as a last resort in patients with inoperable and metastatic melanoma. Vince had been dying of cancer.

TWENTY

Detective Kuni had been on his way home when I called. "I'll send someone right over to take your statement," he said after my detailed description of the place.

"That's it? First the finger, and now the house has been trashed. If this isn't proof that Vince had weird stuff going down in his life, then I don't know what is." It would be nice if he'd come himself and acknowledge that I had something.

"Perhaps, Ms. Pruett. But sending an officer to take a report is the best I can do."

Frustrated, I'd clicked off. True to his word, he did send a uniform over to take the official report. Since nothing appeared missing, there wasn't much else to do. Between the two of us, we secured the front door with a plywood panel we found out back and parted company.

The accident on the Interstate should have cleared. Even if it meant sitting in traffic, I wanted to go home, see Kyle, and sort out the day's events and revelations. The most heartbreaking find of the day, although not entirely shocking after visiting Lorraine, was Vince had cancer. Unexpected was finding a TV reporter's phone number on a notepad in his kitchen. The same reporter I'd seen at the news conference on the road where Vince died.

Deep in thought on how it connected, or if it did, I was on a side road driving to the 402 when a set of lights flashed in my rearview mirror. The needle on my speedometer hovered under the 25-mph mark, worthy of Sunday driver status. I hadn't come upon a stop sign or signal to accidentally roll through.

I pulled to the curb and a short, stocky officer of about forty dressed in a navy-blue uniform approached with no hint of a smile or a soft spot. A baton hung on his left side, his holstered gun on the other. Lowering my window, I had my license and registration ready, as well as my concealed license permit. Floyd perked up at the sound of the officer's gun belt. Kyle often dropped by in uniform bearing doggie treats. We both focused on the window as the officer's frame filled our view.

He bent into my car, his forearms on the window ledge and I handed him my legalities, which he inspected. "Afternoon, ma'am. What brings a private investigator to Riverview?"

The hairs on my arms prickled. He would have had to dig a little deeper to find out I was a PI. Why had he done more than check ownership of my car? "Just working a case." I wasn't above name-dropping Detective Kuni to get out of a ticket, but this could be nothing more than a warning. "Is there a problem, Officer…?" He wasn't wearing a name badge. Wasn't that a requirement?

"Busted taillight. You're going to need to get that fixed. Where's your weapon?"

"Locked in my glove compartment. I didn't realize my light was out. Which one?"

"Passenger side. Must have backed into something. I need your keys or your gun."

Taking my Glock away for a broken taillight was overzealous. Floyd and I weren't that threatening. Best not to argue. I handed him my keys. "May I check my car?"

He opened the door for me as he took the smallest step back and pocketed my keys. “By all means.”

Squeezing out, I was close enough to smell his cheap aftershave with a full days’ worth of perspiration. I held my breath until I was behind my Spitfire. Sure enough, the red plastic covering the passenger taillight had crumbled away. Something sharp and solid had gone through the middle, exploding the bulb. It was fine last night when Kyle and I drove up to identify Vince.

I’d left my car several times today, including when I spoke with Lorraine and at the news conference. It might have happened when I drove up to the construction site if I’d hit a rock just right.

“I’ll definitely get that fixed,” I said.

He gave me a lopsided smile that made my skin crawl up my back. “Good idea.” His radio crackled with a male voice. I couldn’t make out the content since the earpiece was crammed in his ear. He depressed the button on the shoulder cord and responded. “10-4.” His eyes narrowed at me. “Wait here.”

He went back to his car and I leaned against mine. My nerves rattled watching his subdued responses to whomever he was speaking with. His eyes never left me. When he disconnected, he strode my direction.

“We good?” I asked.

He put his right hand on his gun and drew it out of the holster in response. I rocked on my heels. Last time a gun had been pointed my direction, the person pulled the trigger.

“Place your hands behind your head,” he ordered.

“Why?”

“I’m detaining you for breaking and entering.”

“Into where?” My voice inched up an octave.

"The home of Vince Burnotas. Put your hands behind your head before I put them there for you."

A rush of blood hit my cheeks. "I didn't break in there." My mind raced for answers.

"Won't ask you again." His tone left no doubt.

I turned around in a huff. "When I let myself in, with a key no less, the door fell off. Someone had already broken and entered."

He crowded in close to my ear, his chin stubble scraping my jaw. "That's not what the neighbors said."

I almost spun to meet his eye, but thought better of it. All I needed was a resisting charge. "What are you talking about? I'm the one that called and reported it. Call Detective Kuni of Cowlitz County. He'll clear this up."

The officer slapped the cold metal cuffs around my wrist. Nausea swept through me at being trapped like an animal. I swallowed down the acidic mix in my throat. Throwing up on his feet wouldn't help my situation. He walked me back to his car and opened the door. The word "Patrol" was plastered on the side. He shoved me inside and I caught a glimpse of the rest in smaller print. Private security. The top of my head brushed the frame.

"Wait," I said as he slammed the door. I'd been stopped by security? Who was he working for? Before I could compile a list of possibilities, another patrol car pulled up ahead and a very fit and tall officer stretched himself out. He eyed me through the front windshield and if looks had superpowers, mine would have melted the glass between us. I couldn't hear them, but their body language, and constant glances in my direction, said I was their topic.

From the back of the cruiser, I couldn't see Floyd's head, which meant he'd settled back into the passenger seat oblivious to my predicament. What was going to happen to him if they took me to jail? He wouldn't do well at the pound. Could they even do anything with me? Why would they? I needed to call Kyle. Worst case scenario, he could get Floyd. Best case, he might be able to get information and throw his weight around.

But the minutes ticked by and the officers made no move my direction. The longer I sat there, panic settled in and took hold. My breath escaped me like sand through my fingers. I counted to calm down. Ten, nine, eight. Mitz. She must be getting out of school about now. I watched as the officers talked and chuckled. My head pounded. I started over. Ten, nine, eight. No Name kept throwing his head back, laughing, staring at me. Someone trying to take me out by way of a bullet last year had been the ultimate violation. This ran a close second. But I hadn't broken any laws. This was crazy.

Okay—I'd trespassed at the property out on Gee Creek. That wasn't enough to be stuffed into the back of a patrol car. The accusation I'd broken into Vince's place was trumped up. If I'd been a suspect, the real policeman who'd shown up would have taken me in.

The two men climbed into No Name's car and talked some more. It was late afternoon, and the sun had begun to drop in the sky. There'd been no traffic on this side road. I scanned the streets, praying for someone. In answer, a rust-colored Lincoln slowed as it crossed the intersection ahead. A large black man sat behind the wheel. Tyrone? I couldn't be sure. But if that was him, he could be in town looking for Vince. My insides loosened. He also could have broken into Vince's house and trashed it. If that were the case, what had he been looking for?

I slunk low into the seat. Mobsters paid people off. He

could be the reason for me sitting in the back of the security car. Every muscle in my body tensed as he crossed the intersection and kept going. The fact he was gone didn't make me feel any better.

My stomach cramped with thoughts of *what next* crashed into my mind. If these guards were planning to do me harm, it made no sense they'd wait. There were no witnesses. Since they were only security, perhaps they'd called real cops to come. At least they'd straighten this mess out. Another twenty minutes later, no one had shown.

A coastal fog settled over my brain. Then I had to pee. I had to pee so bad I thought I'd wet myself. Between nerves, stress, and having drank too much coffee at Lorraine's earlier, my bladder teetered on the edge of desperation.

I kicked against the door twice before my Fitbit vibrated with a caller ID notification from my phone that was in my car. I craned my neck around to see an unfamiliar Oregon cell number scrolling across my wrist.

There was nothing I could do but watch the call disappear. I laid back on the bench, the hard-plastic grinding into my shoulder blades, and pushed images of water falls from my mind. Floyd would need to get out for a potty-break soon. If he hadn't already. He was a good boy though. He'd hold out if possible. Could I?

What was Mitz doing tonight? Homework was my best guess. I should have taken a picture of her the last time we were together. Although the last time, she'd stormed off. I had a knack for upsetting people. Obviously.

A tear ran out of my eye, feeling sorry for myself. I didn't have time for this. I pressed my cheek against the molded seat and crossed my legs. How many asses had sat here before me? Someone had probably thrown up in here at least once. Or worse.

Dark spots dotted the floorboard. Was that dried blood? I bolted upright. Why was there blood on the floor? I wanted out, a hot shower, a cup of coffee, and a bathroom. Not in that order. This was ridiculous. I threw my shoulder against the passenger door. Feeling angrier with every hit. My fourth heave landed me on the sidewalk in a lump and looking up at No Name. Shit.

He grabbed me by my wrists and hauled me to my feet. I yelped at the pain. "This is police brutality. If you can call it that since you're not even cops," I screamed. "Call Detective Kuni of Cowlitz. He'll tell you why I was in that house."

No Name's face grew dark and menacing. "You're working with Kuni?"

"I told you that before."

His eyes darted to his cohort, who gave him an angry glare. No Name's over eagerness had him missing that part. His buddy didn't appear to like my connection. "It doesn't matter. You broke the law." He spat near my feet.

"Right. I'll make sure he hears my side the minute I have a chance."

"Bad idea. You stay out of this town. Got it? Don't even think about calling him. He can't help you."

Detective Kuni worked for the county. He ranked much higher in the food chain than these rent-a-cops. "This is America. Think I'll call or do whatever the hell I want."

He shoved me back inside, and slammed the door.

"I have to pee!"

He stomped away.

Would I ever learn to keep my mouth shut? All I had

to do was nod and say *yes sir*. How hard was that? Stupid. Trapped again, I groaned and slumped in the seat.

My Fitbit buzzed. Kyle. I sat back and closed my eyes. Willing him mental images of my plight. That I needed him. When the phone stopped ringing, I had a hard time catching my breath. Until it started once more almost immediately. Kyle again. If he called enough times without my answering, he'd wonder where I'd gone. I usually picked up when he called. Unless I was in an interview. My heart sunk. He knew I was on a case. After the phone fell silent the last time, it didn't ring.

I crossed my legs a dozen times and focused on counting, from a hundred this time. By the time the back door flew open, I'd found my Zen and simply opened my eyes and scowled at the two morons peering in at me.

"This is how it's going to happen," No Name said. "You're going to leave and not look back. We clear about that?"

"Crystal." I batted my eyelashes. I'm not sure if the flirty look hit home. It's all I had.

He waited a long minute probably debating whether I was lying. "If we ever see you around here again, you won't fare so well."

The other officer who'd never said a word handed me back my keys and my licenses.

I grabbed them and bit into my lower lip, holding back the rant I wanted to unload that they couldn't intimidate me—because they had.

My nerves pinged all the way out of town and to the dog park where I used the public facilities and Floyd got his break unleashing a pee worthy of a Niagara Falls comparison. While I waited for him, I checked my messages.

The Oregon number was Dora O'Reilly. She was covering a town hall meeting in the city and would try me tomorrow. Fine by me. At this point, I wanted to go home and to hear Kyle's voice. Before I could hit his number, he called.

"Where've you been?" he asked.

When Jeff asked those questions, I got defensive. Kyle's concern comforted me. I wanted to spill everything that had happened, but face to face was better than on the phone. Besides I needed him. His touch. "In Riverview. Heading home. Can you come over tonight?"

"I'm pulling a double, that's why I'm calling. I've got some info on those guys at the track and we should meet right away. Common Grounds in an hour?"

Hot coffee and Kyle. "I'll be there."

I lead-footed it all the way back to Oregon, thankful the accident had cleared, and unable to shake the feeling of being out of control, helpless, and violated. What had I done that had people so concerned?

TWENTY-ONE

INSIDE COMMON GROUNDS, the floors were stained concrete and the walls were covered in a fresh spring green. The place had a very Portland vibe with its long communal tables, a rack of gluten free options, and a dreadlocked clerk behind the counter. My nose filled with the decadent smell of ground coffee and my mouth watered.

Kyle stood at the half moon counter with a wide stance and dressed in his midnight blue police uniform and standard issue ballistic vest. He scanned the chalk written menu above. With his thumbs tucked into his belt, he could have been a character in an old western. My insides crumpled with relief.

He gave me a deep dimpled grin when I drew up next to him. "What will it be, my lady?"

I squeezed his arm, appreciating his muscles. I might be the craziest woman in the world to not let those arms hold me every night. We had gotten our feet wet, so to speak. Trust just took time, at least that's what I told myself. "A large mocha and one of those." I pointed to a chocolate-filled croissant. When peanut butter wasn't handy, chocolate would do.

"Sure you don't want a quiche and salad?" Kyle asked.

It was almost dinner time. "Okay, that too." I smiled.

He chuckled and was probably assessing the potential of my longevity with a diet like that. "Grab us a seat."

I rubbed his uniformed arm again and found us a spot

on the gold velour couch in the corner, away from the other patrons who were busy talking and laughing at the end of one of the four long tables. While I didn't visit here often, opting for my coffee black and day old, this place felt like home. I curled on the couch, resting against the arm, my purse tucked next to me, and relaxed.

A few minutes later Kyle joined me bringing my croissant in a white bag. "Rough day?" He dropped into the black leather chair next to the couch and facing the door.

"You have no idea." I withdrew the buttery goodness and extended the pastry to Kyle.

"I'm good."

He had far more will power than I'd ever manage. I shut my eyes and took a bite. When I opened them, he was watching me. "Do you look like that when you think of me?" His upturned mouth showed his amusement.

What could I say? Me and chocolate went way back. "Okay. I'm ready. What do you have to tell me."

"Ladies first?"

I shook my head and took another bite. I wasn't ready to share.

Kyle's face grew serious. "The guy at the Meadows is Tyrone Johnson. He's thirty-five and has five priors, all for assault and theft, mostly done in his early twenties."

None of that surprised me. "Nothing recent?"

"No. But that's not because they haven't tried. He's stepped up his game. According to my buddy who patrols that area and gets called to the tracks when there's a problem, he does security work for a fellow by the name of Pavel Mikhailov. They call him Mickey."

"That must have been the old guy who talked to me and who knew my dad. He didn't appear too eager to give me his name at the time. Now I know why. Ukrainian?"

"Russian."

"And when you say security, you mean bodyguard?"

He nodded. "Mickey has kept himself clean lately, for the most part. He's had a few racketeering charges thrown at him, and some problems about twenty years ago at the track, but overall he ducks the trouble."

What had my dad been doing with ties to him? The barista approached and set down two large black mugs on the round table in front of us. Each had a leaf design swirled into the foam. We grabbed our drinks at the same time and I balanced mine on the sofa arm as Kyle drew his straight up to his mouth and slurped. "When you say racketeering I think organized crime."

"You'd be right." He set the cup down. "Mickey has ties to a family out of LA that runs books, launders money, and puts up stakes for down on their luck gamblers. For a percentage, of course."

"Stakes?"

"Essentially, he lends them money and then gets a take of whatever they win, in addition to his full investment."

"Like interest."

"More like commission."

The maître d' at the Turf Club had been sketchy about who accompanied Vince in the restaurant the night he won. He might not have been protecting Vince, but Mickey instead. Although Tyrone had said Vince hadn't paid his debt and was buying a round of drinks, unlikely if his loan shark sat next to him. "We know Vince borrowed money from Mickey and appears to have stiffed him. At least that's the gist of what they both said to me. We also know why Tyrone is looking for him. What I don't know is why they didn't want me to search for him and what I was going to get in the way of."

"Best guess would be their collection tactics. I don't expect they'd appreciate anyone interfering in those."

"True. And I can't put stock in anything Mickey and Tyrone tell me. If they were involved, they'd have known Vince was dead. Telling me to not get involved could be as simple as covering their asses and making it look like they didn't have any idea. My trip to Riverview didn't help make anything clearer in that regard either other than I thought I saw Tyrone up there." I launched into my visit to Vince's landlord, Lorraine, who pointed me in the direction of Enterprise, Jackson Wheeler, and the discovery that Vince was sick.

"How sick?"

"Late stage cancer."

"How'd Stephanie take that?" Kyle asked.

"Haven't had a chance to tell her." I stared into my coffee cup.

Kyle took a drink from his. "Who's this Jackson Wheeler?"

"Besides being Vince's former boss, he owns the land in between a waterpark and a casino, which is on the same road and about a mile past where Vince was found." I brought him up to speed on the importance of Wheeler's land to the waterpark deal, how he acted like he didn't know Vince at first, and meeting Dora from Channel 8. "What's weird is I found her number in Vince's house, along with a slogan of the construction company I'd seen out on the property."

"You said Vince had worked for Enterprise. Could have been job related."

"The slogan perhaps, but why the reporter's number? I forgot to tell you too that Vince was arrested for trespassing at Enterprise a while back, but Wheeler dropped the charges." I slunk back into my seat. "I have a call into the reporter to see if she spoke with Vince, or at least what more she can tell me."

Kyle rocked his head from side to side. I recognized that look. My devil's advocate was about to surface. "At first glance, it does sound odd that Mr. Wheeler seems to be involved in these things that touched Vince. As his former boss, not so much. Even if there was something to it all, the fact remains that Vince had a car accident that killed him."

"Unless someone ran him off the road," I said.

"Nothing you've found proves that."

"Maybe, but I have proof that someone doesn't want people out on that property."

His brow wrinkled. "What kind?"

The entire drive here, I'd intended to tell Kyle what had happened the moment I'd seen him. The more we'd talked, I wasn't sure. Flashbacks of Jeff's protectiveness were ever present, and being told to back off or back down never went over well with me. Although after today, even I wondered if I might want to reconsider that. And I didn't want to base our relationship on holding back. "I got detained earlier."

"Detained?"

"I went by Vince's place."

"Okay."

With no questions pelted my direction, I continued to the point of being handcuffed by a security guard.

Kyle straightened in his chair. "He handcuffed you?"

"Yes. They accused me of breaking into Vince's place which I didn't of course. However, I had been out on Wheeler's land and it does say *no trespass*."

"Which you ignored."

He knew me too well. "I had thought that guy, Dylan, who'd found Vince's body, was back there in one of the trucks. I'd seen him drive by earlier."

He put his coffee down and folded his arms over his chest. "Continue."

"Not much to tell after that. They were bringing loads of dirt in and taking loads out. I did end up leaving as directed." Eventually. "From there, I went to Vince's place and that's when I found his house ransacked."

"You failed to mention that part."

"Did I?" Guess I did. "Anyway, I gave my statement to the police. Someone was looking for something although I have no idea what. After that, I left and that's when I got stopped."

"Private security outfits can be overenthusiastic about their jobs. Normally they call us if they have a real case. Sounds like they were making a point that they didn't appreciate your visit."

No Name coming at me with his hand on his gun had accomplished that. "Why not come out and say that? Why lie and make it about Vince's house? Isn't what they did illegal?"

"I would've expected them to detain you at the property at the time of trespass. But like you said, you took off. It is odd that they sought you out, but not necessarily illegal. They might have made it about Vince's house to give you the impression they're aware of every move you're making in town."

I rubbed the palm of my hand with my thumb, feeling restless. There were moments when I wished Kyle didn't know the law and just agreed that these people were whacked. "But there was nothing extraordinary on that land. I don't get it."

"There doesn't have to be. No trespass means no trespass." He massaged his forehead. I'd probably given him a headache. "At this point, where are you? You know Vince was sick. He owed money to Mickey. You've been told to stay out of Riverview, and Vince died in a car accident. From where I'm sitting, the signs points to case closed, agreed?"

I sipped my coffee, buying time. Kyle's look of concern made me shift on the sofa. "I promised Stephanie I'd find out what her dad was doing before he died, and why he didn't return her calls. That part of my mission hasn't been accomplished yet. There are more questions to be answered. For example, why was Vince out on that road? Was he going to a meeting as Marilyn suggested? If so, with who? It could have been Mickey and company if the severed finger was a *meet us now* kind of message. It also could have been someone else entirely."

Kyle shook his head. "Your theories are based on assumptions. There's no proof of anything except that he likely fell asleep at the wheel." He leaned over and put his hand on my leg. Every time he touched me I wanted to melt. "You need to understand that Mickey and Tyrone aren't your garden variety thugs."

My heart beat a little quicker. Part because of Kyle's concern. The other part was he could be right and I was out of my league on this one. My dad had connections to them. Enough that Mickey had referenced a debt to my dad. Had my dad possessed a dark side that I had zero clue about? I couldn't believe that was true. My dad had been a good man. Although he had hid so much. I had to admit there could be a small shady part of him I'd been oblivious to. Even if wrong, I wasn't my dad. "I'm not going to mess with them."

"On purpose, but if you're trying to uncover what Vince had been up to and that includes Mickey and company, they won't like it. They've already told you to stay out of their way. They aren't joking."

I didn't suspect they were either. "They might not be aware that Vince is dead and Tyrone was in Riverview today to check it out."

"They know more about Vince than they've shared. Besides, if you did see Tyrone today, he knows now."

That thought unsettled me. "I'm just trying to help Stephanie fill in the blanks. That's all. I don't want anyone with a mafia connection breathing down my neck any more than you do."

"I hope not." Kyle's lips disappeared into a hard line.

I took another drink of my coffee and let the hot liquid line my throat. Thinking back to the days of Jeff and me, where he and his mother had nearly come unglued at my taking on a murder investigation, Kyle was a welcome change. Even if he wasn't happy with me not being done. "What I do know is Vince owed a lot of money and he might have taken dangerous risks. Even Brandon mentioned Vince was certain someone would pay big on what he knew."

"Or pay him to stay quiet."

"Exactly. How the pieces fall together, not sure, but there could be a connection." I stared into my cup. "I also can't forget about Chuck at the bowling alley. Something happened between him and Vince regarding those pull-tabs. Vince could have had something on Chuck or Wheeler that he could use against them." My head hurt at the different angles. "What feels true is Mickey and Tyrone are at the root. Whatever Vince did, it was because of the money he owed them. Maybe he did fall asleep at the wheel, but I can't dismiss that those mobsters did something to him because they got tired of waiting."

Kyle grimaced. "That's why you should stay far away."

Kyle's radio came to life with a woman's voice. "Officer Jaeger, we have a 12-98 on Broadway and Fifth. Are you able to respond?"

"Roger," Kyle said into a mike that I hadn't realized was snaked behind his ear. "Officer responding." He grabbed my hand. "An officer needs assistance but keep me posted. If you need help, let me know." He squeezed. "Try not to need help."

He searched my face until I relented. "I'll be good."

He released my hand, his warmth lingered, and headed to the door. He trotted down the sidewalk to his cruiser and pulled away, his overhead lights swirling.

Leaning back on the couch, I finished my coffee and nibbled on the rest of the croissant until it was gone, wishing my dad would have met Kyle.

In a million years, I wouldn't have seen myself dating a cop. I'd known Jeff most of my life and then we got married. After he cheated with my former friend, we divorced. I'd met Kyle at the courthouse at some point in all of that. While I thought he was sexy, I didn't know if anything would come of it. But it had, and I believe Dad would have approved. A lump formed in my throat.

I jumped up and brushed a few buttery crumbs from my lap. At the counter, I retrieved the to-go box of quiche, along with another croissant in case my peanut butter stash at home was running low.

Back home, with Floyd resting at my feet, quiche gone, and half a glass of wine consumed, I texted Mitz: Goodnight. Love you. I got a *night* in response. At least she was talking to me. Sort of. She couldn't be mad forever.

I sent ten *Xs* and *Os*. My phone didn't buzz back with a response. Perhaps she could. She had a stubborn streak. Not sure where she got that from. I tossed my cell next to me and closed my eyes.

With Vince being dead, having to relay that information to Stephanie, and today's events, old emotions churned like Class 5 rapids and I didn't want to feel them. It was losing my dad all over again. With Vince's poor decisions and terminal cancer, the comparisons were running rampant with one glaring thing in common—they had both been hiding something. Vince—probably gambling related. My dad—his connection to the mob at the tracks. Not to mention the other revelations I'd discovered during my last case.

Truthfully, I hadn't even begun to process those. With evidence of that *surprise* MIA for the moment, I pretended that the illusion of my dad had not been ruined. If you didn't dwell on it, it didn't exist. Who was I kidding. It had been shattered into a million pieces. His ties to Mickey and Tyrone had only served to scatter the pieces and I wondered if I'd be able to get them back together.

At least Stephanie might be able to forgive her dad more easily than I was managing to forgive mine. If I could find what Vince had been hiding, she could get the process started sooner than later.

Settled into the couch, I almost relaxed when my cell phone rang. Go away. It could be Mitz. I swooped it up.

Claire from Meadows. "Hate to bother you, but there's someone here that used to hang out with Vince."

TWENTY-TWO

GOING TO THE Meadows for information didn't mean messing with anyone. At least that was my justification for climbing into my Triumph after telling Kyle I'd be good and made the drive leaving Floyd at home. Claire had saved my number and felt compelled to call, which was huge. Most people didn't want to get involved. The faster I figured out what happened in Vince's world, the faster Stephanie would have her answers and I could put this case behind me.

The Portland Meadows hopped at night. The two bars were full of individuals from all walks of life. Construction workers dressed in Carhartt pants and reflective vests, businessmen in their pressed suits, and co-ed tables of carefree millennials. Some were here for the beer and free pretzels. Commiserating the day's events. The comradery. Better to drink together than go home and sip suds in front of the TV alone.

Some watched the never-ending loop of races that played on the overhead monitors. Others were getting their gambling fix in the casino. Missing were the blue-rinsed and carefully coifed little old ladies I'd seen in the noon to five crowd. They were likely back home watching Jeopardy and playing cribbage.

Claire stood behind the counter, wearing a "Got Luck?" hooded sweatshirt. Good question. After being stopped today by rent-a-cops, less than I'd thought. I scanned the area for Tyrone or Mickey as I approached Claire, thankful not to see either of them. "Appreciate your call."

"Glad to help." She smiled, her face lighting up. She seemed excited to be part of the hunt for Vince. "The guy who hung with Vince was sitting over there." She lifted her chin in the direction of the bar. "Unfortunately, he left less than five minutes ago."

"Shoot." I'd come as fast as I could, but it was a twenty minute drive on a good day. "Do you know his name?"

"No, but he was tall and younger. About your age, I guess."

That described only a million different people. "How often did he come around?"

"Enough to make me think he and Vince knew each other pretty well."

"Did they spend time at the bar? Place bets together? What?"

"Mostly talked, I guess. I'm not sure how great of friends they were because sometimes the tall guy would storm off, and other times Vince looked perturbed. But generally, the tall guy would come up to him at the bar, they'd talk over a beer, and the guy would go."

None of that helped me figure out his identity. "Did he come around without Vince?"

"On occasion. Again, usually at the bar, placing bets, things like that."

"And you're sure you never overheard his name at some point?"

She shook her head. "I never spoke to him, and Vince never said."

"Any tattoos, anything that would help me narrow it down?"

She thought about it as she shoved her hands in her sweatshirt. "Like I said, he's tall. As in basketball tall."

My thoughts flitted to Dylan, who worked for the trucking company and who might have lied about knowing Vince. Two guys who worked together might drive down here, grab a beer and gamble after their shift. Although why would Dylan lie about that if that were the case. "Blond hair?"

"No, bald."

My stomach tightened. "Bald with kind of a Mr. Clean look?"

She swished her mouth back and forth. "Yeah, now that you say that. Dark eyebrows and good looking."

Brandon? Claire's description fit him right down to the dark eyebrows. Grabbing my phone out of my jeans pocket, I searched Facebook and found Stephanie's profile page where she had several pictures of Brandon. I enlarged his face to fill my screen. "Is this him?"

Claire inspected the image. "I think so. Bald people start looking a like."

They often did. Hair color went a long way in making people recognizable. It was also an easy thing to change. While process serving, people altered their appearance all the time to avoid getting served. A quick change in hair dye, straightening curls, or completely shaving it all off happened regularly. That's why I paid more attention to birth marks and smiles. Much harder to disguise. "You didn't happen to see what kind of car he drove?"

Her face brightened. "That I did. I followed him to the doors to see where he was going."

"I appreciate that." I wished everyone was so helpful.

"No worries. In case you showed up while he was

leaving, I wanted to be able to point him out. Anyway, he headed for a silver Nissan. Four-door, I believe."

Kyle had parked right next to that Nissan Sentra the night we went to Brandon and Stephanie's house. But why was Brandon here? More troublesome, why did he lie when he not only had plenty of knowledge of Vince's gambling habit, but obviously gambled himself? Since Stephanie hadn't mentioned anything about her dad or Brandon hanging out here together, she must be in the dark about all of it. Like I had been until Jeff mentioned our dads doing the same thing. Was this some sort of secret guy's club activity that didn't get shared? "What was he doing here tonight?"

"Not sure. When I first noticed him, he was coming from the bar and he circled the premises. He passed me a couple of times as he went through the slots area. That's when I called you. He paced around, kind of nervous like, then disappeared into the poker room."

"Was he playing?"

She shook her head. "Looking for Tyrone. He'd asked one of the cashiers about him, and she directed him there."

I whipped around toward the poker room near the front door, my gut twisting. That would explain Brandon being edgy. "Is Tyrone in there now?"

"He was. His boss too."

My mind spun on what that meant. Brandon must have known about Tyrone and Mickey. I'd sensed it in our last conversation, even though he'd denied it. He had to be aware that Vince owed them money. I could only speculate what Vince and Brandon had talked about when they hung out together. And why did they hang out? They had been fighting last Thanksgiving. Enough to have Vince calling Stephanie asking her to leave him. Yet even after that, they'd come here to the Meadows and been seen together. It made no sense. Brandon had held out on me. He might even know about Vince's cancer or what he needed to fix. Even what Vince had on someone.

I straightened. Before this night was over, Brandon and I would have a serious talk. "You knew Vince pretty well, didn't you?" I asked Claire.

She smiled faintly. "As well as you can in these surroundings. But yes, we were friendly."

"Enough that you paid attention to who he was spending time with."

She nodded. "Truth is, he reminds me of an uncle I adored as a kid. I did watch out for him. He's a good guy. That's why I worried when he started talking to Tyrone and Mickey."

"Why didn't you mention that before when I was here?"

She shrugged again. "Look, a lot of things go on around this joint. Gambling may be legal in this setting and it's well regulated, but there are elements that fly under the radar. People down on their luck. People trying to work angles. I sell lottery tickets up here, but I'm a good listener, and a keen observer. I know when to stay out of things. Like with Vince. Which by the way, have you had any luck in figuring out where he's gone?"

I'd delivered the news so often at this point, I was starting to feel numb about it. "I'm not looking anymore."

"Then why..."

Our eyes met.

"Oh no. How?"

Starting with the call from Stephanie, I detailed the accident up to my identifying him in the morgue. I kept an eye on Claire's rigid body language for signs she already knew. There were none.

Her eyes misted. "That's terrible. Especially for his daughter." She cleared her throat. "What are you looking for then?"

"I'm trying to recreate his steps before that night. He didn't return his daughter's calls the week before he died. The fact he was deep in debt could have been the cause of that. He was also very sick."

She nodded. "With cancer."

My brow furrowed. "He told you? Because he never said a word to his family."

She swiped her eyes. "He did. Lung cancer. I wouldn't have thought he'd hide that from them. Especially since he said when his meds ran out, that would be the last of it and he'd let nature take its course."

That explained the near empty bottles. "It sounds like you were closer than you've suggested." Like my own dad. Everyone seemed to know him better than me, and we'd been roommates. Fathers hiding secrets was more common than I ever imagined.

"He didn't volunteer the information," Claire said. "It's just when I asked him why he was messing with Tyrone and Mickey, he told me. Which made sense because only desperate people deal with them. Whatever arrangement they made he didn't say. But he was hoping to fix things, and with him dying, as fast as possible."

How did Brandon fit into that? "Do you know what he had to fix?"

She shook her head.

"How about what he owed them?"

"No idea, but I know he'd won last month."

"Right, and he bought drinks upstairs for everyone."

She nodded. "He did take that moment for himself to celebrate….right before he proceeded to bet on another race and lost it all."

I shook my head in disbelief. "Would Mickey have killed him if he didn't pay up?"

Claire stiffened and whispered, "They have ears everywhere. We shouldn't even be saying their names, but you said he had a car accident."

"I said he ran off the road. He might have fallen asleep at the wheel. I'm just not convinced it's that simple." I didn't have a fully developed theory, but the whole thing hadn't sounded right to me from the beginning. "Less than a year ago, he hardly gambled. Suddenly, he's desperate. That desperation has him tied with thugs and getting arrested for trespassing at his former employer." Which reminded me of Dylan, who might have more details about that trespassing issue.

Claire was easy to talk to and a good listener. But better to not share my recent experience in Riverview, or the fact that someone had been in Vince's house looking around. If Tyrone hadn't seen me that day, I didn't need to announce I'd seen him. In case those ears were close. "It may be that none of it's related, but there's something weird about it all. I owe my client, his daughter, a detailed report on what."

"You are right about the timing. When I think back, I'd only seen Vince monthly before late last year. Then it was daily. Him and that tall fellow were here often."

"About that young guy, has he been around this past month?"

"Tonight was the first time since I'd seen Vince last."

I lifted my chin toward the poker room. "Are Tyrone and Mickey still in there?"

"They went upstairs a few minutes ago."

So much for getting in and out of here unseen. I didn't get the feeling much got past them. I didn't plan to stick around to confirm.

A customer came up to the counter and I stepped aside. The ring of machines echoed from the slot room, and a rowdy group of men whose eyes were glued to a race on an overhead screen near the bar caught my attention. A line of horses crossed the finish line and a roar went up from the table. At the other end of the room, an older couple sat drinking beer and playing Keno, the older man with his mini hand-held oxygen concentrator.

I tried to visualize my father here at the tracks, playing the races, throwing back a drink. Talking with Mickey. I couldn't. I didn't want to. Like I didn't want to believe Brandon was a loser—as Vince had implied. I wanted to protect Stephanie from the truth, but I couldn't. At least not forever.

STEPHANIE'S HOUSE BASKED in the warmth of amber streetlights. I glided into her empty driveway, the Sentra nowhere to be seen. Brandon hadn't come straight home from the tracks. It was late and Stephanie might be asleep. Although when I'd been married, I didn't pass out until Jeff had crawled in next to me.

Up or not, a late-night knock would startle her, and that wasn't my intent either. Instead, I called.

"Hey, what's up?" She sounded congested when she answered.

"Shoot, did I wake you," I asked.

"I wasn't sleeping." She sniffed. She'd been crying. I remembered too clearly my own nights of tears after my father died.

Brandon not having come home to her rankled me. "How're you doing?"

"I'm managing. For the most part."

"It's hard. I can only tell you it gets better…over time." I didn't want to tell her I still grieved for my father, even now, angry at him or not.

"Thank you."

"Brandon is being helpful, I'm sure?" I didn't want to come right out and ask where he was.

"When he can. He had to go to Corvallis tonight. His friend's house had a pipe burst, and he offered to help him."

Corvallis was two hours south of Portland and the opposite direction of the Meadows from their house. "With everything that's going on, he left you? When was that?"

"This afternoon. We had a fight. I'm sure he was anxious to volunteer. I've been too demanding with the pregnancy and not feeling well. It's no biggie. He'll be back in the morning at some point. He has to work at the dealership at noon if nothing else."

My shoulders tensed that he'd lied to his wife. His being at the Meadows an hour ago meant there was no friend, or busted pipes. For Stephanie's sake, there'd better not be someone else. Sharing my suspicions wouldn't help her blood pressure or her marriage. And I didn't know what I'd even tell her until I'd spoken to Brandon. "Don't be silly. You have a right to be demanding. You're carrying his child."

"I guess. Enough about me. Are you calling because you found out more about my dad?"

"I'm not ready to provide you a full report yet. But I did find out he was sicker than you knew. He had late stage lung cancer."

"My grandfather died of that. I told Dad to stop smoking which he did. Clearly not soon enough." She spoke so matter-of-fact on the subject, she might have already suspected on some levels. There could have been signs at Thanksgiving that she'd ignored. She could also be too exhausted to feel anything.

"Look, I'll let you go. If you see Brandon before I do, let him know I'd like to chat. Either way, I'll try him at his work tomorrow."

"What for?"

"To clarify that last conversation with Vince he had."

She paused. "It wasn't about anything important, I'm sure. They never got along well."

Her pause had been filled with sadness. The argument had caused the distance between her and her father. From what Claire had said, the two men had reconciled to the point of meeting at the Meadows in the months before Vince drove off that embankment. Why had they kept it from Stephanie? "That could be, but I intend to fill in all the blanks for you."

She sniffed again. "All right."

"Are you going to be okay tonight? I'm close. I can swing by and keep you company if you'd like."

"I'm good. A little alone time isn't a bad thing."

Being alone when your partner was lying put a whole different spin, except she didn't know about that. I hung up and popped my car in reverse. I was overdue for a little alone time myself.

Tomorrow I'd get to Riverview, and not only to find Dylan. A bridge spanned between the two worlds that Vince traversed. Finding the connection felt like the key. But after being warned away, I had to figure out how to accomplish that.

TWENTY-THREE

THERE WERE A few things I vowed I'd never do again in my life. Waxing owned the top spot. Only once did I let some chick approach me with a bowl of hot goo and paper strips, and that was one too many. Not far behind, asking my ex-mother-in-law, Arlene, to borrow her car.

There were times, however, when vows had to be broken. The warning to stay out of Riverview, coupled with my Spitfire Triumph being non-discreet, left me no choice.

After leaving another message with Dora at KGW reminding her to call me back, and with Floyd back in bed after his outside rituals, I rang Arlene's bell the next morning at nine o'clock.

She answered, dressed in a light-blue velour jumpsuit, freshly showered, and looking bright-eyed and bushy-tailed, as my dad used to say. She'd no doubt been up for hours. "Why, good morning." She scanned my burgundy Nike jacket. I'd traded in my signature gray hoping I wasn't as recognizable in Riverview. I also wore my wavy brown hair down and fluffed around my face. She tilted her head. "You didn't kill the fuchsia already, did you?"

Arlene never missed a beat.

"It's alive and thriving." I could have added "surprisingly" for her benefit, but I only smiled. "Got a minute?"

She shook her head, probably not believing me and

wondering how Mitz had made it through the baby stages. Admittedly, she had helped with that. "Come in."

I followed her through her entry hall complete with framed photos of Mitz and my wedding day with Jeff perched on a long oak table. "Going to get you some updated pictures at some point," I said.

"These suit me fine."

I'm sure they did. While she hadn't brought up the topic since helping me recover from my gunshot wound, she'd made it clear she didn't approve of her son and me divorcing. Something about that whole till the end of time, or death, or ripping each other's hair out part. Truthfully, Jeff and I had gotten along well enough most of our years together. That hadn't been the problem. The fact he didn't like me working for my dad had never set well, but infidelity was the deal breaker.

As we rounded into the kitchen she said, "What brings you here? I'd offer you coffee, but I'm finishing up and heading out for some errands."

Since Arlene hadn't launched into the topic of potentially being a grandmother for the second time, Jeff hadn't come clean about giving up a DNA sample or Linda's re-emergence in our lives yet. I didn't plan to enlighten her. "No worries. I'm in a hurry myself and was hoping you'd be willing to exchange cars today."

Her back was to me as she dried her breakfast dishes and put them into the cupboard. "You want me to drive your tin can?"

Ouch. Even if she had a point, she hadn't come right out and said no. "It's been running well, so I don't anticipate you'll have any problems. I really need to get somewhere."

"You can't take your car because?"

I winced. "I'm working a case and I need to be incognito."

Her head bobbed up and down as she turned toward me. "Incognito, huh. What have you gotten into now?"

Telling Arlene about my cases never went well. No way was I going to tell her about the maggoty finger, Vince's house being trashed, playing chicken with a couple of mobsters, or being tossed in the back of a car by a rent-a-cop. I couldn't believe I'd let that happen myself. But I may not get the car if I didn't share some details. "Do you remember a Stephanie Burnotas from our high school?"

"Little red head. Pretty as could be with her freckly face. Jeff had a thing for her. Of course, I do."

"Yeah, her. He did?" I should have known there was more to the story when Jeff had remembered her.

"In kindergarten, if I'm correct. Until you moved in next door and you became the center of his attention."

Her memory was impressive. "Her dad went missing a few weeks ago and she asked for my help."

"Oh dear. Have you found him?"

"Unfortunately, yes. He died in a car accident."

Arlene raised her hand to her chest, covering her heart. "Poor thing. She must be devastated. Her mother and she were never close after she married Brandon. I can't imagine having to go through that kind of heartbreak alone."

Stephanie hadn't mentioned much about her mom. I'd chalked that up to her not thinking her mom would care what happened to her ex-husband since they'd been divorced for years. "She's not alone. She has Brandon, and they've been married for ten years." Although he had some answering to do on his whereabouts last night. "It's been that long since she and her mom have spoken?"

"Oh, I'm sure they've talked. Not often though. Even after she found out she was pregnant, it hasn't healed. From what I understand, Brandon hasn't amounted to much and he likes to keep Stephanie to himself. At least that's what her mother believes."

Interesting that Brandon had been quick to say Vince was the controlling one. "How do you know her mother?"

"She's in our bunko group. She's been no fan of Vince's either. She's bitter towards most men and never has remarried."

Was that also Arlene's reason for staying single all these years? I also was in no hurry to get on any registry lists, but I wasn't bitter. Clearly Vince had issues, and after learning of Brandon lying to me and being at the Meadows, Stephanie's mom could be justified in her feelings towards men. At least those men. "So, your car. Are you good with the switch?"

"I suppose. You'll put gas in it before you bring it back? I'm only heading into downtown. I won't be using much of yours."

"Of course. Thank you." Perhaps mothers never stopped mothering. Was I destined to drive Mitz crazy like this? If her storming off was an indicator, the answer was yes.

We exchanged keys and I thanked her again. I was almost out of the kitchen when she asked, "Has Jeff seemed off to you?"

Oh-oh. I turned her direction. "What do you mean?"

"He seems preoccupied. Distant. He says everything's fine. I don't believe him. I know my son. He's not telling me something."

I chuckled, struggling to sound natural. "You think he'd tell me if he had a problem?"

She scanned my face. I was not going to be the one to tell Arlene about the DNA test. No way. "You two talk."

"About Mitz. That's all." I glanced at my Fitbit before my expression gave it away. "Need to go." I walked over and gave her a quick hug. I'm not sure what compelled me to do that. I usually only reserved those for birthdays and holidays. "I'll have your car back soon."

As I rounded the corner for the front door, she stood with her mouth agape. I'd confused her into not asking more questions. I'd have to employ that technique in the future.

HEADING BACK TO RIVERVIEW, I had one thing on my mind. Dylan. Had I known he'd disappear into thin air yesterday, I might have stayed on his tail. But then I would have missed the news conference, and the connection to Dora's name on the notepad.

Problem now was where to start. He could be in any big rig wandering the city, working at the bowling alley, or a number of other places since I wasn't privy to Dylan's habits. It'd be smarter to be looking for the car he drove versus popping into places and announcing my presence in town.

At a stop light, I logged onto the Department of Licensing website. Before it turned green, I had Dylan Schaefer's make, model and plate number. I swung through the bowling alley lot slunk in my seat, his Kia Sport nowhere to be found. Next, I cruised past Enterprise. His mini SUV sat between a couple of 4x4s. He must be out in a truck.

Driving back out to the property could invite trouble, and he might not even be there. I pulled into the Country Café and parked next to a large van. One person I'd encountered might have a suggestion as to his whereabouts if they were willing. I dialed their number.

"Enterprise Trucking, Gladys speaking."

"Gladys, hey, this is Kelly Pruett," I said, and reminded her of our recent chat about Vince leaving room for a response. Judging by her willingness to help before, the friend angle might work again. This time I got silence in return. "Dylan Schaefer's working today and I'm trying to find him," I continued, undaunted.

She hesitated. "Okay."

"You wouldn't happen to know if he's running trucks out to the waterpark, would you?"

She cleared her throat. "I don't handle the schedules and Mr. Wheeler isn't here."

That might be her official response. I didn't get that much passed by Gladys while she sat at the front desk. "There's no need to bother Mr. Wheeler. It's just I got the impression that you cared about Vince. What I didn't tell you is his daughter is pregnant and had been looking for her father for weeks. I was hired to help her do that. Sadly, I found him too late. Now I'm trying to backtrack his steps from before his terrible accident. Dylan might be able to help me with that." I paused. "Please."

The silence said she was contemplating my story. Or she could be torn. I should've laid the desperate pregnant daughter part on thicker.

Finally she said, "Well, I can tell you, your visit put things in an uproar yesterday."

"How so?"

Her voice dropped to a whisper. "Right after you left, Mr. Wheeler stormed out. Said he was running out of time."

"Any idea what he meant?"

"No. I can't say any more." Her voice tightened.

I couldn't lose her before getting Dylan's whereabouts. He'd lied to me about working for Enterprise and perhaps knowing Vince. There must be a reason for that. "Thank you for sharing that much. But truly, any information you could share would go far in easing his daughter's pain. And she is in pain, Gladys."

She cleared her throat again. "He was a good man."

"Vince?"

"Mmmmm. Always had a joke for us ladies in the office when he came through. Good hearted."

I'd only been investigating what felt like desperation around Vince. Of course he was a good man. That's how I'd remembered him as well. "Absolutely. That's why I want to help his daughter. Are you sure you don't know where Dylan is working today?"

She sighed. "The guys have been running the waterpark route all week. Mr. Wheeler has been prepping that land for sale and they've been working it hard. It's at least a place to start."

Without any further pleasantries, the line disconnected. If Dylan was at the waterpark, I'd have to go back out Gee Creek Road to find him. The security guards could recognize me even in another vehicle. My stomach pinged at the notion. Or would I have to?

I did a property search for Wheeler's land and pulled up an aerial view. Yay for Google Maps. Within minutes, I had a picture of not only his land, but the proposed land for the waterpark, and the parcel where the casino was being built. The casino that had its own separate access from the other side. If I circled around and came in from that direction, I should be able to reach Wheeler's land undetected by security. Hopefully they were too busy spit polishing their make-believe badges to even worry about me.

TWENTY-FOUR

A WORK ROAD snaked the side of the casino like Google Maps predicted, right down to a makeshift shed that had been constructed to house machinery. It was scary how accurate those eyes in the sky were. I'd have to remember not to sunbathe in my backyard so other Google surfers wouldn't get a shock.

My speedometer needle barely moved as I eased onto the gravel path and made my way around. Even with his short squatty legs, Floyd could have outrun me at this pace. But in the likelihood people were out on the property, stealth was key if I didn't intend to announce my presence.

A few minutes in, I approached what must be the middle section. The carved sign dangling from an arched entry above a rusted gate indicated I'd found the right place. The signage and gate hadn't been visible from where I'd been yesterday because the hill had blocked my view, but Wheeler's land had been a farm at one time. A weather-beaten tractor sat off to the left. I could make out where a home had once been looking out over the river. Wood from an old barn was piled high. That must be getting removed, along with the dirt the tractors and bulldozers had been moving out. From the layout, the area with the excavation going on would have been a pasture or fields back in the day when the farm was alive and active.

Wheeler's land spanned larger than I'd first thought. Much larger than the *sliver* that had been referenced. And I was at a dead end unless I opened the gate. While I didn't see a *no trespass* sign, that didn't make me feel any better. They might not count on the public coming in this direction since mostly construction guys from the casino were on this side of the property. No sign didn't mean I'd been invited. After the incident of being trapped in the back of a patrol car, quite the contrary.

But I'd come to find Dylan and I wouldn't stop now. The upside to hoofing it in would be no one could hear my car. The downside would be if security saw me and decided we needed another chat. With the amount of peanut butter in my diet, I couldn't outrun them. I'd have to take my chances and drive in. If I had Kyle's 4x4, I'd have driven around the gate posts. Arlene's car sat too low to the ground. I might high center if I tried it.

Tucking my purse under the seat, I got out to move the gate. It creaked in protest and weighed about half as much as me. With a few pushes, I managed to slide it open enough for Arlene's car to drive through.

The dirt road led me around a bend. Another two hundred yards, a bulldozer came into my line of sight. The man behind the controls had the claw scooping dirt from a mound at least a story high. The machine twisted to load one of the two dump trucks backed in and ready. Déjà vu from the last time I was here, except for one major difference. That day didn't have a couple of men on the ground wearing white jumpsuits and gloves. The activity had picked up here.

Whatever the reason for their presence, their dress didn't blend in with my idea of simply clearing land for sale.

Between the noise of dirt dropping like rocky waterfalls into the back of truck beds, and being so wrapped in conversation, no one noticed me idling nearby. But I needed to get somewhere less obvious and was considering my options when the car of my recent nightmare flashed into view on the narrow road coming in from Gee Creek. My throat closed.

The security patrol car moved at a fast clip as it dodged potholes and small boulders in its path. Had I been busted already? No one knew Arlene's car. I hadn't stopped to announce my arrival in town. Wait. Gladys. Had she turned me in? I had to think. Calm down. Their being here might not be about me at all. To make sure of that, I had to hide, and fast.

Four employee vehicles formed a line to the left of the digging activity. Swallowing hard, I depressed the gas pedal enough to move, but not to kick up dust, and eased next to a large white work-truck.

I killed the engine, cracked the window and ducked. I strained to hear talking or someone approaching my car and prayed for a little luck that wouldn't happen. My gun was secured in Arlene's glove compartment and my pepper spray in my purse, but having either out might cause more problems and I had to believe the security guards wouldn't mess with me. At least if they did, there'd be plenty of witnesses this time.

The patrol car turned off its engine closer to the dig site. Anxiety had me boiling and I unzipped my jacket. But if I was the target of his visit, he would've pulled in behind me. I popped my head up. The white truck hiding me also made it hard to see from my vantage point.

Unbuckling, I flipped onto my stomach and slid through the front bucket seats. My unzipped jacket caught on the buckle. I moved forward. My coat yanked me back. With a huff, I slinked out of it and proceeded, only to miss my hand on the back bench and hit my chin on the cushion. Mitz would have flown over the seats in one leap. Ten years ago, I might have done the same. This getting older crap was a real bitch sometimes.

When I finally made it into the back, I peeked over the headrest. The uniformed guard was speaking with someone in a white suit. A twinge of fear hit me. It was Officer No Name. A woman exited his car and strutted up next to him. She was dressed in tailored blue pants, and a silk V-neck blouse. Her brown hair was up in an elegant chignon, tendrils draping down her neck. There was no mistaking the Bausch & Lomb aqua eyes. The city owned the land being sold for the waterpark, but I'd assume an employee of the mayor's office would be handling anything to do with that. What would Olivia Chambers be doing out here? And why was she with the security officer who had harassed me? Did he work for the city?

The man in the white suit extended his arm and pointed toward the land behind where he stood and swept it out in front of him. He stopped in my general direction, and their focus followed his hand. I dropped flat. Not sure if I'd been seen, I laid frozen, afraid to move.

Minutes passed with my heartbeat rushing in my ears. No one came. The roar of the bulldozer kicked up. No Name and the mayor's wife might have left, but I couldn't be certain. I listened for the sound of car doors closing, or gravel crunching under tires. The dozer's engine made it hard to tell.

I'd give it a little longer and get out of there. I stared at the cloth ceiling of Arlene's car. Glanced at my watch.

My eyes darted to the window as the shadowy figure of a tall man appeared. He had come around the car to the passenger rear window. From my position, all I could see was his work jacket as he pounded on the glass, sending my stomach into a nosedive. The man bent down. Dylan.

Wiggling my fingers, I gave him a sheepish wave and climbed out the back door. Feeling chilled, more from nerves than being coatless in the cool morning, I wrapped my arms around me.

"Hey, stranger." I smiled like we were old friends and my lying flat in the backseat of a car was just part of a normal day.

His hard-set jaw said he didn't view me as a friend or normal. "What are you doing here?"

"Funniest thing. I took a wrong turn." It sounded lamer out loud than it did in my head.

He rolled his eyes. "That's what security said you might say."

Damn. "The security guy came here to tell you about me?"

"Yep. Said there's some woman ignoring keep out signs and asking questions. We're to call him if we see you."

I shifted feet. "In my defense, there were no signs by that gate I came through." I didn't add that I actually had to open the gate to come through it. "But you obviously saw me."

"I did. This town doesn't take to strangers. In case you haven't noticed. When you crested that hill, I assumed you were a pretty girl who got confused. That's why I came over." Dylan softened, giving me a full body scan landing on my chest again. I'm pretty sure he pumped his eyebrows.

Being a letch was his norm. Lucky for me, I could use that to my advantage. "I appreciate that you didn't rat me out." I tilted my head and smiled, ignoring the reflex to slap him.

He cleared his throat, his tone shifting to something more official. "Honestly, didn't realize it was you, but I have him on speed dial. You're going to need to do better than you took a wrong turn."

"How about you tell me why you lied to me first."

"About?"

"Enterprise, to start. When I met you fixing a ball return you said you'd never even heard of Vince. But he did work for Enterprise."

He folded his arms over his chest. "Before my time. You asked if I knew him, which I don't. Although I've definitely heard of him."

Past dealings taught me that people were only big on semantics when they were hiding something. "Okay. What've you heard?"

"What's the difference? He's dead. I'm even the one that found him." His face grew a few shades whiter and he swallowed hard.

The image of Vince's bloated body had not left either of us. At least I'd seen a cleaned-up version. My voice softened. "I'd heard that. I'm sorry. That must have been rough, but it makes a lot of difference. His pregnant daughter is looking for answers. What had you heard?"

He shrugged. "There was a rumor a while back that he broke into their offices and got fired. That's really about it."

"But Wheeler didn't press charges. Any ideas why not?"

He chortled. "No, but I bet he didn't."

"What makes you say that?" My Fitbit buzzed. Kyle. I'd catch him later.

Dylan crammed his hands into his coat. "How about we talk about this over a beer at lunch in a couple of hours." He leaned against my car.

I smiled again. He was relentless, but I couldn't fake interest in him that long. "I do love beer. How about you tell me first?"

He shrugged again. "Mr. Wheeler doesn't want anyone in his business. And I don't just mean the four walls of Enterprise Trucking."

"Including law enforcement?"

He nodded. "Why do you think he has his own security personnel?"

Wheeler must have put No Name on my tail after our meeting. "Do you know anything about why Vince broke in or if he was looking for something?"

Dylan shrugged. "Beats me."

He wasn't proving to have much information on Vince. I looked past him and at the work going on. "What's up with those men wearing white jump suits? Seems overkill for shifting dirt."

"We're moving out the old and bringing in the new. At one time, the land was a sheep farm. As they say, it was rode hard and put away wet. That's all we've been told."

"Rode hard?"

"Abused."

"By sheep?" Kyle's number buzzed on my wrist again.

"I guess." He glanced at his watch. "Talking about hauling, my load is probably ready for me about now."

I frowned. This trip had been a bust. He never did answer my first question. "I don't understand why you didn't tell me you'd heard of Vince."

"Because I like my job."

"I get that, but I keep getting the run around. No one wants to be connected to Vince, yet no one says why."

He stared at me; his arms folded over his chest. "I can't help you."

"Can't or won't?" Kyle called again. It wasn't like him to blow up my phone. If I didn't answer soon, he'd think I was crammed in the back of a patrol car again. But he'd have to wait. Dylan and I were at an impasse and I couldn't blink first. I also didn't want to push him too far and make that security car a reality.

Finally, he huffed. "His name's a four-letter word."

"You must know why."

"Only that the waterpark is important to this town, and nothing can stand in the way of that."

"Meaning if Vince was messing around and causing a problem in that regard, people wouldn't take too kindly."

"Who would?"

I'd take that as a yes. "What was he doing?"

"Not sure what or if he was. I don't care. Keeping my nose down secures my employment. Anyone who's asked about Vince, can't say the same."

That piqued my interest. "Other people have asked about Vince?"

"It's a small town. People talk. We were told last night this job needs to be finished by tomorrow. Guess the deal is closing Friday. This place is going to be crawling with even more rigs real soon." Dylan stiffened and looked around.

His sudden alertness made me nervous. Activity had picked up in the short time we'd been talking. "Is there really that much dirt that needs to be taken off this property?"

He turned towards the mounds of soil. "So they say."

Dylan didn't seem that clueless to only go by what he'd been told. For whatever reason, he didn't want to share his opinions. At least with me. "Thanks for the chat."

He nodded. "About that beer?"

"Gosh, wish I could, but I have to pick up one of my four kids from school."

He straightened. "Four?"

"Yeah. Me and their daddy stay pretty busy."

He coughed. "I need to get back."

What a shame. I ducked into my car and pulled out of the property the way I'd come in and re-secured the gate. While I was out of my car, Kyle called again. I'd call him as soon as I was off the property.

The security patrol worked for Jackson Wheeler. I'd at least gathered that from my conversation with Dylan. Gladys said that after I'd left, Wheeler was riled up and said he was running out of time. That probably had to do with the land deal being done this week. But why remove all the dirt? How did it being a sheep farm cause a problem? Jackson Wheeler and I required another chat on those subjects and why he'd lied about his connection to Vince from the beginning.

Before I drove out onto the main road, I grimaced at my phone. If I ignored Kyle's calls much longer he might send out the troops for my rescue. I punched in his number.

He picked up before a ring even sounded in my ear. "Oh my God. You're alive. Where are you? Are you okay? Is Floyd okay?" His torrent of words hit me like a wave.

I'd never heard Kyle sound desperate. A lump lodged in my throat. "I'm fine. Why? What's happened?" My mind raced trying to figure out why he was upset.

"I heard the report over my radio and I just thought..." His voice was tight.

"What report?"

"They described the vehicle as a Triumph Spitfire. I mean, how many of those are there?"

My chest constricted. "What's wrong with my car?"

Kyle drew in a deep breath as he struggled to get a grip on his emotions and tell me what had happened. "It exploded."

My phone nearly fell out of my hands. "Where's Arlene?"

TWENTY-FIVE

The thirty-minute sprint to Portland was a blur. Kyle had called back to confirm the sizzling bonfire parked curbside downtown had been my car and a sixty-two-year-old woman had been transported to Legacy. No other casualties—and no other details available.

My frantic calls to Jeff went unanswered. By the time I arrived at the hospital, my stomach had lodged in my throat and my hands were shaking. The nurse in Emergency directed me to the fourth floor. Arlene had been admitted, but they wouldn't say anything else.

The elevators opened onto the floor in front of a nurses' station. Jeff was at the end of the hall, pacing in front of a room with the door shut, and two guest chairs up against a white wall, his tennis shoes squeaking on the floor. I'd had enough Formica in my life this past week to last a lifetime.

His face scrunched in distress as I rushed toward him. His teary expression said it was worse than I'd imagined. My anxiety shot past ten. She must be laying near death. Or she'd lost her arms—or legs. My heart squeezed. How could I live with myself if she was maimed? Even worse, if she died from her injuries? Jeff and Mitz would never forgive me. I'd never forgive me. Please be okay. I have so much more to say that I haven't yet.

Jeff locked eyes with mine. "My God, Kelly? What's going on?"

I wish I knew. "Is Mom okay?"

When I was within arms-reach, he moved in with an all-body embrace that caught me off guard and had me blinking back tears as his relief flooded over me. "I think so." He held me tight; my arms wrapped over his shoulders. After a few seconds, I let go. He didn't. I patted his back. He cleared his throat in my ear, released me, and checked his emotions. We might be divorced, but over twenty-five years of an intertwined life anchored our friendship. Tenuous as it often was. "The doctor and nurse are with her. Thankfully she wasn't in your car when it exploded."

That didn't mean metal hadn't flown off and hit her. "Where was she?"

"Inside the drycleaners. She ran out when she heard the explosion and tripped. Cut her hand bad, and she's been having a hard time breathing. They think it's anxiety."

Understandable. My own anxiety and guilt had threatened to blow a hole in the roof. My throat loosened a little at hearing she hadn't been burned or worse by the blast. "I'm glad she wasn't seriously hurt."

Jeff shook his head. "Don't even want to think about what the outcome would be if she'd been sitting in the driver's seat. Or you and Floyd. Or Mitz." The lines of pain deepened in his face at the images in his mind before his eyes flashed with annoyance. "Your car was a piece of shit, I just didn't realize it was that bad off."

The worst case scenarios tightened my throat again. We had all lucked out. But my dad had given me that car. It might be old, but it wasn't a piece of junk. Certainly not so much that it would explode. "Me either."

We stood in silence. Waiting. My brain swirled. Was

it possible for a car to combust on its own? Mechanics wasn't my forte, but it didn't sound like the transmission. It could have been a faulty gas line. My dad told me once about Spitfires having issues over the years—electrical, I think. I didn't remember him ever mentioning that the issue resulted in explosions. Unless my car hadn't combusted on its own.

An ache in my shoulders marched into the back of my neck. If that were the case, Tyrone or someone in Mickey's employment jumped onto the likely suspects list. In the movies, mafia types blew things up all the time. The finger in the garbage proved they were capable of violence. They had warned me to stay out of their business. Tyrone must have seen me both in Riverview that day and talking to Claire last night. He might have had time to mess with my car at some point in between. I wasn't sure when he'd made me. Claire had referred to ears everywhere. Perhaps eyes, too. I didn't see a tail on my way home, but my car had been parked in the driveway all night. The idea of someone outside, messing with my Spitfire, and me oblivious shot another dose of anxiety through me.

The other option was that Jeff was right and my tin can had been on the verge of destruction for some time. Whatever it was, it did not bode well.

The ding of the elevator brought my attention back. Kyle stepped out and took long strides down the hall towards us. His hard frown registered a mixture of irritation and concern. He came right at me, gathering me in a hug, lifting me off the ground for a few seconds before setting me down, and squeezing. The explosion had sent as many emotions charging through him as it did Jeff. I hadn't had so much one on one contact in one day with the men in my life as this. My own emotions had me struggling not to melt on the floor.

He let go and turned to Jeff. "Your mom going to be okay?"

Jeff had been watching us and flopped into one of the guest chairs. "Waiting to hear."

Kyle nodded and then searched my face. "We need to talk."

"Okay."

"Alone."

I glanced at Jeff. "We'll be right back. Text me when the doctor's out."

Jeff nodded and Kyle grabbed my hand and led me to the elevators. He punched the floor for the cafeteria. We found the coffee vending machine, grabbed a couple of hot blacks, and settled at a corner table. A jar of peanut butter would be great. Coffee would have to do.

Kyle hadn't said much up to this point. He locked his gaze on me. "I can't tell you how it nearly killed me when I thought I'd lost you."

My face flushed. The depth of his concern stirred emotions that I secured behind walls. Of course, Mitz loved me, despite her not talking to me right now. But to be cared about so deeply about whether I came home or not. I took a long drink. "I'm fine. Arlene will be fine."

His shoulders slumped. "She's lucky. Because what happened today was no accident."

I rubbed my eyes not wanting my fears to be justified. "Are you sure? It's an old car. Has trouble starting sometimes. Do you really think it's possible…"

He shook his head as I spoke. "The explosion came from under the car. What's left has been taken to Seizure World."

"Seizure World?"

He took a sip of coffee. "It's what we call the storage lot where cars are taken after an arrest, or in your case, for evidence. Arson and ATF have taken over the case. It'll be a day or two before we get the full results, but my dad was in munitions in the Army. I grew up learning about explosives. I also thought I might train for the bomb squad at some point."

The words *what's left* resonated and I had no idea about his dad, or his aspirations when it came to law enforcement. Like his previous marriage that ended badly, there were things he didn't volunteer information about. "It was a bomb?"

"Fairly certain. Cars don't go boom on their own. They can burn, and if that was the case, it would melt in one spot. Before I came here, I stopped to look at it myself. ATF agrees it doesn't match a gas leak or something along those lines, where the flames would travel a particular route. It was a quick burst in one location, designed to take out the driver's side. They think some of the remnants of the bomb remain inside the engine. They'll tear that apart."

I gulped past the lump in my throat. "Driver's side?"

"Whoever put it there wanted you out of the picture. If arson and ATF agree, a homicide detective will get assigned." Tension bunched around his eyes. In one sentence, he aged before my eyes. I might be doing the same before his.

During my last case, I'd almost been killed. Twice. I hadn't expected that to happen again. If someone wanted to take me out, how about look me in the face. I shook my head. I may be acting bold for my psyche's sake. My insides banged against my ribs like a kid going to town on his new drum set. This was supposed to be a simple missing persons case—for a classmate no less.

Kyle rested his hand on my arm. "Who might have wanted that to happen?"

Brandon was unaccounted for and didn't want me investigating. Based on my reception thus far in Riverview, I wouldn't win a popularity contest there. Did that rise to the level of having me wiped off the face of the planet? My earlier unsettling theory dominated. I didn't answer.

"You took my advice yesterday, right, and you left Mickey and Tyrone alone?"

I stared at the table.

"Correct?" He withdrew his hand and straightened in his chair. "Okay. Spill it."

Even though I didn't like his questioning me, I cared for Kyle. That alone was reason to tell him the truth and it was guaranteed to upset him. "I got a call last night that someone was at the racetracks that hung out with Vince." Thinking back, I could have had Claire describe the person over the phone and texted her a picture of Brandon for confirmation. But I didn't regret going. I might not have learned what I did about Vince otherwise.

His eye twitched. Yup. He was mad. "You said you were going to stay away from there."

"No. I said I wasn't going to mess with Mickey and Tyrone, and I didn't. However, they may have seen me talking to Claire." I looked away. I was using those semantics I'd accused Dylan of earlier.

Kyle folded his arms over his chest. "Did you learn anything so earth shattering that it was worth putting a bullseye on your back?"

Kyle had been frantic, thinking I was dead. I resisted the urge to walk away and anchored my butt to the seat.

"It was Brandon that hung out with Vince and knew of his gambling problems. He went there last night to seek out Mickey and Tyrone, but left before I got there. I'll find out more after visiting him at the dealership where he works this afternoon."

"Bad idea."

"I'm in the market for a new car anyway. This way I'll accomplish two things while I'm there."

He shook his head.

I shared his concern, but Stephanie deserved the truth. If he had heard her desperate phone messages to her dad, he wouldn't be able to walk away either. "Look, Brandon was in touch with Vince far more often than he's let on—even after his argument with him last Thanksgiving."

Kyle stared at me for a long minute. I stared back. "You're not going to like what I have to say next. You need to give this case a rest."

I leaned back in my chair creating distance from him. "I don't like being told what to do."

"Normally, I wouldn't. This is different. People don't go around blowing up people unless they're onto something."

"Exactly. I'm close. I can't let up." I had to make him understand.

He gave me an *I think you might be crazy* look.

My tough-girl façade crumpled and I pressed the heels of my hands onto my closed eyes for just a second. My shoulders slumped I said, "Honestly, I'm not sure what I'm close to finding out. Everyone has been a dead end. Vince was in deep and I've kept you updated on all that right down to the terminal cancer he had. But that's it."

Kyle gave me a lop-sided grin. "That's it, huh?"

It was scary that he knew I was holding back. "There's

the land, of course, which got that security patrol on my ass. Although I don't get why. It's just a lot of dirt. Or how Vince, working for Enterprise as a driver, or breaking into their offices, fits into any of this. At least not yet. And yes, that is all I know."

He nodded and my phone dinged.

Jeff. "The doctors are out of the room. I need to see Arlene."

I stood without finishing my coffee. Upstairs, we walked into the room to a fragile Arlene laying in the bed with cords attached to her chest and heart monitors beeping. Her always perfectly styled pixie cut was disheveled. One hand was wrapped in a bandage and an IV drip was connected to the other. I'd never seen fear or devastation on Arlene's face until that moment. I never wanted to see it again. She quickly masked it with a stoic stare.

My heart broke. From the side of her bed, I laid my head on her chest, hugging her. I stayed there for longer than anticipated. I was so glad that she was alive. She meant more to me than I ever realized.

She placed her hand on the middle of my back. "I'm fine, dear. I'm fine."

A few sniffles, and a struggle to gain my composure, I straightened. "I'm sorry this happened." Jeff and Kyle were somewhere behind me. They were a million miles away as far as I was concerned. Arlene and I were the only two people in the room.

"Just a cut on my hand. The doctors say I can go home in a day or two. They want to watch my heart."

Putting myself in danger was bad enough. I had Mitz to think about. If I didn't piss him off too much, even a life with Kyle. But putting the people I loved in harm's way... And I did love Arlene. Admitting it often might mess with the *at odds relationship* we had perfected so well. I pushed. She pulled. We had quite the balance going. "I'm glad it's nothing serious."

"Me too. How's my car?"

I grimaced. "In much better shape than mine."

"You should have gotten rid of that piece of junk a long time ago. It barely wanted to start today, and when it did, it made weird noises."

I looked back at Kyle who nodded. It didn't take a bomb expert to deduct that the bomb had been tied to my ignition. It faltered. Long enough for the car to get somewhere and to park. Thankfully long enough for Arlene to be far away. Whoever put it there had meant business if they intended for it to detonate the moment the engine turned.

The notion sent a wave of nausea through me. With Floyd often riding shot gun, we both could have died today. My eyes brimmed. What was I doing? Trying to make Mitz motherless? And my sweet boy Floyd...

Arlene's face slacked with exhaustion. A few minutes later, the nurse ordered us out of her room so Arlene could rest. I squeezed her hand before I left. Neither of us said much else. Neither of us were used to feeling these emotions.

In the hallway, Kyle waited by the elevator while I gave Jeff a quick hug. "She's going to be fine."

Jeff nodded.

"I'm glad you haven't told your mom about the DNA test yet."

He ran his hand over his beard. "Yeah. I'm waiting until I hear back. She doesn't need to be worrying for nothing."

"When are you supposed to hear the results?"

"Tomorrow. Linda's been in touch."

A nerve pinched behind my shoulder blade and worked its way into my neck again. If the results were positive, how was I going to get used to her being back in my life, even if it was on the outskirts? I shuddered. One thing at a time. "Keep me in the loop."

"I will. I'm going to stay a while longer in case Mom needs me. Mitz is in school for a couple more hours, and I'll pick her up and bring her here later. Don't forget her program Friday night."

No matter how upside my world, having Mitz and school programs grounded me. Kept me in what was real. "I won't. Hopefully Arlene will be out by then."

"I pity the doctor who'd try to hold her back from being there."

I chuckled. Me too.

Kyle grabbed my hand as we rode down the elevator. "Everything okay? You two seemed to be having a serious discussion."

"Fine." I hadn't brought him up to speed about Jeff and Linda, and the potential for Mitz having a half-brother. We hadn't had time, and now wasn't the place. Besides, I was at a loss of what to say about it yet.

Outside, Kyle's patrol car sat parked next to Arlene's.

He opened my car door. "Did you want to grab another coffee at the café down the street?"

We hadn't finished our conversation, but I couldn't miss my opportunity to see Brandon. "Later, okay? Brandon should be at work by now."

His face flushed. "Jeff was right about you."

I spun around. "You and Jeff have talked about me?"

He put his hands up in surrender. "Not recently. We'd

chatted in the waiting room when you were being treated at the hospital during your last case."

I'd feared that when I'd seen them sitting together that day. "Great. What did my ex have to say?"

"He said good luck ever trying to get you to back away from anything. You're very much like your father."

I straightened. "I'll take that as a compliment."

"He sounded like a great PI. And you're rivaling him. But Kel, please do as I ask and let this case rest for a few days. The lab will have more info on the explosive soon and then we'll know what we're up against. This is an active police investigation at this point. Blowing up cars and attempted murder is a crime."

Of course it was, whether I wanted to think about it or not. "I can't promise you anything. Just please, don't be Jeff."

He scowled. "Thanks for that comparison. If not wanting you dead is a negative trait, we need to reassess where this is going."

"I didn't mean that."

He rounded his cruiser and opened his car door. "Yeah, I know what you meant. I'll be in touch."

He dropped into his car and I watched him back up and drive away. I was far too much like my father than might be good for me. Why did I always have a way of alienating the people I wanted to keep close in my life?

TWENTY-SIX

"BRANDON JACOBY TO the showroom floor. Guest waiting." The announcement echoed off the walls of the dealership and blasted out into the vehicle filled lots.

After leaving the hospital, I'd come straight to find Brandon. With my back against the U-shaped reception desk, I waited for him to appear. The twenty-something girl with shimmering platinum hair behind the counter assured me he was moving some cars before she'd grabbed the intercom. When passing through the rows of various models, I hadn't seen him. However, a used blue sedan had caught my eye and it would be the perfect excuse for my visit if he did answer her call.

He was taking his time. Instead of standing there, I meandered the bright and shiny in the showroom, wondering if I'd ever feel compelled to plop down the asking price for a new vehicle. Doubtful. In my business, that would be stupid. Besides the possibility of drawing attention, it could be destroyed as easily as my Triumph. Not that I expected my car detonating to be a regular occurrence, used and cheap would be my best bet.

An alarm system might be handy too, regardless what I bought to replace my ride. Did they even have bomb detection alarms? A siren that alerted me to someone touching my car would work. The whole idea had my stress level inching up again and I fought to not give into it. If Mickey and associates wanted me dead, Brandon might have information on why after his conversation with them last night. There'd be time to lament at how close of a call it had been to losing Arlene, or making Mitz motherless, later.

Brandon waltzed through the double glass doors laughing and chatting with one of his sales buddies at the same time I'd circled back to the counter and faced the receptionist to avoid eye-contact and to have some advantage.

"I'm Brandon," he said, approaching. When I swung around, he had a *got one on the hook* slimy smile.

His happy face slid away with his recognition. "Hi, Brandon. I'm Kelly. I'm in the market for a new car and figured you could help me with that."

"Seriously?" he said, his voice low.

The platinum girl's blue-eyes widened. That couldn't be her real hair. I smiled at her and then at him. Despite Brandon not telling me the truth, getting him fired wouldn't help Stephanie's blood pressure. "Yes. My car is on the fritz." A mild description, like saying Mike Tyson love-tapped his opponents. I scanned him for any signs that he already knew my transportation status. None. "I'm desperate."

His eyes narrowed. He wasn't sold yet. "What did you have in mind?"

"There's a four door in front. Can we take that for a test drive?" A win-win situation. Get me far away from his bosses so not to cause a problem in his job and giving me alone time to grill him.

He shifted from one foot to another. "Give me a second and I'll get the key. In the meantime, Kimmy here will photograph your license."

With images of *Full House* reruns in my head, I

yanked the ID from my wallet and handed it to Kimmy who had it scanned and returned to me within a minute. When Brandon re-appeared, he had the keys. I followed him out and he drove the car off the lot. "This is a 4-cylinder. Great gas mileage. It's an older model, but new enough you can get an extended warranty."

"Uh-huh. Can I drive?"

He gave me a sideways glance. "Ah, yeah. Sure."

He swung into a furniture store parking lot. Once we swapped seats, I eased out onto Canyon Road and turned for the highway. I punched the gas. The engine stalled before it kicked in. "It's a little gutless," I said, giving him my own sideways glance which he didn't catch.

"It takes a beat to kick in. Once it does though, hold on. It's a smooth ride."

"Cool, but I'm not really interested in the car."

His shoulders slumped, making his six-foot frame shrink into the seat next to mine. "Figures. Why are you bothering me here at work then?"

"To get the truth, for a start."

"About?"

We dropped onto Highway 26. Traffic crawled, and I slid behind a logging truck. I was in no hurry until I had the answers I'd come for. "Where were you last night?"

He opened his mouth and his cheeks turned bright red. If he could have channeled Moses, he would have split those cars in front of us like the Red Sea to get this ride over with.

He was taking too long to answer. "Please don't start some bullshit about being in Corvallis since you were at the Meadows hours after supposedly leaving to help that friend you told Stephanie about." His mouth chomped closed. That's what I thought. "Did you even go home this morning?"

He tilted his head back onto the rest and closed his eyes.

"It's not what you think."

"What do I think?" I cocked an eyebrow.

"That I'm having an affair." He didn't move his head, but he reopened his eyes and locked onto the ceiling.

I'm not sure I did think that. I'd seen *after the fling* guilt before all over Jeff's face. Most married men reeked of remorse when they cheated—or at least after they'd been caught. Not that I'd let Brandon off easy. "That's half of it. The other half is you knew all along that Vince owed money to Mickey. That's why you didn't want me to snoop around. I'm guessing that's why you went to talk to him last night."

He turned to me. "I assure you I'm not sleeping around. I love my wife."

The only time I'd seen him interact with Stephanie, he'd been genuine and attentive. "Let's assume that's true for the moment. What about the rest?"

He shrugged.

An admission in my experience. "Why care if I asked questions of Mickey or found out about the gambling? If Vince owed him money, what difference does it make?"

"It's not."

"What do you mean? It's not important?"

His head nodded forward, his chin resting on his chest. "You're going to tell Stephanie."

"About?"

"Everything."

A tingle started at the base of my neck. "She's my client, and my friend. But I need more information and you can give me that."

He let out a defeated breath. "I'm screwed whichever way I go."

I'd felt that way more than once in my life. "I'm willing to help you if I could understand the situation. I promise you'll have the opportunity to come clean with Steph before I say a word." I had to give up something if I wanted his cooperation.

"I did it."

I took an exit to swing back around and hit more traffic. "You did what?"

"Borrowed the money. It wasn't Vince's debt to pay."

My grip tightened on the steering wheel. "What the hell, Brandon? Your debt?"

He nodded.

"How much?" I asked.

His face grew taught, perspiration beading on his forehead. "A quarter million."

A pain shot into my stomach like I'd been kicked. "How did that happen?"

"I didn't borrow that much." He punched the dash, making me jump. Although I'd be pissed if I owed that kind of money. And hopeless.

"Then how did it get that high?"

"Mickey keeps doubling the damn thing every time I talk to him. The original loan was thirty grand."

"For what purpose?"

His hands balled into fists again. "I'm not making money selling these damn cars. We weren't supposed to have kids. We'd agreed. But Stephanie got pregnant, and I panicked. I wanted to do something right. Something good for us. A guy here at the dealership told me about a tip on one of the horses. I took money out of our savings and made the bet. It was a sure thing."

Obviously not. "Thirty grand?"

His face wrinkled. "I took fifteen from our savings and wagered that originally. When I lost it all, I freaked. Everyone at the tracks says Mickey can help if you're in a jam. That's when I borrowed the thirty with the plan to put the money back into our savings and bet the rest on another race."

A grimace of disgust crossed my face. "Another sure thing?"

He moaned. "Getting involved with him was the stupidest thing I've ever done."

"You think?"

"There's more. The race did pay, but Mickey expected I'd bet the whole thing because he offers stakes. He expected when my pony came in, I'd have my investment, plus interest, to repay him. And there would have been had I bet the whole thing—that and plenty more. But I played it safe."

"And Mickey did the math."

He nodded slowly.

"Why not take that money at least, along with what you'd put back in savings, and give it to him? He might have let you walk away."

He laughed—a sound full of regret. "I wanted to. Even though Stephanie would be furious, I could survive that. What I didn't count on was the surprise that waited for me when I got home that night. Steph had gone crazy decorating the baby's room. Top of the line everything: crib, rocker, furniture. She'd gone to the bank that morning and when she saw the money, she thought I'd been on a selling streak. She went to town. By the time she was done, there wasn't much left." His eyes were rimmed red. "I couldn't make her take it back. Mickey doesn't accept partial payment anyway. He's made that clear. Once the penalties and interest started, it was over."

"But a quarter million?"

"Thirty doubled is sixty. Double that..."

"I get the idea. How did Vince fit in?"

"At Thanksgiving, I told him about my troubles at the tracks. We argued because he didn't want me approaching Mickey."

Something didn't line up. Stephanie hadn't found out she was pregnant at Thanksgiving. "You've had a long-standing gambling problem, haven't you?"

He looked away. I could do math too. "I have it under control now."

Right. "Go on."

"Anyway, the next day I told him I had borrowed from Mickey and he was livid. He called Steph and told her she should divorce me. That she deserved better." He rubbed his hand over head. "I've been hearing that my whole life. It made me more determined to win and turn this around."

"But it didn't turn."

"No. And Vince let me wallow in it for a while. After he tried to get Steph away from me, he realized I wasn't going anywhere. When he found out she was pregnant, he tried to call her, but she wouldn't answer. She was too upset from his earlier rants about leaving me. Then earlier this year, out of the blue, he said he'd help me clear the debt."

"Was it the pregnancy that changed his mind?"

"It might have helped, but he said he was sick and things in his life were clearer than they'd ever been."

Traffic started to move. "How did he think he could help? He didn't have that kind of money, did he?"

"He wouldn't say. Only that the less I knew, the safer I'd be. I did know he was gambling and that he'd won a little. But like I said, Mickey didn't take partial payments."

Which explained why after Vince's big win he made more wagers, even if he had a moment of being human and celebrated. "Why go to Mickey last night? Doesn't he already know Vince is dead?"

"He didn't act surprised; he's hard to read. Regardless, I'd much rather go to Mickey than have him show up at my home or work. As expected, he wants his money, but I bought myself a few weeks. Told him I have to help my wife bury her father, and some life insurance policies will be paying out."

I perked up. "There are?"

He shook his head, his eyes red again. "No, but I have to keep him off my back until I can figure things out."

Good luck with that. Quarter of a million wasn't going to drop from the sky. "Staying away from home isn't the answer."

"I couldn't face Stephanie. I swear, I slept in my car here at the lot. I'd never do anything to hurt my wife." His eyes brimmed.

He already had. The news of his addiction would devastate her, as much as realizing the man she thought was taking good care of them was destroying their future. Even I was on Vince's page about Brandon being no good, but Stephanie... "She needs you now, more than ever."

Why we choose the men in our lives we do, was a question for the ages. We really might be drawn to men like our fathers on some level. Vince and Brandon with the gambling. My dad and Jeff with the indiscretions. Kyle seemed to have my father's protective streak. Although his definition of me being safe most recently was to quit and my dad's was to keep me in the dark. That wasn't proving to be a good thing as it pertained to Mickey and Tyrone.

"I need her too," Brandon said.

I nodded. "My car blew up this morning. Someone tried to kill me. Tyrone at Mickey's direction is the likely candidate. Although I can't figure out why Mickey would want me dead."

His brow creased. "That's not good." He thought about it. "But it doesn't make sense. You don't owe them money."

"That's for certain." Not that things always made sense. Like canceling *Fringe*. Or putting potato chips on a peanut butter sandwich. They could want me dead because as Stephanie's friend, my death would have served as a scare tactic for Brandon by hitting close to home. Like the finger in Vince's garbage.

We pulled back into the lot. "You really are in the market for a new car then, yeah?" he asked.

"I will be when I find out if insurance covers what happened." That was going to be a fun conversation. "I'll come back when I know. It'll need to have more guts than this one." Brandon missed that jab too. But I'd do whatever I could to help Stephanie. Directly or indirectly. At least I'd try.

He nodded. "I'll get you a good deal."

"Thanks. When are you going to tell Stephanie?"

He rubbed his hand over his shiny dome again. "After the funeral."

"You may not have that long. I can give you until I figure out this case and then I'll have to give her a full report." At the rate I was going, he might have a little time.

He groaned. "Fine."

We exited the vehicle and I tossed the keys over to him. "Stay as low key as possible. That means no more nights away from home. Got it?"

He nodded. I couldn't protect him from Mickey. If they wanted to use me as an example, I could only imagine what they were prepared to do to him if he didn't pay. But I wanted to be able to find him if necessary.

As I drove out of the lot, I thought of Vince. Had he been used as an example too?

AFTER PARKING ARLENE'S car in her garage where no one would have easy access, and setting her car alarm, I went home where a tail-chasing Floyd greeted me at the door. After he had a romp in the backyard and a bowl of kibble, I made myself a spoon full of peanut butter, dipped in jelly, and poured a glass of wine. At the kitchenette table, Floyd curled at my feet and I closed my eyes, savoring the spoon and letting the tension of the day drain out of me.

When my phone rang, I didn't recognize the number and groaned at the intrusion. Floyd looked up with droopy eyes and flopped back down. Voicemail could get it. Recognition struck me. Dora. I swooped up my cell and dislodged the peanut butter spoon out of my mouth. "This is Kelly."

"Kelly, Dora O'Reilly returning your call. Sorry it's taken so long to get back to you. It's been a wild news day. A car exploded downtown."

I almost chortled at the irony. "Really?"

"Yeah. Crazy stuff. Thank God no one was killed. Only minor injuries."

Hearing her talk about the incident made me shift on the chair finding it hard to get comfortable. I gulped down some wine. "That is wild."

"Anyway. You said you had something that might be important?"

That's right. "My friend's father died recently. He lived up in Riverview and your phone number was written down on a notepad in his kitchen. The name is Vince Burnotas. Does that sound familiar?"

"Burnotas?"

"Yeah." I spelled it for her.

"Doesn't ring any bells. I'm sorry to hear he died, but any time I do a report, there's a listing of my number at the bottom of the screen telling people to call if they have something they want me to check out. He could have jotted my number down for future reference."

She had a point. I had no idea when he'd taken down her information. It could have been a year ago, or right before he died. Regardless, what did he think he might want her to investigate? "I see."

"Wish I could be more helpful."

Another dead end. "No worries. I really appreciate your calling me back." I closed my eyes. Mitz. "Does your offer stand about doing a studio tour?"

"Absolutely. I have time tomorrow if that would work. I'm off for a few days after that."

I set down the wine glass. "That would be awesome. We can be there around three after my daughter gets out of school."

"Perfect."

I ran my hand over Floyd's back. Excited for my field

trip with Mitz tomorrow, I voice texted Jeff to make sure that would be okay and got a quick *she'll love it* in response.

Easing back into the chair, I put the spoon back in my mouth, the idea of stepping back from this case flitting through my mind. I wanted so much to make things right with Mitz. I acted all tough but having her mad at me had me feeling like a failure. As much as giving up, which I was on the verge of. If I did, I could spend more time with Mitz. I could drink more wine. I could sleep.

Despite being irritated with Kyle for telling me what to do, he might be right about letting it rest. I couldn't admit defeat, but I was in over my head when people were willing to chop off body parts and detonate vehicles.

My head hurt thinking about how close Arlene had come to dying. Time and distance might make things clearer. Besides, I'd done what I'd initially been hired to do. I'd found Vince. The authorities believed it was an accident. Who was I to argue that?

I'd also uncovered some details of what Vince had been doing before his car crashed—including trying to save Brandon's worthless ass and dying of cancer. The stress alone of that could have had him drinking and driving, and not concentrating on that backroad. All things I kept telling myself to make me feel better as I climbed the stairs to my bedroom, Floyd at my heels.

At my dad's closed room, I rested my hand on his door. Many times, I'd asked what he would do. This time, I didn't need an answer. He'd never step back. It wasn't in him. Despite Kyle saying I could rival my dad—I wasn't him by a long shot. I didn't cheat on my spouse. Do favors for the mob. Or keep my daughter in the dark. Especially one who worked in the same office. I rubbed my right eye as it twitched.

Keeping my rage pent-up at my father had been an accomplishment over the past few months. The ache in my jaw indicated it was seeping out with some vengeance. I flopped into bed, cramming it away. He was human. I'd gone over that countless times in my head. But I couldn't avoid my feelings forever. At some point, I was going to have to reconcile his betrayal. Somehow. Just not tonight.

Around midnight I drifted off. My desire to bury myself under the covers and never come out would be a colossal disappointment to him. I wasn't sure one part of me cared.

TWENTY-SEVEN

MY EYES FLEW open at nine in the morning. Arlene's near miss, as well as my own, had taken its toll. That, and finishing two glasses of wine before bed. I groped for my cell on the nightstand. Kyle hadn't tried to reach me.

I flung my arm over my head. He was still irritated. Texting to tell him I was stepping back from the case for a bit crossed my mind. But I didn't. While having us back to the way we were, before I insinuated he was like the man I'd divorced, sounded good, I didn't want his approval. I winced. The lies we tell ourselves. No more than I wanted my dad's.

With a huff, I rolled out of bed and got Floyd out, started coffee, and threw a load of laundry in the washing machine downstairs. I checked in with Jeff. Arlene had improved, but they wanted her for another couple of days. I could use her car for at least forty-eight more hours before I'd have to figure out what to do next.

The rest of my day went fast. After making sure Arlene's Oldsmobile hadn't been tampered with through the night, I swung by my office, Floyd in tow. Neither of us enjoyed spending time behind these walls after what happened last year. Giving it up might eventually arrive, but my dad had worked from here for thirty years. I wasn't ready to let it go. Or the good memories we'd shared here. Whether he'd kept major portions of his life and himself hidden, I couldn't be wrong about who he really was. I couldn't let myself believe anything else. I parked in a spot right outside my office window and kept an eye on Arlene's car as I sat at the front desk.

The mail produced some checks and a few bills—Portland General Electric and Century Link. Carla from Baumgartner & Sokol was the only message on the machine. She had several trial subpoenas that needed served by the end of next week. I'd grab them after the weekend, glad that no matter how this or any case went, I had process serving to fall back on.

At two-thirty sharp, I had Floyd in the back seat, and Mitz in the passenger side. We backtracked it to Jefferson Street in Portland, where the KGW studios were located.

Our ride had been void of any communication until I couldn't take it anymore. "You still mad at me?" I signed at a stop light.

"No, Mama. Just disappointed."

Disappointed? Might as well pierce my heart and get it over with. "I only think what's best for you. I hate that you're disappointed in me for that."

She signed, "I didn't mean you. Jaycee made fun of me because I can't get my ears pierced yet. I told her my mom cared what I did and wanted to be there with me. She laughed and said I was just a baby." She lifted her chin. "Real friends don't do that, Mama."

"They certainly don't." I gave her a smile filled with pride and sadness that she was learning some life lessons so early about people and friendships. I bumped her arm. "Have I told you lately how incredible you are?"

"Oh Mama, you and Daddy tell me that all the time. I'm not. I'm..."

Special came to mind. Incredible. "Awesome."

She shook her head. "Normal. That's all I want to be."

Who was this eight-year-old sitting next to me? Somehow in all of mine and Jeff's madness, Mitz was holding her own. We weren't screwing her up too bad. "That might be your goal, Ladybug, but you'll never be ordinary. I'm sorry. Awesome is the lowest rung you'll ever occupy."

She laughed, flashing her gappy smile my direction. "You're funny, Mama."

Nothing would ever feel or sound as good as her laughter.

We spent the rest of the drive with her telling me about the program on Friday night. She'd been practicing her pogo trick for weeks and could hardly wait for the big performance. She kept asking where we were going. What we were doing. I only smiled in reply as she rattled off guesses so not to spoil the surprise.

We made the drive around the brick-laid half-circle and parked on the street. She bounced out of the car and ran ahead of me to the retro-futuristic two-story building with its window cowls. She waited for me at the door and together we walked into the bright lobby. Her eyes lit with wonder at the TV screens and KGW Channel 8 logo blazoned on the back wall. Mission accomplished. We approached the reception.

"We have an appointment with Dora O'Reilly." I clutched Mitz's hand.

We were directed to the overstuffed armchairs near the windows, both of us beaming. You'd think we were entering the Willie Wonka Chocolate Factory we were so excited. A few minutes later, Dora walked out wearing her reporter gray trousers. Instead of her KGW black jacket, she had on a red polo shirt with the logo stitched on the left side.

With having a deaf cousin, Dora jumped in communicating right away. "You must be Mitz?"

Mitz nodded with more enthusiasm than I'd seen in a long time. "I've seen you on TV."

"You have? Well, I'm going to show you where some of the magic happens," Dora signed.

Mitz did her version of a squeal and put both of her hands in front of her, palms pointing back toward herself, and circling them down, back, up, forward, down, back, up. The sign for happy.

My cheeks ached from smiling so big.

Dora laughed. "Looks like you're ready to go."

The small entry into the studios belied the true size of the building which was a reverse L-shape. Dora gave us the full tour and talked to Mitz about potential careers at the station. Mitz had twenty questions about being an interpreter including how old she had to be to get started. Could she start now. We all laughed. Dora had every answer.

An hour later, we ended where we began in the lobby. "Thank you so much, Dora."

"It has been my pleasure. You have a wonderful daughter."

Mitz eyed a vending machine in the corner. "Mama," she signed. "Please?"

I dug a dollar out of my purse and handed it to her and turned back to Dora. "This means the world to her. And to me." I kept an eye out as Mitz walked over and contemplated her choices of junk food. We'd grab a salad for dinner before I took her to Jeff's. Maybe we wouldn't.

She nodded. "It was a good thing we met that day on Gee Creek."

"Definitely."

"You never did say why you were out there," she said. "Were you following the story on the waterpark?"

I shook my head. "I was following someone and your caravan drove by." I thought back to that day. I hadn't told her what I did for a living at the time because I was focused on her story. Later, I'd only said Vince was my friend's father. "I'm a private investigator. Vince Burnotas' daughter hired me to find him. He's the man I'd called you about who had your number in his drawer. He went missing nearly a month ago now and as I mentioned, he was found dead this past week out on Gee Creek Road."

Dora tilted her head. "When did you say he went missing?"

"From all accounts, the first week of April. He left a tavern located in town after telling his girlfriend he needed to meet someone."

Dora put her hand on her chest. "Who was he meeting?"

"Don't know. And while he was found in Gee Creek, he never said where the supposed meeting was to take place. Because no one called in the accident, we don't know if the meeting even happened. The only thing I'm fairly certain of is he worked for Enterprise Trucking, which I'm sure you're aware is owned by Jackson Wheeler."

Dora's face paled. "I think he was going to meet me."

My heartbeat quickened. "You said you'd never heard of him."

"I hadn't. About six weeks ago, I'd done a preliminary story on the waterpark. The next day, I got a call. The man refused to tell me his name, but said he had a story to sell. He asked if I was interested in information that might shut the waterpark down."

"You wanted the waterpark not to happen?"

"Not necessarily. My original story had to do with the impact the construction would have on the watershed and the nearby wildlife. That access property hadn't been sold yet so there was real concern. The caller said he had irrefutable proof that things were happening out there that weren't good for the environment. When I asked him how, he said he might be a former employee of one of the contractors out there."

"Vince."

"Like I said, he didn't give a name. He called me the morning of the 7th, I have it on my calendar, and wanted to meet that night. We arranged it for eleven at the end of the road where the news conference was held."

The timing was right. "Why there?"

"I asked the same question. He insisted. Said I could see for myself and he'd hand over the proof then. He'd asked about the Crime Stopper reward. Seemed very focused on getting paid for whatever he had."

The fact the man was interested in a payout confirmed for me it was Vince. "No clue what that something was?"

"None."

I wrinkled my nose. "You went by yourself?"

"I don't go anywhere without my cameraman. Besides that he's my boyfriend, I wouldn't be much of a roving reporter if I didn't have a way to get the images back to the station."

True. "But you didn't meet the man?"

"He never showed. I took a flashlight and looked around to see if I could find what he'd been talking about. Nothing seemed out of place. Truth is, for as many people who don't want the park, there are those that do. I figured it was one of those pro-construction types unhappy with my previous reports who thought it would be fun to send me out there late at night."

"Wish that had been the case."

She nodded. "I feel terrible that I didn't see the wreckage as we drove out. If I could have helped him, I would have."

"Don't feel bad. Unless you saw him drive off the road, you wouldn't have even known where it happened without stopping and looking over the edge."

She dropped her chin to her chest. "Maybe."

I understood. She was part, if not the only reason, Vince had been on that road in the first place. If she could have, she would have tried to do something. I liked Dora O'Reilly.

Mitz ran back to me clutching a bag of chips. I ran my fingers through my girl's red curls. "Ready," I signed.

She nodded and I reached out and shook Dora's hand. "You've been more than helpful. I don't mean just the tour."

"Sorry I can't tell you more."

She had told me more than she thought. So much for taking a step back. Vince Burnotas had something in his possession that he'd planned to give Dora the night he died. Where had it gone?

TWENTY-EIGHT

I DROPPED MITZ at home with Jeff with a promise to see her tomorrow night for the talent show, and called Detective Kuni on my way up to Riverview. He picked up after the second ring.

"Long time no chat, Ms. Pruett. What can I do for you? You been working on Mr. Burnotas' case?"

The warmth of his voice settled my nerves that had frayed even further since leaving Dora. My head already knew, but even my body sensed travelling to Riverview wasn't a great idea. "Yes. And I need some more information about the accident if you've got a second."

"Happy to try."

"Was an inventory kept of what was taken out of or found around Vince's vehicle at the scene?"

"I'm sure there was. Let me grab it."

He put me on hold and I tapped the steering wheel of Arlene's car. If the response was yes, and he had the contents, I'd head straight to the police station.

He came back on the line. "Got it. Looks like nothing you wouldn't expect. A few candy and fast food wrappers. Scratch offs and pull-tabs. I already told you about the ticket found on him."

"Nothing else odd or suspicious?"

"Doesn't appear to be. You looking for something specific?"

"Not sure. I learned today why Vince was on that

road." I ran down my meeting with Dora O'Reilly and that she and Vince were scheduled to meet at eleven the night he died. "Unfortunately, he was a no show and he didn't provide Dora a clue of what he planned to give her."

"I see. Well, the car has been thoroughly gone through at this point. Ms. O'Reilly could have been confused by the message."

I chewed on my lip. "Except the man wanted to sell a story, and mentioned being a former employee."

"Wish I could be more help then."

I wasn't ready to give up. "Since his vehicle was in water, is it possible something could have floated away?"

"The glass was broken. It's not impossible, but a perimeter search was completed."

"How far out does the search go?"

"General practice would be closest proximity to the car up to the banks. After that, anywhere wreckage or car parts landed."

"With the creek water moving toward the river, wouldn't they search out there?"

"Only if parts were found that far. The Traffic team believed this was a case of falling asleep at the wheel. They wouldn't go beyond routine procedures."

I rolled down the passenger window giving Floyd some fresh air. I could use some myself. "Thank you. That helps me with what to do next."

"Do I want to hear what that is?"

Arlene's car clock read four-thirty. "Probably not," I said.

"Tell me anyway."

Most construction crews would be off about now. The security detail that I intended to avoid might not be. In the interest of common sense, it might be good for someone to know what I was up to—and I couldn't call Kyle. "I believe there's something to what I learned from Dora. Vince's death could have been an accident, but it wasn't as simple as an evening drive that took him out there. Vince had something to sell and I want to find it."

He cleared his throat. "Our department is pretty thorough, but if they have something in their heads..."

He didn't finish the sentence. He didn't have to. I was surprised at the admission. Cops didn't go around slamming their own departments to outsiders. It might be the connection with my dad, but every time the detective and I spoke, he treated me as his equal. And he reflected my thoughts exactly on the subject.

"Just don't get in the way," he continued. "Riverview is odd in its politics and community loyalty."

"I've noticed."

"I don't want to hear about you being arrested for trespass. You might not fare as well as Vince did on having the charges dropped. My advice is stick to searching from the public road, and you'll stay out of trouble."

"Absolutely." I was telling my dad I'd be staying home all night all over again, even though my plan had been to sneak out with Jeff. Except the detective couldn't believe I'd be able to search from any road. "Who would I be trespassing against if I'm down on Gee Creek Road anyway?"

"The city owns the land that's being sold for the waterpark."

"I guessed that much from the news conference, but to who? And would they care?"

"It's a conglomerate of investors, which is a big deal around these parts. I wouldn't test them to find out."

Olivia Chambers came to mind. "How's the mayor's wife fit into all of this?" I asked. "She was at Mr. Wheeler's office that first day I came into town, and yesterday she was out on the property with a security guard."

"Olivia? She's quite active in the mayor's office and helped spearhead the sale by gathering the investors. It's her family that owns Hildebrand. They're slated to build the waterpark, so she's motivated."

"Hildebrand Construction?"

"Yes."

"Wouldn't that be a conflict of interest for her family to get the contract if she was coordinating the selling of the land?" That could be why Vince had written the trucking company's name on the notepad along with Dora's number. A conflict like that could be a big story to sell to Channel 8 news.

"Ethically it is, but legally, once the city sells it, the investors who buy it can make any decision they want as to who they choose to build."

"Unless she'd only sell to those people who would choose Hildebrand?"

He clicked his tongue. "A possibility. However, you'd have to round up any other potential buyers who felt slighted to prove it. Could be hard to do."

"What if Vince found that proof?"

"There's no evidence of that."

Not yet. "How about I check in with you when I'm done canvassing the main road. That way you'll know I'm out of your town."

He agreed. "I have a dinner event, but at least leave a message. Also, we'll be releasing Mr. Burnotas' body tomorrow. We'll need Ms. Jacoby's direction of where she wants his body to go."

My heart pinged. When you're in an emotional blur, even the simplest choices become huge. When I had time, I'd research options for Stephanie to help her decide. "I'll be in touch."

"Look forward to your call."

I hit the 402 toward the end of town and rested my hand on Floyd's back leg. "Hey buddy, I think it's time to put your skills to the test."

Floyd tilted his head and thumped his tail twice as if he understood. I'm pretty sure *Lady, what took you so long?* flitted through his mind.

BY THE TIME I parked at the end of Gee Creek Road, it was well after five. On my way past the construction entrance, I hadn't seen any trucks coming or going. My route through Riverview had been direct. I blended in with people headed for home, and I hadn't seen any security patrol cars on my way through.

After I'd hung up with Detective Kuni, I'd swayed between paranoia, checking my rearview mirror to make sure no one had followed me, and calm, certain I hadn't been seen and that Mickey's people hadn't trailed me from Portland. For the moment, I felt relatively safe from them.

Or was I? Organized crime's tentacles could be anywhere gambling occurred. And that was more places than I'd imagined. I had to look no further than Tip Top Tavern or the bowling alley for that. While Mickey might have nothing to do with the card room or pull-tabs, I'm sure he had connections in every dark recess. Regardless, I had to stop debating criminal elements and focus on the task at hand. It wouldn't be dark until eight. If I hurried, there'd be plenty of time to search for anything Vince had left behind.

The question was where to start now that Floyd and I were out of the car. Better question—what was I looking for? Dora said her caller had indicated the information could shut down the waterpark construction. Photographs of inspectors taking bribes or papers of illicit transactions of some kind could do that. None of which would do well out in the elements.

This could be a huge waste of time. I strapped Floyd into his harness and made sure I had a few treats in my pocket for him. We had to at least check, or I'd be up all night wondering.

Waist-high grass had been beaten down into a pathway off to the right of the roundabout. We started there. The trail led into dense brush and the creek area. Our starting place needed to be where Vince's car had gone down, which meant doubling back.

The underbrush and thicket intertwined to form a flat, albeit springy, walkway. Floyd took the lead. Before we'd made a hundred yards, my foot dropped down to midcalf and splashed into freezing water. I yelped. The Swamp Thing took hold, attempting to pull me under. Too many horror movies after midnight. Floyd bounced back toward me. "I'm okay." I ruffled his head. I'd just broken through some branches. I recovered, and yanked my foot out, minus my tennis shoe. Shoving my drenched foot back into my sneaker, and tying the laces tighter, we pushed on with Floyd ahead.

Fifteen minutes later, with another drop through the flooring with my other foot, and pants soaked to my knee, we made it back to the horseshoe-shaped portion of the creek where Vince's car had crash landed. I shivered, as much from the irony that the horseshoe hadn't offered much luck for Vince as my cold jeans plastered to my skin. Deep ruts where the wreckage had been pulled from the water marred the narrow shore and the embankment where it had been hauled to the main road. One hell of a chain and set of hydraulics would have been used to accomplish that task.

The accident happened a month ago, and the water at that time had been deep enough to cover a vehicle. Now, the spring run-off had dwindled. The water had receded, exposing more of the brush around the creek line.

I removed Floyd's leash. "Stay close, boy."

He meandered, nose stuck to the ground, looking for something dead to roll in, his expertise. Detective Kuni said they'd searched this area but hadn't found any unexpected contents from Vince's vehicle. Nothing was appearing to me either. We made the round-about and started back toward the river.

Floyd froze and pawed a piece of brush. Odds were a dead bird or rat. My lip curled. More than once he'd covered his body in rodent triggering a late-night bath in ketchup. It's all I had at the time. It worked its magic, but the vinegar smell had lingered for weeks. I didn't plan to relive that moment anytime soon.

"Come on, boy." He didn't listen. I ran to him before he opted for roadkill cologne around his neck. "Leave it, buddy. Watcha got?" He ignored me again, continuing to work the area with his nose and paw. I grabbed his harness and held him back enough to get between him and the bush. My heart pounded at his eagerness. I bent down and lifted the limbs. And frowned. "Really, bud?" He'd found a half-full bag of Doritos.

He promptly sat and stared at me, jowls slack, eyes

bright. He lifted his chest up, expecting the bag as a reward for his efforts.

"No way, my friend. But you're a good boy." I retrieved one of his cookies from my pocket and snapped it in half, giving him part. He took the piece in one swallow.

The chips might have come from Vince's car. More likely, teenagers hung out here during the summer and it was left over from that. This would be a decent swimming hole. Even Detective Kuni had mentioned that with it being isolated, kids had been known to come down here to party. Jeff and I had been to a few keggers down country roads in our time. I winced. Our time. As in back in the day. Geez. You'd think I was ancient. Thirty-two wasn't old, but this case had me feeling every one of those years.

Floyd recovered from not getting his lost treasure and took off again. After about thirty minutes, I sat down on a log near the main river. Other than the Doritos, and a few leftover items too gross to mention from thoughtless partiers and lovers, I hadn't found any smoking gun, as they say.

Another dead end in a string of them. Sitting made my legs stiff and the shivering returned. Time to go. But Floyd didn't want to give up. He'd gone ahead and down the shore of the river heading toward town. His swaying tail disappeared into the overgrowth. I forced myself up and traversed his direction by way of downed limbs across the wet slog. "Floyd, come."

I hadn't gotten far when the sound of branches cracking came from behind me. I stopped. Turned. No one in sight. Another crack.

Had I been followed? I'd been so careful to get here. Were cameras up on the main road that had alerted someone to my being there? I hadn't seen any on my way in. I scanned the trees overhead. Nothing. The road and Arlene's car weren't visible from my vantage point.

More branches snapped. I didn't think to grab my pepper spray—better yet, my gun. If whoever it was knew I was onto them, they might go away. "Who's there?"

No response.

I crouched, not seeing Floyd. Or hearing him. My mind was playing tricks on me. If someone was out here with us, he would have barked. Where was he?

Before I could get a fix, he leapt out of the brush with more energy than I'd ever seen him possess. "Floyd," I yelled. He bolted past me. Birds lit from the trees. The question wasn't who, but what. Two deer took off in a lope the opposite direction. Floyd howled at their heels as they disappeared. I ran my hands through my hair as my stomach slid back into place. "Between you and them, I almost had a heart attack."

Floyd didn't see the problem as he hurried back to where he'd disappeared before all the ruckus.

Taking a couple of calming breaths, I followed and noted the amount of garbage along the shoreline. This was part of the watershed for the town. I'd have thought the city would want to keep that clean.

When I caught up with Floyd, he came out of the bushes with a Subway wrapper in his mouth. "Drop it," I commanded. He did, blinking at me with anticipation. I called him to me and he got another treat. Bringing Mr. Nose was turning out to be a bad idea. I was almost afraid to see what he'd bring me next now that this game ended with food.

I frowned. "Look, if we're going to search anymore, then you need to focus. We're supposed to be finding something that Vince had. Something he was going to give to Dora. Do you understand?"

He shook his whole body in response, beads of water flying at me like a spray hose. He had no clue what I was talking about. What had I been thinking? We were about to turn around, when a piece of taillight glass in the underbrush got my attention. Picking it up, I tossed it in my hand. It could have been part of Vince's car. If it had been, then the creek had carried it quite a way from the original accident. Farther than the police had searched. I scanned the general vicinity not seeing any other car parts.

We headed back the way we came, following the river. The other side of where I had parked led towards the waterpark and Wheeler's land. If the river was moving toward the Pacific Ocean, I doubted anything would have floated that direction from this part of the creek.

But I wasn't savvy when it came to tides and I didn't know where I was in the tributaries. It was possible something could have floated that direction.

This time, I led the way. Floyd trailed, darting back and forth, over-stimulated by the scents of fish, the disappearing deer, and no doubt the goal of scoring more garbage and thus treats before this day was over.

Which would be any minute because I wasn't finding anything else. This whole idea was turning out to be a bust. Like Floyd, I'd been nose to the ground and only coming up with empty wrappers. Detective Kuni was right. Dora could have misunderstood. It might not have even been Vince who had called her. There must be other former employees who were desperate for money. Thinking about it, did it even make sense? If Vince had something that could shut down the waterpark, he could be using that to blackmail someone. That would get him more money than a Crime Stopper reward, which was what Brandon needed. So why would he be willing to turn that over to a news reporter? Unless the blackmailer called his bluff. Who was he blackmailing?

Wheeler seemed likely, but with the cold creeping up my legs, it was hard to think. Time to wrap this up. By way of the shoreline, we were past Arlene's car, and a good quarter mile into the waterpark and farm property when I had to stop. A landslide of dirt had come down the cliff and created a mound near the river. A small clearing had been made in the trees that lined the farm property above the river's edge. Trucks had been removing dirt. I'd seen them take it away. Some must have fallen over the cliff.

When I looked to find Floyd, he was gone. "Damn it, boy, where'd you go now?"

I retraced my steps fifty yards. His tail stuck out like a flagpole, his butt in the air, in a row of vine bushes filled with thistle. He'd be a joy to get clean. Exasperated, I yelled, "Come here."

He refused. Whatever he'd found held more interest than any treat in my pocket. I waded into the grassy mire and grabbed hold of his harness. "Let's get out of here."

His head came up with a white wrapper in his mouth. Not again. I reached to grab it, but it hadn't contained food this time. It was an envelope. Soft and fragile from the elements, an animal had helped it along in disintegrating by ripping a hole into the middle. I pulled Floyd out of the thistle, then shook the contents of the envelope. A vial of brown stuff dropped into my hand.

I glanced at the area where it had come from, but dark shrouded the ground underneath the vines. With my cell's flashlight mode, I illuminated the space and a cartridge of some kind caught the light. Threading my hand through the brush, I retrieved a video, the twisted film hanging out. The same animal that had made toast of the envelope had gone to town on the cassette. The camcorder that had been flung against Vince's wall. I closed my eyes. This was about the same size. Unfortunately, even if it had fit, the cassette was useless in its current state.

Whatever had been on that tape might be gone, but the vial remained intact. The same kind of vials I'd found stashed in a box in Vince's spare bedroom.

I kissed Floyd's water droplet covered snout, my irritation dissipating. "I think you found what we were looking for."

This had to be what Vince was bringing to Dora. Whatever *this* was.

Floyd sat at attention, as if he knew he was the man of the hour and got the rest of the treats in my pocket.

A few minutes after giving him a *good job* massage and removing a few dozen pricklies from his fur, as well as a dozen from my arms for going in after him, we hiked to Arlene's car. I set him up in the backseat. He had a musky outdoor smell. Giving him space to dry and conk out, I climbed into the driver's side.

With the heat blasting towards my pants, I stared at the vial and shook the powdery substance. Was it drugs? Gun powder? It looked like the bronzing stuff I hauled out during the summer to make people think I spent time in the sun. Cocoa? Yeah right. He was out there making hot chocolate. Only way to know was to be brave. With a twist of the lid, I lifted off the cap, braced, and sniffed.

Mildewed. Musty. Dirt. Dirt?

I snapped the cap back on and screwed it tight as

Dylan's words flowed through my head. The dirt on Wheeler's land. They were cleaning it up. Piles of it were on the bank of the river. The men had been in white suits. Did the dirt need testing? Is that why Vince had a vial of it? Did he want Dora to get it tested? He might have already done that. That could be what was on the tape. What kind of testing did a sheep farm need?

Phone in hand, I hit my web browser to ask Google. The icon only spun. I needed to get out of this gully to higher ground for better cell service. I kicked my car into drive, and rolled a few feet feeling a clunk as the tire rolled. Another couple of feet. Another clunk.

Flipping the gear into park, I hopped out, and rounded the car. And frowned. The passenger side front wheel was flat. On my way down, I must have hit a screw from the job site.

I'd never changed a tire. This should be loads of fun. The sun hung low in the sky. With the number of trees in this area, it would get darker here sooner than above. My legs were frozen. I had to work fast.

Wrestling the tire and jack out of the trunk, I shimmied the spare over to the front of the car. When I squatted down, the culprit hung out of the sidewall. It wasn't a screw. A wood-handled knife, its brand, OCD, blazed into the grip, had been jammed into the rubber. OCD. Was that a joke? Every cell in my body jettisoned like a pinball machine. I leapt up, my eyes scouring the area. Floyd and I hadn't just heard a couple of deer.

A strong shudder shook me. Someone had been down here, watching us. Why had they only slashed the tire? I was easy pickings out in that brush. Whatever the reason my tire was the only casualty, the message was loud and clear. I wasn't safe. Anywhere.

TWENTY-NINE

EITHER I'D BEEN followed right from the moment I left my house, or I hadn't gotten through town undetected. Whichever, that's what I got for feeling too confident. I had to get out of here in case whoever had messed with me came back.

After retrieving my gun from Arlene's glove compartment, I set it next to me while I worked. My sweaty hands slipped off the tire iron. I had to put my whole body into it to get the bolts to loosen. A nail ripped to the quick when lifting the spare, causing a few choice expletives to fly out of my mouth.

Ignoring the pain, I tightened the last bolt, praying the tire wouldn't drop off on the highway. With the jack and the flattened tire in the trunk, I sped up the road and eventually out of the gully. My breath started to even out as I made the final crest where the sky was lighter than at the bottom of the road.

The heat blasted and I waited at the stop sign, ready to turn right onto the main road when a car approached, the silhouette of its bank of lights dark against the setting sun. Head bent, I pressed my chin against my chest, as the security guard flicked on his blinker and turned in front of me. He glanced my way, his mouth moving, but didn't look like Officer No Name or the other man who'd stopped me a couple of days ago. He also didn't show signs of recognition. The choice to wear my hair down had at least been a smart one.

He accelerated away and my shoulders lowered an inch. Even if those other two rent-a-cops had warned their team about me, they didn't know Arlene's car. He was also driving the way in which I'd just left, confirming that security had not slashed my tires. Although that didn't help me in narrowing down who did.

Kids who liked to party back there could have seen my car and didn't like my intrusion. If my car hadn't been detonated yesterday, I might have bought that theory. Now, it didn't feel innocent. I just wasn't sure it was related to Mickey and his thugs. After trying to blow me up, they certainly wouldn't follow me all the way to Riverview only to slash my tires.

If Jackson Wheeler had sent his security goons like the one that had driven past, they'd have waited for me at my car, not slashed and run. Maybe it had been kids screwing around. A half mile later, my muscles remained knotted. I couldn't relax, even if there were no headlights behind me.

My phone dinged with my Google request. Cell service had resumed.

The Tip Top Tavern was ahead on my left. The parking lot was nearly filled to the max. Popular place—and one I'd be able to meld into. I found a spot smack between a minivan and a Honda Civic and kept my engine running while I grabbed my phone and read through the list of sheep farm articles. How to start one. Quality of feed. Not what I needed. I re-Googled, sheep farming dirt.

Seconds later, I had another slew of reading material which hit the target. Because dipping sheep for pest control used to be commonplace, soil contamination often resulted. DDT, dieldrin and arsenic occurred in sheep farms as they were elements used in the process. Used extensively between 1940 and 1960, at the time they were thought to be harmless. These elements were most problematic when near groundwater.

Setting my phone in my lap, my stomach flipped with nausea. I didn't know what dieldrin or DDT were, but arsenic poisoning sent a chill through me. If my ninth-grade history teacher Mr. Schwartzman had it right, arsenic had brought down Napoleon, among others.

They were dumping chemical-laden dirt from Wheeler's land down the embankments into the river. Groundwater. My leg muscles cramped. I'd taken a whiff of that dirt. I forced air through my nose—as if that would undo any damage done to my lungs.

I picked up my phone to read more. My legs ached because of my wet jeans. Nothing more. But poisoned soil covered Jackson Wheeler's farmland. He must be removing the dirt for the sale of the property. Why dump it into the river basin? Could it be accidental overflow? It might not be. How much did Vince know about the land and what Wheeler was doing to take care of it? Or what he wasn't doing? That would explain the test vial. How did Vince breaking into Enterprise have anything to do with that? Was he looking for something there?

The only way to find out was to talk with Jackson Wheeler. Except the Enterprise offices would've been closed for a couple hours by now. It might have to wait until tomorrow. I could use the night to pull myself together and figure out next steps anyway. Although Dora at KGW would want to know about this and she might have some insight. I dialed and got voicemail. I started to leave a message, and then hung up. I'd try again later so I could tell her personally.

A fist hit my driver's side window. I jumped, my seat-belt digging into my chest and anchoring me in place. Floyd startled and barked but didn't get up. Marilyn Corder, her fiery red hair glistening in the last of the sun, grinned and gave me an old-school *roll down your window* gesture. My heart pounded. I hesitated to remove the glass barrier between us.

She hit it again. "Open up."

I slid the window down a crack. "There are better ways to get my attention." Had she also put a knife in my tire?

"What are you doing here?"

"Passing through."

She gave me a thumb down. Was that a commentary or a direction? "Roll down the damn window more."

I complied curious to know the source of her agitation. "What's wrong?"

"You need to get out of here." Her copper hair had more of an orange tinge. Her makeup a little whiter. The Joker jumped to mind. "You've got the town buzzing about you, and not in a good way."

Dylan and Gladys had said as much. And if it hadn't been kids, people didn't generally go around putting knives in tires for no reason. "I'm getting the gist of that. What have I done other than try to find Vince?"

The lines around her mouth deepened. "Which I heard you did. Damn fool."

I wasn't sure if she was referring to him or me. Either way, I'd half expected misty eyes like the first time we'd met, and she'd thought Vince might be hurt. Nothing. Her initial concern might have just been an act. "I'm assuming after you learned about his death, you returned to his house again to find that pull-tab ticket worth $5,000." I eyed her up and down. She was small, but she could have trashed Vince's place. She'd exhibited enough rage at Vince for leaving her high and dry at the bar that night.

Her eyes narrowed. "How do you figure that?"

"Come on. He owed you money. By all accounts, he wasn't often lucky. I'm sure he must have told you about the winning ticket at some point. That's why you came to his house that day we met in the first place, right?" I took a shot in the dark.

Her face turned a deep red. "He told me about the ticket. It came up because he said it was a drop in the bucket and not going to solve anything. Of course, I was looking for it when I thought he'd given me the shaft at the bar."

"With Chuck shutting down games at random, is it even valid?"

"He had me buy it a few days before his accident, and last I'd seen at the bowling alley, it's still going."

Maybe Chuck wasn't doing anything flaky after all. Vince had just taken any losses personally.

"He owed me a thousand dollars," she continued. "Even if it was unrealistic to expect he'd leave the ticket behind, I was under the impression he'd gone home after he left me. But there'd be no point going there after he was dead."

"Someone broke in and tore his house apart."

Anger flashed in her eyes. "You thought I'd do that?"

I shrugged. "Well…"

"I may be lots of things, but I'm no vandal or thief."

"I don't know who to believe any more." I was also tired of dancing around subjects in this town.

"I'm sorry I bothered to warn you."

She stepped back from my car. I hadn't expected to talk with Marilyn tonight. My sliced tire had me rattled. But I had more questions. "Look, I'm the one that's sorry. I appreciate your telling me that I should go."

She sniffed. "Hmm."

"I've found out what Vince needed to fix."

She leaned over the window, showing more cleavage than I needed to see. "And?"

"He was in deep debt at the racetracks. Did he ever talk about that? Or mention someone by the name of Pavel or Mickey Mikhailov? Maybe Tyrone?" I didn't see the point of explaining who really owed the money.

Her shoulders slumped. "No. But it would explain why he'd been so moody and upset. He'd started to drink more. Gamble. Desperate to win. I've already told you all that. But that night he told me his luck was running out."

His luck had done that. "Did he ever mention a woman named Dora O'Reilly?"

She bristled at the name. "The news reporter?"

"You know about her?"

"Only seen her on TV. She's done some reports about the waterpark. Why would Vince mention her?"

"That's what I'm asking."

Her jaw tensed. "No idea. I can tell you people don't like her any better than you. If you're teaming up with her, you're asking for more trouble."

I hadn't asked for anything, but it did seem to find me. Vince too. "You told me when we first met that you didn't want Vince to lose his job. That he talked about some deal related to his work. I found out he'd been arrested for trespass earlier in the year at the Enterprise Trucking offices where he worked. Even though his boss

Jackson Wheeler dropped the charges, he also dropped him off the schedule."

She shook her head. "He never said anything about that. Doesn't surprise me about Wheeler. My nephew worked for him a few years back and told me more than once Wheeler would do any job for good money. Based on that right there, I wouldn't trust that fool farther than I could throw him."

After reading about the likelihood of his poisoned land, I had to agree.

She tilted her head. "Guess doing anything for money could be said for a lot of people in this town. Including Vince." She sniffed. "I need to get back inside. My friends think I'm smoking and they'll be looking for me soon."

She turned her back on me and walked to the tavern. Despite her rough exterior, there might be a heart in that woman because she didn't have to update me—even if she hadn't told me anything I didn't already know about how people felt about me in this town. I'd been warned enough times to have my own warning label attached to my forehead. I had to be on the verge of getting to the bottom of things. Now to get to the bottom of them before my tire wasn't the only casualty of a sharp blade.

THE SUN HAD disappeared and the streetlights lit up the road ahead of me by the time I pulled out of the tavern parking lot. Enterprise Trucking sat a mile ahead on the opposite side of the street and the plan was to return there tomorrow. But a light in the back office radiated through to the front. It could be a nightlight, except the Dodge Ram with the license plate *BigWheel* parked in the front stall nearest the door said different. Jackson Wheeler was there.

Without thinking it through, I made a U-turn in the next driveway and circled back. My pants were soggy. I was cold, famished, and ready to go home. Floyd, proud of his earlier find in the creek, snored in the backseat. Bed would be a good place for both of us. But I had questions for Mr. Wheeler and he might not be available tomorrow. Worse, he could have better safeguards in place than last time I'd visited so I couldn't even get to him. Safeguards like Officer No Name. Right now he was by himself. It might be the best opportunity to get answers.

Detective Kuni expected a call when I left town. I wouldn't confront Wheeler without bringing him in the loop. Obviously, Wheeler had been concerned enough at my original poking around to send security to harass me. Tonight's topic would focus on what appeared to be his illegal dumping activities and what did Vince know about those. Easing next to Wheeler's truck, I turned off the engine and called the detective. Another voicemail—he was probably at that dinner event he'd mentioned.

"Hey, detective, just wanted to give you a heads up that I'm at the Enterprise Trucking office. Give me a call when you get this."

For a beat, I thought better of going in. But if I could get those answers now, I wouldn't need to come back to this town again. That by itself would be a bonus. And I wouldn't go in unprotected. I retrieved my gun out of the glove compartment and stuck it in my purse.

I fluffed my hair and unzipped my jacket part way. The last time Wheeler had commented that he'd make time for a pretty lady. Things had changed, but hopefully he'd feel the same with my knocking well after hours.

"Back shortly," I said to Floyd as I hit the lock.

The front glass door was locked. I knocked and cupped my hands around my eyes to see in. A shadow moved in Wheeler's corner office. I rapped harder in case he didn't hear. More movement in the office, but nothing my direction.

He could have music playing or have headphones on. He didn't seem the type to be jamming to Pandora, but it was possible. My dad was slightly younger than Wheeler and I'd seen him with my earbuds a time or two. The door had a mail slot. I bent down and held the flap open. "Mr. Wheeler, it's Kelly Pruett. Are you in there?"

A chill spilled out of the opening along with no response.

"My car has a flat. I need some help." Not a complete lie. The damsel in distress might at least get his attention.

Another elongated shadow shifted around in his office.

"Mr. Wheeler, I can see you're in there. Please."

Scuffling. A thud, followed by low guttural sounds. Was that a moan? "Are you okay?" A groan, louder this time. "Mr. Wheeler. Do I need to call 9-1-1?"

Glass crashed to the floor in his office. Most likely a lamp because his office dimmed. Something was wrong. Seriously wrong.

With fierce shakes, I willed the door to open. It wouldn't budge. In one leap, I landed at the base of the stairs and sprinted the width of the long building and rounded the corner into the dark alley toward the back. A vibration rattled under my feet. The metal grill of a vehicle careened straight toward me. No time to think. I lunged toward the building. Smashed into the cement wall. The arm that had taken a gunshot months ago took the brunt, shooting pain into my fingertips. I crumpled and screamed. My head hurt. I'd hit it against the wall. The only thing that saved me was the driver swerved off its trajectory, perhaps deciding I wasn't worth destroying their vehicle in the attempt to take me out.

Aching, but alive, I scrambled to my feet with two choices. Chase the vehicle that had nearly flattened me and had already turned onto the main road or find out what was wrong with Jackson Wheeler. I sprinted to the back of the building.

The back door hung wide as I made the last corner. Not sure who'd just taken off or what I'd find, I retrieved my gun and held it in front of me, ready to blast anyone who jumped out.

The door put me in the lunchroom where an eerie calm filled the space. White tables and chairs. A vending machine. An old microwave with hand smudges on the handle. A two-door refrigerator, running. A white-faced clock keeping a strict cadence.

The lunchroom door opened to a hallway. My heartbeat pounded in my ears as I tip-toed my way through the room and peered out. The hallway led into reception where I had been that first day.

I traversed the Formica, my damp shoes squeaking like a dog toy. So much for stealth. At the office edge I hesitated and called, "Mr. Wheeler? Are you okay?"

His groan was barely audible this time. To hell with it. With gun in hand, I ran toward his office. If someone else was here, they were going to have to tackle me at this point. As I crossed the threshold, my breath stuck like a bone in my throat. Jackson Wheeler laid spread-eagle on the floor, blood pooling around him, a wound from his chest gushing with every beat. He wasn't dead. Yet.

I hit speaker on my cell and dialed 9-1-1. At the same

time, I ripped off my jacket and peeled off my T-shirt. I told the operator where I was and how to get in.

"Put compression directly on the wound," the woman's steady voice directed me.

I was ahead of her. With my balled-up shirt, I found the gaping hole in Wheeler's chest and shoved it in. The palms of my hands, one over the other, holding the T-shirt in place, I prayed the bleeding to stop. On my knees, in only my bra and jeans, I rocked. Adrenalin jettisoned through me like fireworks. Pressing on the massive wound. I searched Jackson's face. Ashen. Slack.

Panic gripped my chest. I remembered this look. It had haunted my dreams since I'd last seen it walking in on my father in his office where his sudden stroke had toppled him to the floor. I'd knelt beside his lifeless body, giving him CPR for the fifteen minutes that it took for help to arrive. I thought it would never come. Now I could hear the wail of sirens approaching, echoing the wail inside my head. I chanted the same thing as I did for my dad not so long ago. And to no avail. Don't die. Don't die. Please…don't die.

THIRTY

CURLED UP AGAINST the backseat of Detective Kuni's sedan with Floyd nuzzled up against my leg, and a blanket over my lap, I closed my eyes and continued the rocking I'd started earlier while applying pressure to Wheeler's wound. Unsure how I'd made it to the detective's car, I wrapped my Nike jacket tighter around me and zipped it to my chin. At some point they'd removed me from Wheeler's bloodied body, directed me to get my coat back on, and stay out of the way as a medical team rushed in and took over.

Wheeler's life teetered on a high wire and the ambulance had arrived and whisked him away. He was now in the hands of the critical care team at the Medical Center. The coppery smell from my bloodstained hands made the acid boil up from my stomach.

Wiping my hands on my damp jeans, I texted Mitz. "Love you, Ladybug."

Within seconds, I had a love you back and asking for Facetime. My eyes brimmed. I couldn't let her see me like this. "I'm on a case. Excited to see you tomorrow," I texted. I shouldn't have written her at all, but seeing Wheeler had thrown me into the past and losing my father again. I was desperate for a lifeline.

My next text went to Kyle. "Sorry." The last time we'd spoken was in the hospital parking lot where he'd driven away angry. Even if his anger hadn't lessened, I wanted to know he was there. With an olive branch extended, he might call. My cell laid silent on the seat next to me.

Time disappeared. My eyelids were heavy by the time Detective Kuni slid into the front seat and shifted his body to face the backseat.

"Not sure he's going to make it. You at least gave him a chance by slowing down the bleeding."

I searched the soft folds of his tanned and tired face. How many calls did he have to deal with after he'd gone home for the day? Had he interrupted his dinner because he knew I was here? "Any idea who did that to him? Did you find the weapon? I didn't see anything around his body."

"Not yet. My team is tearing the place apart. Most likely, the attacker took it with them." He pulled a pad out of his overcoat. "Hope you're up for a few questions."

I'd expected this. "Exclude me as a suspect?" I said. He was only doing his job, but I lacked the energy for it.

"It's a necessary formality. How is it you came to be here?"

I straightened in the seat. "I didn't plan to stop tonight. I was driving by, saw his back light on and seized the opportunity. That's when I called and left you the message."

"Was anyone with him when you first arrived?"

"His was the only car parked up front, but I didn't even see him, only shadows and movement in his office. That was before the crash of what sounded like a lamp, followed by his moaning. That's when I went running."

"What were you coming to talk about?"

The adrenalin easing out of my body started my body shaking.

Detective Kuni started his car and turned the heat on high.

"I found something that came from Vince's car." I handed him the glass vial I'd tucked into my coat pocket earlier. I'd have handed him the tape if I'd thought it could be saved, but it was trash. "I wanted to know what he had to say about this."

"That's what you turned up by searching from the main road?"

I grimaced. "Sure."

"What is it?" He started to unscrew the lid.

My hand flew up. "Stop. It's dirt, but it's likely toxic."

He pulled the vial to arms-length and retightened the lid. "How do you know that?"

I repeated Dylan's comments about trucking the dirt off the land in time for sale, as well as my Google search of sheep farms.

"I'll get this tested. See what the lab says about it."

I nodded. "If it does turn out to have chemicals, then Wheeler has some explaining to do. A bunch of that dirt has been dumped down the embankment of the farm's edge and is sitting near the river."

Detective touched his thumb to the side of his nose. "Cheap bastard. Would rather pollute the area than pay the dump fees."

"Are those expensive?"

"Exorbitant. Especially if the material is tainted. Only special dump sites will even touch it in that case."

I started to warm with the heat kicked in and unzipped my jacket to my collarbone. I caressed Floyd's fur to ground me. "But he was selling the land and the deal was closing Friday. I would have thought it was all done by now."

"Word is papers were signed but the transaction records with the county tomorrow at five o'clock. However, the deal isn't done until the county says it is. The buyers could pull out up until that point. That's why there's a waiting period."

I shifted to my hip, resting against the seat with my shoulder. Jackson had darted out of his office telling Gladys he was running out of time. Cleaning up the land could have been what he'd meant. With me on the trail, he might have been afraid I'd uncover what Vince had. "You think Jackson could have been attacked because of the land deal?"

"Any time there's this type of growth in rural areas, there are conservationists that don't want the expansion. Around here though, big business and most town folks do. He'd already signed, so the attack seems too late if that has played a part. By all accounts, Wheeler stands to make a bundle. I don't see him wanting to back out of it. A deeper search into his financials will be in order if he doesn't make it. Until then, I'll be asking around. For the moment, we're in a waiting game."

"Interesting," I said, more to myself than the detective.

"What's that?"

"Vince had that vial in an envelope in his car and was planning to meet that news reporter I told you about the night he died. He must have known, or suspected, the dirt was bad. A month before that, he's breaking into Enterprise offices where Mr. Wheeler miraculously doesn't want to press charges. Meanwhile, there's a rush to get the dirt off the land. Vince suddenly drives off the road the same night he's going to turn that dirt over. Now someone's tried to kill Mr. Wheeler. Sounds connected to me."

He rubbed his chin. "When you put it that way, it

does. But what's Vince's motive? Why would he go to such troubles?"

"He was helping out a family member who got himself into debt. I figured he was blackmailing Wheeler. At least I believed that right up until the point where I found him on the ground. There must be a partner. Maybe there's a double cross going on. Or…"

"Ms. Pruett."

The detective's voice was strong and commanding, stopping me mid-sentence. "What?"

"Tonight's events, and this vial, they'll allow me to get Vince's accident re-opened. I'll also be checking on the connection to Mr. Wheeler and I'm curious about this debt you talk about. Your role in all of this, however, is done. I can't afford to have you causing any complications or jeopardizing yourself. I've got it from here."

I'm not sure I had a choice on the jeopardizing part. It's not like I was asking to be targeted. "But…"

"No buts. It's not up for discussion."

My face flushed.

He ignored it. "I mean it. Tell me more about the car that left the scene."

He continually reminded me of my father. He wasn't a man I argued with. Did I want to stay on this case anyway? I'd done what Stephanie had asked. I had to think of Mitz and get myself extracted from this town and its people that had started to resemble the movie *Deliverance*. "Fine. As for the car that nearly made wallpaper of me, other than being certain the occupant attacked Mr. Wheeler, I can't tell you much else."

"How can you be certain of that?"

"Why else would he have been driving like a madman and without headlights on if he wasn't trying to get out of there unseen? I'm sure he didn't expect me to show up. I rounded the corner of the building in a sprint after I'd heard the sounds coming from inside. The rumble got my attention before I even saw the car. I managed to get up against the wall. Barely." I rubbed my sore arm. The rush of adrenalin had masked my injury. Now it ached. "The vehicle was out of sight by the time I recovered. Getting to Wheeler was my priority after that." I slumped into the seat again. "Can Floyd and I go home?"

Detective Kuni gave me a small smile, the one you give your sick kids when you know they need to get under the covers to feel better. "I don't see why not. I've got your number. Can you drive?"

Teleportation would've come in handy, but I'd crawl back to Portland if I had to. "Yes."

Extracting myself from the detective's cozy car, me and Floyd climbed into the chill of Arlene's. It helped to wake me as the drive to Portland dragged on like a bad movie. I never wanted to return to Riverview regarding this case again. Detective Kuni was right. He'd take it from here.

Stephanie had wanted information on what her father had been up to the week before he died and why he hadn't called her. Now I could tell her. He'd been busy collecting toxic dirt. Jackson Wheeler had been tossing dirt down into the watershed to avoid fees. Clearing it off for a big pay day no doubt. Vince had dirt, literally, on his boss that he intended to use. And he was dying of cancer. Knowing his daughter was pregnant and her stupid husband had landed them in serious debt with some bad dudes had motivated him to wrap up loose ends while he was able. But even with his illness and the stress, I couldn't agree with the police's Traffic Division that he'd just fallen asleep at the wheel. Something else happened. Regardless, Detective Kuni could handle it from here, right?

I'd had enough of Vince Burnotas' life in my world. If I backed away, I could ignore that someone had tried to blow me up and put a knife in my tire. And what would have happened had I walked in on Wheeler being bludgeoned with something so sharp it had ripped into his chest? A ripple of anxiety went through me. Was I convinced Tyrone or someone in Mickey's employ was involved? Yes. They were connected somehow. They could know about the dirt. Maybe what I wasn't supposed to mess up for them was that they took up Vince's blackmail of Jackson Wheeler. But I was off the case now. Mickey, and whoever else wanted me to leave things alone in Riverview, would go away if they saw me fading into the woodwork. I wouldn't think about if they could be one and the same. My life could go back to normal.

I didn't look into the rearview mirror to avoid my lying eyes. Quitting wasn't an option. I had to see this through to the end. Wherever that might lead. The thought about Mickey being the one who wanted me to leave things alone in Riverview settled in.

As I hit Portland on the Interstate, the blue Legacy Hospital sign where Arlene was recovering illuminated the clear night sky. Arlene should be checking out tomorrow if Jeff's last update was correct. Unless something had changed.

I looked atrocious, and felt worse, yet found myself taking the hospital exit and parking near the entrance. The double automatic doors opened into the sterile hospital and I hid my hands and went direct to the nearest bathroom and scrubbed until they were clean enough to perform surgery. I pulled my hair into a ponytail attempting to look more put together than I felt, and made my way to the fourth floor.

The nurses' station was empty as the elevator doors opened. Probably making their rounds. I snuck to Arlene's room without interruption.

From the doorway, the rhythmic sound of her breathing said she was fast asleep. With no intention to wake her, I listened and closed my eyes. After tonight, I had to be certain that everyone I loved was okay. Despite our issues, that included Arlene. The feeling my profession had once again impacted the ones I loved weighed on me. If I hadn't been exhausted, I would have stayed longer, but I had what I'd come for. I turned to go.

"You don't need to worry about me," she whispered.

I stopped. "I know." I waited for her to continue with more. Anger? Forgiveness? Anything.

She didn't. It was as if she'd woken from a dream to assure me. There were times that Arlene shocked the hell out of me. In those moments, I missed my mother. A part of me yearned to be reassured. That I was doing okay. That Mitz would be fine. That I was doing it right.

My mother didn't say as much in words as in action. Reassurance came in the form of a longer hug, brushing my hair, one-sided conversations where I rambled on about my fears that I'd never be pretty. Or skinny. Or normal. Her simple smile melted those concerns away like sugar in water. Unlike Arlene where everything had been a struggle to even feel normal in her presence. But somehow she managed to show me she cared.

I ignored the ache in my heart. My mother was a woman I didn't allow to stay in my thoughts or I wouldn't be able to function. Thinking I'd lost Arlene had made that harder to keep away.

Like the issues with my dad, I'd have to deal with my mom's loss some day; the gaping hole in my psyche that I covered up and pretended wasn't there. Like the disappointment around my father. Any shrink who'd get a hold of me could retire on the extent of therapy I'd need. Tonight wasn't that night. Despite often feeling broken, for the most part, I kept it together. I had to. If for no other reason, Mitz.

I made the drive home, processing the shock of the past couple of hours. Pulling Arlene's car back into her garage, I grabbed out the envelope with the cassette and stuck it into my purse. Floyd ran around her yard and did his business. We secured the garage and started down the stairs to my house.

Midway down, my legs locked. An SUV with California license plates sat in my driveway. A woman stood at my door, knocking.

So much for life returning to normal. Who was I kidding. Chaos was my norm.

"She's not home," I said.

My nemesis, Linda, turned around. "Got a minute? I think we should talk."

THIRTY-ONE

I COULD HAVE left Linda's skinny, straight blonde hair down to her waist, ass standing at the door. I could have ignored her altogether and gone into my house through the basement. Better yet, I could retrace my steps back to Arlene's and drive into the night. All options were tempting. Except I couldn't run forever. Like the crack of lightning before the rumble of thunder, the minute Jeff had told me about the DNA test, this day was inevitable.

Without a word, I climbed the front stairs. Floyd sniffed at her feet and then ignored her while I unlocked the door. He didn't feel like giving a traitor the time of day either. Good boy.

Linda followed me inside the entry. I dropped my purse on the floor, ignoring the contents falling out, and slipped my shoes off. She followed me through the living room—a room we'd grown up in. Staying up to watch MTV. Talking about boys. Doing homework. She'd been a part of my childhood. The sister I didn't yet know I had. A twang hit my heart at the memories.

Floyd found his bed. I tossed her the remote. "You're going to have to wait. I need to get out of these clothes."

"I've got time." Her voice was just above a whisper as she found her old place on the sofa and flicked on the television. Perhaps she didn't relish this moment coming either. Any decent human would feel guilty. Decent people didn't screw their friend's husbands. I didn't look back as I climbed the stairs.

Under the steaming stream of water, I tried to let some of my tension swirl down the drain along with the remainder of Jackson Wheeler's blood. I scrubbed my hands and arms with soap, trying to rid myself of the images of him bleeding out. It was no use. After emptying the hot water heater, I emerged a half hour later with the same knots in my back and shoulders. And only slightly more able to deal with Linda by the time I walked into the living room. She was put together in straight jeans, knee-high suede boots, and a mid-thigh wool sweater. I opted for gray sweatpants and a navy sweatshirt, my damp hair up in a bun.

"Thanks for letting me in," she said as I plopped in the oversized chair across from the couch.

"Did I have a choice? Because if I had a choice, I'd have expected a phone call asking me when it was convenient. Not you showing up on my doorstep and expecting me to make time."

She grimaced. "I didn't think you'd answer."

She had that right. In the two years of not seeing her, she hadn't changed much. It was always about her. "What do you want?"

"Has Jeff told you what's going on?"

With my mouth closed, I ran my tongue along the outside of my teeth. How much did I want her to have to tell me? The answer came down to how long I wanted her sitting in my living room. "Pretty much everything. Have you found out whether it's his or not?"

She glanced at her lap. "I don't know yet."

"Then why are you here?"

"Because if the result is what I believe it is, Mitz is

going to have a half-brother. That means you and me seeing each other. How is Mitz anyway?"

"You're making a lot of assumptions. Don't you live in California?"

"I may be moving back." Of course, she would. I would. Most people would. "I mean, it would only be fair to my son, Seth."

Wouldn't want to be unfair to Seth. "And if he isn't Jeff's?"

"My parents are here. It'd be nice for them to see their grandson more often."

I folded my arms over my chest. "Sounds like you have it all figured out."

She nodded, her eyes misting, regret filling her perfectly symmetrical green eyes. "You know I am sorry. About everything. About Jeff. About that night."

I reminded myself to breathe. "So you've said."

She searched my stone face as I refused to give up anything.

"I do mean it. You were my dearest friend. My oldest friend."

I strangled down the *ha* that wanted out. "That sure played a part when you slept with my husband."

She winced, flush creeping up her neck.

Did she really expect that I'd have forgotten and open my arms back up to her? That we'd be buddies again? Yet, the fire I'd felt before didn't burn the same hole in my gut with her sitting right across from me. "Look, to be honest, I've played this moment out in my head too many times to count. I've had many things to say and quite a few names I've called you." I rolled my eyes. Some things I wasn't proud of. "Right now, I don't feel anything. Really, you did me a favor. I love Jeff. Always will. But we weren't right for each other. Even if it wasn't pleasant the way it all went down, it all worked out because if it hadn't, I might have stayed with him for Mitz's sake."

"But you can't forgive me that easily, right?"

I laughed. The sound held more pain than I'd have liked. She was right. Because it wasn't Jeff that I mourned. "No, I can't. You were my friend. Knew all my secrets. All my weaknesses. All my hopes. I trusted you with it all. I can get over Jeff. In fact, I've moved on. Met a nice guy." Even if he wasn't talking to me. "But your betrayal."

"I'm so sorry."

I swallowed hard. Trying not to let the emotion get a hold of me. "It is what it is. For a long time, I thought it was me. That I was too busy raising Mitz, and adjusting to her being deaf, that I hadn't been there enough when you needed me. So you took it out on me in a way you knew would cut me the deepest."

"It wasn't you. I truly don't know why I did it."

I put up my hand to stop her excuses. "You're right. It is all on you, and on Jeff. I was a good friend. Hell, I was a great friend. When your drunk boyfriend at the time came on to me at that Christmas party at your house, I told Jeff I didn't feel well and we got out of there."

"He did? That son-of-a…"

I tilted my head to the side.

She shut her mouth.

"The point is, being drunk isn't an excuse. Whether Jeff is your son's dad or not, that's not a free pass into my life. I'll always support Mitz. If she has a half-brother, so be it." At least I had some experience on the subject that might help my daughter. "But that doesn't give you any leverage in my world."

She stood, her eyes serious, her face tight. "I understand. You're very disappointed in me and my betrayal of our friendship."

I got to my feet, feeling much better with that weight off me. "See the thing is, Linda, I'm not. I'm done. There's a difference."

She walked to the front door, wrapping her shawl jacket around her. She stopped as she glanced at the envelope in my purse, the videotape hanging out of it. She nodded at the package. "Didn't remember you being so old school."

How did she remember me? I'd been many things. Old school was absolutely one of them. "Not mine. It's destroyed video of who knows what for a case I'm working."

She picked it up and inspected the tape. "It's twisted, but you can fix that. And it's damp. Let it dry. It'll be okay if it was only exposed to water, but not sitting in it."

As kids, she'd had a knack at repairing our audio cassette tapes when they got screwed up. "Really?"

"Might be worth a try. Sometimes things seem damaged beyond repair, when all they need is time," she said, looking at me.

I met her eye, aware the comment hadn't only been meant about the video. "Sometimes even when they are mended enough to function, it doesn't mean they're ever the same."

She shrugged and closed the door behind her.

I leaned my back against the door and locked it. I couldn't think about her anymore. I swooped up the tape from my purse and walked into the kitchen. How did one dry out a videotape?

PRETTY MUCH ANYTHING can be found on the internet. Including how to deconstruct a tape and let it air dry. I'd almost ran for my hairdryer, and that would have sealed the fate of the video. By air drying it through the night, there might be a chance at retrieving the information.

Far later than I intended, I crawled into bed. I sunk into the coolness of the sheets, desperate for sleep to take me. My phoned chirped with a text. Kyle.

Want company?

A little late, buddy. Where you been? I texted earlier.

Sorry. Wanted to respond. It's been a crazy day and I just got off duty.

That didn't usually stop him from touching base. His day must have been as bad as mine, but I couldn't find the energy to be supportive. I wouldn't be any fun. It's been a day for me too.

I heard. I'm at your front door.

An unexpected relief flooded over me. In sock feet, and my sweats, I rolled out of bed and ran down the steps with Floyd right behind. We opened the door to Kyle. He didn't say anything. Just walked in, grabbed me in his arms, and laid a warm body-tingling kiss on me.

If this was his way of saying he'd gotten over my comparing him to Jeff, I liked it. When he stepped back, I asked, "How'd you hear?"

He bent down to greet Floyd. "Detective Kuni called. Told me what happened and that I should check on you."

Apparently, I had my own guardian angel in the detective. "Did he give you an update on Wheeler?"

"He's still in surgery. Sounds like the weapon was a type of hammer. Half-inch in diameter. Rounded. He had injuries to the back of his head that were consistent with the same weapon, and which might have taken him down initially."

"A hammer? That means the attacker got close."

"Very. And took him by surprise." He moved back in for another hug and scanned my face. "How are you? I understand your trying to stop the bleeding is what has him alive at this point."

I took Kyle's hand and led him upstairs. "I'm okay. I'll be better once he's out of the woods. I want a chance to drill him when he is." In the bedroom, Kyle stripped down to his boxers and T-shirt and crawled in next to me. Lying next to his warmth, I updated him about the dirt. "But according to the detective, I'm officially off the case."

"I like Detective Kuni. You are going to let him handle it from here. Correct?"

"He's a good cop, no doubt, and yes, he makes a good point."

"But?"

I had no desire to reignite our disagreement from the hospital parking lot. "I'm as tired as anyone of being the target of mafia types and weird town people."

"Hmmmm." It was a sidestep to agreeing with him. His lack of response said he didn't want to argue either. "About mafia types, I found out some information on the bomb."

I flipped to my side. "What?"

"Ammonium nitrate was used, which is a component of fertilizer. I would have expected Mickey to be using

C-4 or TNT, but he may have needed to get creative on short notice. He can't be ruled out."

If Kyle could have seen my face, he would have seen the deep crease between my eyes. "I'm definitely not ruling him out." Mickey warning me not to mess with his collection efforts had been clear. "Except Jackson Wheeler owned farmland. Having access to fertilizer doesn't seem like it would be too far of a stretch. Since his rent-a-cops were screwing with me earlier in the week, he knew I was investigating not only Vince, but stuff around the waterpark and the land. He might have been afraid I was going to find out what Vince had on him the night he died. But enough to want me dead?" Although if he'd had anything to do with Vince dying out there, that question answered itself.

"You said the sale was big money. People do crazier stuff for less. Greed being one of them."

"True, but here's why I'm stumbling. While I was searching at the end of Gee Creek, someone put a knife in my tire. It could have been Wheeler, I suppose, but why just the knife? Why not attack me directly? Unless it was kids being juvenile delinquents, and believe me, I haven't ruled that out either."

Kyle laid on his stomach and propped himself up on his forearms. "You didn't hear anyone coming or going?"

"Branches snapping got my attention. Turned out to be deer passing through. Other than that, no."

He shook his head. "That doesn't exclude Wheeler. He might have been trying to find out what you knew and screwed with you on his way out."

"Timewise, it's possible. It's just that he was attacked next. What could make sense is if Mickey took over the blackmailing of Wheeler. If Wheeler pushed back, the attack on him could be the equivalent of a severed finger in Vince's garbage."

We laid in silence. Both contemplating. My head hurt.

He laid back down, shifted toward me, and caressed my arm. "You may be right but enough talk tonight. You need some rest. We'll figure it out tomorrow with fresher minds."

I put my hand on his and squeezed. I had more to tell him. To bring him up to speed about the DNA test and about Linda coming by. About the videotape. More on my theory that Jackson Wheeler was being blackmailed by Vince and how Mickey and Tyrone might play into that. I turned toward him again, his hand on my hip. He was right. It could wait until morning.

I melted into Kyle's touch. I'd been keeping a flimsy wall between us. Afraid to let him know me. Afraid of truly caring for someone else. Linda showing up tonight had been a reminder of what I'd lost. But was I ready to risk my heart fully again? Did I want in or did I want out of this relationship? Being half-way was only going to cost me.

When I pulled him my direction, he searched my face. I kissed him hard. He found my neck with his lips, my stomach with his warm hands, and he buried us under the covers.

THIRTY-TWO

THE NEXT MORNING, I woke to sun streaming through my bedroom window that Kyle had opened a crack. It was going to be a warm spring day. Friday. If he had the day off, I'd see if he wanted to accompany me to Mitz's event tonight.

We hadn't talked much more last night after some much-needed *physical* therapy, and I had plenty to update him on. While I was officially off the case, I had the video to check out. It would be nice to have Kyle's assistance with that.

Retrieving my sweats from the floor, I trotted down the stairs and into the kitchen where I expected to find Kyle sipping coffee. Instead, Floyd was curled at the base of the kitchen sink. A sign that Kyle had been there, and Floyd had awaited handouts. My cup sat next to the coffeemaker, which held half a pot. Kyle had propped a note up against the mug rack next to the videotape I had strung out to dry.

"You looked too beautiful to wake. Got called onto duty until tonight. Will call you. PS. Looks like a fun science project." He drew an arrow pointing to the tape. "PSS. Love you."

Love you? My insides thumped as my cheeks warmed. I wasn't ready for that one yet. I mean, I liked him. A lot. But love?

I poured a cup of coffee, flipping the note over. He

might not mean anything by it. It was more like a see ya later. That lie was half-way believable if the words didn't have their own lead in. PSS. The part of me that liked to run scared was sprinting for the hills.

After a long drink of the hot coffee, I grabbed the tape, and plopped down at the dining table. I'd think about what those words meant later. Rotating the VHS tape in my hands from side to side, I examined the film. It looked dry. I straightened the crease in the film and using my pinky, rewound it into the case. Another inspection from top to bottom and it was the best I could do. Time to try it out.

Upstairs, I found the key to my dad's office in my nightstand. The old school guy he was, his TV had a VHS recorder attached to it. The last time I'd opened this door was six months ago to get my gun. The second time I thought about opening it, I wanted to pack his belongings away and get rid of them. The father I grew up with and who I'd come to learn about were so different, and I felt I knew even less after uncovering his connection to Mickey and organized crime. But I also knew him to be a loving and smart man. The man that raised me on his own and who loved Mitz to no end. I held onto that. But starting to move on and donate some of his belongings might be in order.

Later. I'm glad I hadn't acted on that instinct or I might not have the VCR to use. Inside the room, I opened the blinds and the light revealed a layer of dust covering the flat surfaces and the television. I flicked on the set, and turned the channel to components, choosing VCR.

The TV and VCR rested on a cabinet filled with tapes. I fingered through them. At some point I'd seen an adapter in the drawer. A VHS tape that looked normal but had a compartment to slip in a smaller cassette.

A few run-throughs with my fingers over the tops and I found it. I sat down on my dad's bed. Floyd had come upstairs and laid in the hall outside the door. My phone rang. Stephanie.

I would have liked to get through the tape before talking with her, but I also wanted to confirm Brandon had made it home last night like he promised.

"Hey, Steph. How you feeling this morning? Brandon get home safe and sound from Corvallis?"

"Kel-Kelly." Her voice trembled.

My stomach jolted. "What's wrong?"

"Brandon got a text this morning. He doesn't know I saw it."

I gripped my cell. "Who was it from?"

"I didn't recognize the number. But it said, 'tick-tock, tick-tock. Your wife was sure cute yesterday walking around the neighborhood.' What do you think that means?"

Tyrone. Damn him. Brandon had said they had an arrangement. Was Tyrone making sure Brandon understood he was being watched? "How did Brandon react when he read it?"

"He was in the shower when it came in. He might not have yet because he had an early morning staff meeting, and he looked stressed about seeing his bosses today. I didn't want to mention it and upset him more. He was in such a hurry."

I crushed the heels of my hands into my eyes. "It could be someone screwing around with him from work." Although I didn't believe that. "But stay inside today, okay? And when Brandon gets home, you need to tell him that you've seen it and see what he says." I'd warned Brandon. Circumstances were now going to dictate that he come clean whether he'd planned on dragging his feet or not.

"Okay."

"Please don't stress. Things are going to be fine." Soon.

I hung up with a promise to call later. I couldn't stop thinking about that text threat. It was one thing to come after me, or Brandon, even Vince, but don't screw with the fragile pregnant woman. My blood boiled at the thought.

With the adapter open, I slipped the tape inside and shoved it into the VCR. The quicker I put pieces together, the sooner this would be over. I pushed play. The machine squeaked coming to life and the tape squealed like a bunny in trouble. It wasn't going to work. I ran my hand through my hair and reached for the off button. The squeal stopped before I hit it and the image of the back of Enterprise Trucking's building filled the screen, followed by Vince's face. His mouth moved. No sound. It took a moment to realize the volume had been muted.

I rewound the tape a click, turned up the sound, and hit play again.

"So this is another day in the life, Little Pea. It's not glamorous. I do what I can to get by. As you've seen on other videos, it's been a lot of driving truck. This here office is where I come and go to get my routes."

Vince's voice sounded strong, but dark circles shadowed his eyes. It might have been a long day, or the cancer had taken hold. I'd seen a stack of those other tapes at his house labeled *A Day* and had thought nothing of them at the time. Stephanie would be excited to hear that he'd left a diary of sorts for her and the baby.

"It's not a bad gig," he continued. "I wish I was going to be around to meet you, and take you places. Drive you around in my dump truck. Be your Papa the right way. It's just not looking like that'll be the case. Please know I—"

Vince stopped abruptly. His image disappeared; the screen turned white. The camera was hanging at his side and the lens focused on the linoleum squares. The image bounced. He was walking, quietly. I couldn't even hear him breathe.

"Don't tell me what I need to do," a man said. He had a rich, deep voice. Not Vince. Jackson Wheeler?

"If the investors find out they're buying a piece of property next to a toxic landfill, they'll pull out. If not worse." A woman's voice. Stern. Haughty. Had I heard it before?

"It's not like they couldn't clean it up if they had to. What's the difference?"

"Don't be stupid, Jackson. These men don't mess around and they prefer to live in the shadows. They're already going to be pouring millions into the development. If the environmentalists get hold of the information, the ensuing protests will make them run. I don't want to think about how angry they'll be if they think we've wasted their time and tried to put one over on them."

"No one will find out. My buddy at the EPA has been greased like a pig. He's already approved everything. Shit, I don't even need to remove it. They'd be none the wiser."

"If it ever came out, it'd be a political nightmare. They're the type of people who would come after us. Have you seen the *The Godfather*?" The woman made a sound like she'd shuddered.

The sound of movement. "Ahh, baby. Don't you worry.

I'm not like your poor excuse for a husband. I'll get it done. No one's coming after us."

The sound of wet mouths, kissing, slurping. My stomach turned.

"They better not. I haven't put everything on the line for nothing. This town needs this sale. I need this sale."

The man laughed. "Only so you can get far away and your family can break ground."

She giggled. "I won't leave you, sweetie. You know you're more man than..." A loud thud. The woman's voice dropped to a whisper. "What was that?"

"Probably nothing."

The sound of scurrying, the film bounced again, the sound of a drawer being opened and partially closed, the screen went black, the stifled creak of a door being pushed open.

"What are you doing out here, Burnotas?"

Vince cleared his throat. "Sorry, sir." I detected a quiver in his voice. Nervousness. "I needed to get my paperwork for tomorrow's haul. Gladys said she'd have it ready for me."

Muffled footsteps. "Well, did you find it?" Jackson must have crossed to Vince because his voice was clearer on the tape. Papers moving around. Another drawer opening.

"I've already looked in there." I detected a higher pitch in Vince's voice. He must be hiding the camera from Mr. Wheeler. "Found the papers."

"Good. Now get out of here. Next time you come after hours, announce yourself, will you."

"Sorry, sir. I didn't mean to intrude."

"No intrusion. Just finishing up some work and don't like to be startled."

"Yes, sir." Footfalls fading away. A back door slammed.

"Who was that?" the woman said, her voice tense and agitated.

"One of my employees. He's no bother." Jackson's voice grew distant and then a door clicked closed. He and his kissing buddy must have gone back into the office. I didn't want to imagine what they were doing in there.

I didn't budge from the edge of the bed as the tape continued until it ran out or the battery died on the camera. Either way, the screen went blank after thirty minutes.

Vince had recorded the entire conversation. What started as a day in the life became a way to blackmail Jackson Wheeler. He'd been forced to leave the camera behind in Gladys' desk, which meant he would have had to come back for it. The reason for his trespass became clear.

Somehow, he'd been able to conceal the video when he'd been caught on the premises at the later time. As a gambling man, Vince might have revealed his hand right then to Jackson and told him he had proof that he'd paid someone off in the EPA to hide the contaminated land element, and that he was in cohorts with a married woman. Given what was jotted on Vince's notepad, I suspected he knew who that married woman was. Just like I might. I popped the tape out and secured my dad's room.

Faced with the threat of Vince having that information, Jackson might not have pressed charges. That would have allowed Vince to walk off with the video tucked on his body, or he'd had time to go to his car and leave it there. How it went down might never be known unless Wheeler recovered to enlighten me.

While my gut said I'd heard that woman on the video's voice before, I wanted to confirm. I made a call to Dora. I'd planned to tell her last night about what Floyd and I had found. Now I felt it best to wait until I had it wrapped up tight.

"Wanting another tour so soon?" she said, chuckling into the phone.

"No. Although that was wonderful. What I really want is a copy of that recent interview segment on the water-park you did. Any chance you can email that to me?"

"No problem. What are you looking for?"

"Confirmation. What do you know about the mayor of Riverview and his wife?"

"Only that they're big on trying to change the face of Riverview. The town has been dying for a long time. They've been getting investors involved to revitalize the town. The entire waterpark area was Mrs. Chambers idea."

That matched with what Detective Kuni had said about her spearheading the sale. It was starting to make sense. She'd sell the land, and then let her family be the recipient of the windfall in constructing the project. She had a lot to lose if this deal didn't go down. "Who are the investors?"

"They're a consortium of people from all over the country, and a few outside of the country from what I've found. Very rich. Very powerful."

"Any possibility of dirty money or organized crime being involved?" The woman's reference to *The Godfather* meant only one thing to me.

"Possibly. Wherever there is big money, there's the risk of that. Why?"

Mickey and Tyrone. Their connection was starting to come into focus as well. "At this point, just curious.

I have found out some info and I'll give you an exclusive if it turns out I'm right. But from the way it sounds, there'd be some real upset investors if something happened to the deal."

"I look forward to it. And you're right. With lots of money floating around, I'm sure. Not only for the buyers. The seller is making tons—not every day you have that kind of money being thrown at you—and the increase in tourists will bring a boom to the smaller businesses and property values in town. The waterpark is a win for everyone."

If I was right about the voice, it was biggest for one in particular. "Thank you for the insight. I'll look for that segment."

"It'll be to you shortly."

True to her word, within the hour I had the news conference coverage in my email.

I moved the footage up to the point where Olivia Chambers was answering a question. "Absolutely. When Charles Chambers decides he wants something, nothing stands in his way."

I hadn't noticed it before, but when the mayor placed his hand at her back, Olivia had pulled away.

She continued, "After years of envisioning this waterpark for the benefit of the Riverview community, it is about to come to fruition. The people of this city should be proud of what he's accomplished on their behalf."

I listened to the news conference three more times until I had no doubt. Olivia Chambers was the woman with Jackson Wheeler on that VHS tape. Instead of her husband, she should have said when Olivia Chambers wants something, nothing stands in her way—including running Vince Burnotas off a narrow road and nearly bludgeoning Jackson Wheeler to death.

THIRTY-THREE

After seeing the video and confirmation of the voices I'd heard, I had only one option—get the tape into the hands of Detective Kuni. Olivia Chambers incriminated herself as far as knowledge about the land. From there, one could, like in one of Mitz's favorite movies, follow the yellow brick road. Vince had been blackmailing Jackson, who in turn would have told Olivia about it. She'd made it clear she wanted to get to the top or have her husband Charles get there and bring her with him. There'd been talk of his running for governor after all of this. And her family business would benefit from the park. If Vince threatened to destroy all of that by making the toxic land public and killing the sale, as well as her affair with Wheeler, she might be willing to kill him.

I didn't know what had made Olivia turn against her lover, Jackson, but something had. Her attack on him was vicious and personal. Detective Kuni would get to the bottom of it all.

After a quick shower, I dressed in a short-sleeved V-neck that read *Good Vibes* and a pair of jeans. I could use all the positive affirmation I could get today. It was noon and the temp had warmed to seventy. Floyd would need to stay behind. Mitz's event was tonight. I bent down to rub Floyd's ears. "You can come with me later, okay, buddy?"

He flopped to his side in response, exposing his belly.

He needed extra attention if I planned to leave him, and he deserved every bit of it. Had he not found the envelope with the dirt and VHS tape, I wouldn't be solving the case right now.

Making sure Arlene's car wasn't compromised, I hit the road and found a convenience store. After getting a cup of coffee, I texted Detective Kuni. I'm on my way to Riverview with something you have to see. Can we meet? I patted the videotape in my purse.

The detective responded. I'm heading to the hospital to check on Jackson Wheeler. Be there in 45.

Meet you in the lobby.

I punched the accelerator. This roller coaster car I occupied was almost cresting the track. This ride couldn't end soon enough.

Detective Kuni would be another twenty minutes. I paced the hospital lobby a couple of times. Waiting. My last time around, I spied a vending machine and pushed the black coffee button. I didn't know Wheeler's status, or what room he was in. All I could do was wait.

I looked up from the vending machine and Gladys the receptionist from Enterprise Trucking was crossing the lobby to the front doors. Leaving the cup to fill, I ran towards her. "Gladys."

She turned, her face deep with worry. "Yes?"

"It's me. Kelly Pruett. The PI working with Vince's family."

Relief flooded her expression and she yanked me in for a hug. "Oh my gosh, thank you for what you did for Jackson."

Would she feel the same by the time all was said and done? “It was nothing.” I patted her back.

She pushed me to arm’s length. “Are you kidding? You saved him.” Her face crumpled. “Now it’s a wait and see.”

“Have they moved him out of ICU?”

“No. He’s in Room 909. He made it through the surgery. He’s still in a coma from the blood loss, but his brain waves are good. They’re monitoring him.” She let out a shaky breath.

I rested my hand on her arm. Unsure what to say. I didn’t have any love for Wheeler. He and Olivia had likely had something to do with Vince’s death. Even if he made it, I wasn’t planning to celebrate any homecomings for him. “I’m sure he’ll pull through. He’s a strong man.”

“I hope you’re right. I’m terrified to go to work though. What if his attacker comes back?”

The probability of Olivia randomly attacking Enterprise employees was slim to none. “I think you’re safe. The attack seemed to be targeted.”

Her eyes brimmed with tears as she nodded.

“Can you think of anyone who would have wanted to hurt him?” I asked.

She shook her head. “Like I told that handsome Hawaiian detective, Jackson is a good man. So many people have already been by here to wish him well. I can’t imagine him upsetting anyone. The detective wouldn’t say—do you know if they have a suspect?”

They will soon. “They’re working on that. Is Mr. Wheeler married?”

“Divorced. For years now. No children either.”

“Have a girlfriend?”

She shook her head. “Enterprise is his family.”

I'd have felt sorry for him if I didn't know better. "Olivia Chambers come by often?"

She turned a shade of pink and looked uncomfortable at my question. "On occasion." She glanced at her watch. "She's upstairs now. That's why I left. They don't let many people up there at one time."

My stomach clenched. "Mrs. Chambers is up there now?"

"Yes." Gladys looked at her watch. "I should get to the office. Everyone is a mess."

I ran to the elevators. Detective Kuni hadn't shown yet, but Jackson might not have that long. If his attacker was in a room alone with him, he could have very little time. I willed the elevator to move faster to the ninth floor.

When the elevator opened, my heart sunk. Unlike the hospital where Arlene was admitted, I didn't have free access on this floor. A shiny metal double locked door blocked my path.

I started to text Detective Kuni to find out how far away he was. Then stopped. If I told him Olivia Chambers was in with Jackson, he wouldn't understand the implication. I didn't have time to write a novel.

I had to take my chances with the nurses' call button. I started formulating a plausible story to get me in when the shiny doors started their slow open. An elderly couple plodded out. The woman crept, hunched over, her husband's arm wrapped around her. Their patient must not be doing well. I offered a genuine grief-stricken nod as I passed them on my way through and then put my head down.

The nurse station was quiet. A doctor standing in a room off to the far left flipped through a chart. An orderly cart with linens sat in front of another room. A nurse in light blue pants and a smiley face covered scrub was heading into another room, the light above that door flashing.

If anyone stopped me, they might send me back downstairs. Saving Wheeler wouldn't garner me any free passes when it came to hospital policy. Best chance was to not give them the opportunity. Room number signs directed me to the right and I made my way down the echoing hallway. His room had partially closed blinds covering the glass window and a closed door.

I peeked through the window before busting in. Jackson Wheeler was laid out with a breathing apparatus taped to his mouth, IV drips pumping life-saving fluids into him, and a pallid complexion that said he straddled two worlds. This week had been far too full of Formica floors and disinfectant smells. I didn't see any signs of Olivia until a manicured hand reached for Jackson's arm.

I stepped away from the window before she saw me. I forced myself to wait and see and tapped the camera icon on my phone. The videotape of the land deal was all the proof of her involvement I had. While it was damning, it didn't prove she'd attacked Wheeler. I didn't want to cause a scene in an ICU unit unless necessary. If I caught her in the act, it wouldn't only be her word against mine.

Olivia Chambers stood over Jackson and patted his arm. Her hand was moving towards the tubes. I leveled the phone near the window. Was she about to finish him off? To hell with proof. I had to stop her.

I shoved my phone in my purse and stepped toward the door. A man's hand reached out of nowhere and gripped Olivia's arms. He crowded behind her, his chin on her shoulder. Mayor Charles Chambers. Why were they both standing in Jackson Wheeler's hospital room?

Olivia gave a no-teeth smile at her husband and grasped both hands onto his arm. She leaned into him. She acted distraught at seeing Jackson's condition. Was the mayor that big of an idiot that he had no clue what was going on?

They stepped away from the bed at the same time. Shocked, I was staring at them when they walked out of Wheeler's room. I stuffed the envelope containing the videotape deeper into my purse.

Olivia gave me a fake lip-only smile when she came out. The mayor gave me a nod.

I couldn't let them walk away. Tackling her in the hallway wasn't an option either. Jackson looked like he was doing okay. "How is he?" I managed.

The mayor frowned. "He's on life support. Are you a relative?"

He obviously didn't know Jackson Wheeler well enough to know he didn't have any family. "No."

"I recognize you," Olivia said.

I bet she did. I'm sure Jackson had told her all about me looking around the land. Getting closer to the truth. The image of the knife in my tire screeched into my mind. OCD on the handle. I'd believed it was the brand. Did it stand for Olivia Chambers'...desk? It had to. Which meant she'd been down on Gee Creek Road watching me before going to Jackson's office. She might have gone there concerned I'd gotten too close. It made complete sense. "I think we met briefly. In passing."

She nodded. "I do hope the dear man makes it." An actual tear squeezed out of her eye.

She was good. "Indeed." I tried to sound less sarcastic than I felt.

She tilted her head. "Excuse me?"

Guess I failed a bit. "I mean. How do you know Mr. Wheeler?"

The mayor wrapped an arm around his wife's waist. "He's been a generous contributor of my political campaigns."

"I see." He'd been generously taking his share of his wife's affection too. Not that I cared about his failing marriage, but I had to stop myself from tapping my purse. Wheeler's getting in good with the husband could have been his way of securing the land sale. The mayor had been oblivious. Like Jeff and my dad's infidelity, I guess we all only saw what we wanted to.

"You never said who you are?" he asked.

"I found Mr. Wheeler after he'd been brutally attacked." My eyes didn't leave Olivia's face.

Her top lip twitched. "Then you're the one to thank." Her voice dripped honey; her eyes were cold.

I'm sure she wished me dead, as she had Jackson. "No thanks necessary. I was there to confront him about some issues around the land he's selling."

"What did you have to tell him?" the mayor asked. "Perhaps I can help."

Olivia swayed, grabbing her husband's hand like a vice. "Honey. I am so exhausted. We must go." Her foot twisted to the side and off her red high heel pumps. Those pumps that no woman could possibly walk in unless they were a runway model or Olivia Chambers.

Wheeler's injury was supposedly caused by a rounded hammer. I had seen the hole in his chest. It seemed smaller. Could it have been caused by a shoe heel? I shuddered.

"You're right, dear. Another time." He propped his

wife up and escorted her down the hallway. She shot a dark glance back at me.

She had her husband duped with her Oscar worthy act. I wanted to drop her right then and there. Instead, I clutched my purse closer. Detective Kuni would get her for me and if Jackson Wheeler pulled through, he'd get him too. It appeared Olivia's visit to him this time had been to cover her ass. She wanted people to think she cared. If she came back without her husband, that might be another story. Except she wasn't going to get the chance. When this tape was seen, her life would be over. It was going to feel good to see her arrested.

As if on cue, the elevator dinged. The mayor and Olivia Chambers stepped in and Detective Kuni stepped out.

THIRTY-FOUR

DETECTIVE KUNI STOPPED at the nurse's station and became engrossed in conversation with the doctor I'd seen when I came up. He flashed his credentials and lifted his finger for me to wait as I walked back to meet him. Patient confidentiality. I stayed in the hallway until he finished.

He motioned me to the double doors several minutes later and we stepped through them and into the waiting elevator.

"How is he?" I asked, hitting *L* for Lobby.

"The doctor said he's turning the corner. Looks like he's going to make it and they expect he'll gain consciousness soon as his vitals have been getting stronger."

That was good news. He should pay for his crimes like Olivia would have to. "As you saw, the mayor and his wife just left. Did you know they were both close to Wheeler?"

He nodded. "The Chamberses are community minded. Anything for Riverview and of course they'd have dealings with him with the waterpark."

He didn't know the half of it. "They've had more than that, or at least Olivia has." I was about to tell him what I'd found when the elevator stopped on the third floor and a nurse stepped in. We rode the rest of the way in silence.

We found a couple of chairs in the corner of the lobby and I hustled back to the vending machine while he took a seat facing the door. The coffee I'd left filling earlier wasn't there, as I'd expected. I grabbed us two fresh cups.

Detective Kuni was pulling his notepad out of his jacket when I set the cup down on the low table in front of him. "You said you had something for me," he said.

"I do." I sat across from him and yanked the envelope with the VHS tape from my purse and handed it to him. "By the way, did you find the weapon that took Wheeler down?"

"No. As mentioned before, we've ascertained it was circular in nature. The doctor believes it's consistent with an upholstery hammer."

"How about the heel of a stiletto?"

His right eyebrow raised in question. "Possibly." He jotted the idea in his book and stared back at me. "What makes you suggest that?"

"You'll understand when you watch the tape that's inside." I gave him the run down. "I think you'll be convinced like me that Olivia felt this deal was imperative. Wheeler had been paying off the EPA, but she was concerned that he was not getting the dirt off the land fast enough. Might have been why he took to shoving it over the side. Anyway, she clearly had a lot to lose. Like you said, she was instrumental in gathering the investors, and her family stood to make millions when they were awarded the waterpark contract. With Vince having this video to hang over both their heads, it's not a far stretch to think they'd do anything to stop him. I don't know why Olivia turned on Mr. Wheeler. Pretty brazen to be showing up here with her husband though."

"Agreed. If this shows what you say, then it will be enough to bring Olivia Chambers in for questioning, at the least, and to get a warrant to search her home."

I relaxed into the chair as Detective Kuni verbally flipped through the list of what he thought next steps would be.

He continued, "I can't imagine she's kept the shoe, if that does turn out to be the weapon. We'll make sure that warrant includes her car as well. It's far harder to remove trace blood from upholstery and carpeted surfaces."

I nodded. "What kind of car does she drive?"

"A Jaguar." He continued to make notes.

The vehicle that had almost run me down was a big sedan. The noose was tightening around Olivia as Wheeler's attacker. Had that same Jag been used to run Vince off the road as well?

"I have another theory I wanted to share," I said.

Detective Kuni looked up. "I'm listening."

"Ever hear of Pavel or Mickey Mikhailov or his muscle, Tyrone?"

"Yes. Why?"

I launched into the story of Brandon's debt, Vince's attempt to bail his son-in-law out, and how that tied to the vial of dirt I'd found. We'd talked about that connection right after the attack on Wheeler, but I wanted to remind him. "On the tape, you'll see that Olivia is talking extensively about dirty money being involved. When I'd talked with Mickey originally, he kept telling me to stop looking for Vince because he didn't want me messing up what he had going on."

"You think they're connected?"

"I do. I think there's a possibility that he found out Vince was blackmailing Jackson and that was about to mess up the bigger and more lucrative land deal that he was involved in."

"Hmmm, that doesn't sound like Mickey."

"Silencing Vince or?"

"Just being involved in that kind of deal at all."

People surprised me all the time by acting differently than I'd ever expect. "How do you know him? His reputation precedes him even up here?"

He slapped his notebook closed. "More personal than that."

My stomach tightened. "Don't tell me you borrowed money from him?" I blurted.

He guffawed, like I'd told a bad joke. "No. That case I worked on with your father years ago involved him."

My face felt flush for making such an assumption about the detective. "I see. What did he do that time?"

"It's not what he did, it's what your dad did to help him."

"Mickey had said he owed my dad a debt. I'd assumed it was for something illegal, especially after Mickey mentioned my dad working within his system."

"It wasn't like that."

A small amount of relief crept in at those words, but it was hard to completely forgive. "All I know is my dad gambled. He cheated on my mother. Pretty much lied to me my entire childhood. I started being a real PI six months ago thinking I wanted to make him proud. But if he was involved with men that had something to do with Vince's murder, then I'm not sure what I want."

The detective shook his head. "You believe the worst because of the tape, and I'm assuming you're referring back to the severed finger?"

"Even you said that was indicative of organized crime. That's Mickey and his goon in a nutshell, right? Then with Olivia and the dirty money involved in the land…"

He drew in a deep breath. "I agree, the finger fits his

MO. I will not sit here and tell you he is a great guy. I will tell you this. Your dad, and that favor that Mickey refers to, runs deep."

"How so?"

"Your dad went undercover at the tracks years ago when a group of trainers and owners were killing horses for insurance money and doping some before races. It was a nightmare. The police believed Mickey was the ringleader, but Roger believed it was an inside job. He and another gentleman spent some time at the tracks and began to investigate it."

Jack—Jeff's dad. That had to be the timeframe he was talking about. "Okay, so I know some of that."

"Well, your dad did unravel it all, but not before one of the trainers kidnapped Mickey's daughter. The police continued to look at Mickey and suspected he staged it, but Roger was the only one that believed him and stepped in to help. Your dad contacted me and we worked it together. Roger found Mickey's little girl in a training facility several miles outside of this city. She was hog tied and near death. If it wasn't for his tenacity and working the inside angle, which no one else could have done as effectively, that child would have died. Of course, Mickey was cleared of any charges. He owes your dad everything."

When Mickey had warned me off the case, he told me his debt was done. I wondered if a debt like saving one's daughter was ever repaid. I slunk into the chair. "So my dad wasn't a gambler?"

"Only as far as his undercover required."

"He was a hero," I whispered.

"To Mickey he was. And to many others over the years. Because he had many of those kinds of cases, I'm sure he wasn't as forthcoming to you. Being a father, I can attest that was solely out of being protective. He was human though, Ms. Pruett. Fathers do the best they can, and he was as solid as they come. When he took on a case, he finished it." The detective's face softened. "You are like him."

I closed my eyes. Tears stinging them. Part was relief that I had not been wrong and that I had held onto what I knew of my father. The good things. Part was shame that I had considered the notion that my dad was a criminal for even a second. But that didn't clear everyone. "That doesn't mean Mickey isn't involved in this land deal."

Detective Kuni rested his hand on my forearm. "I've never known him to be involved with other investors. I will certainly check into it though. Unfortunately, dirty money is everywhere. Olivia Chambers is going to have to answer a few questions."

We sat in silence for a few more minutes. Detective Kuni's phone rang. He answered and listened. "I see." His face was crestfallen. "Thank you."

He hung up. "I asked the doctor to let me know when I'd be able to talk with Mr. Wheeler. He just reported that he's taken a turn for the worse."

My insides crumpled. "We saw him just over a half hour ago."

"He's suffered an embolism. He's alive, but it's weakened him."

"Could Olivia have done something to him when she was in the room?"

"It's a possibility. It's equally possible that his injuries are catastrophic." He stood. "Thank you for the tape. I need to get this processed and pay Olivia Chambers and the mayor a visit."

I gathered my purse. "Glad I could help."

Outside, I stood and breathed in fresh air.

Detective Kuni ducked into his tan four-door and swung it wide out of the parking lot. A combination of sadness and relief washed over me. I didn't like Jackson Wheeler, or what he'd done; I didn't want my life-saving efforts to go to waste either. On the relief side, my involvement in the case was over. Olivia Chambers would soon be behind bars. And my dad was a hero. He'd saved a little girl. How many more cases had he been a hero in? My dad might never stop surprising me.

I needed to get on the road so I could be a hero in my own story with my own daughter. Mitz's program was in a few hours. No way would I be late, and I had one very important thing left to do.

VINCE BURNOTAS' SHABBY little house had that recently condemned look with the plywood the officer and I had used to seal the entry a couple of days ago. It wouldn't be hard for Lorraine to get it looking rentable again, but she clearly hadn't started yet.

The house key should work on the back door. I had come for the tapes and the photo albums. Memories of my dad and my life with him were solidly in my mind. I wanted Stephanie to have more than that of her dad to hold onto sooner than later.

The rear door opened into a tiny laundry room. Even though it was warm outside, the inside felt icy and sent a shudder through me. I closed the door and made my way to the back bedroom.

The case was done, and life could go back to normal. Normal couldn't start soon enough. I scanned the boxes for the tapes. On my drive over here, relief had settled over me. Back in this house, in this room, I felt unsure again. Had I missed something?

Olivia would be arrested, supported by the evidence I provided. Because of the embolism, Jackson might not make it, but because everything had already been executed, the sale would continue. If he lived, Jackson would have to answer for the tainted soil. It was too early to see how that all would play out.

Vince was dead because Olivia didn't want him to destroy her plans of political grandeur or her family's windfall with the waterpark contract. Simple greed. Right? But why had she gone after Jackson Wheeler? I shook the thought. I hadn't come here to contemplate any more. I had come for Vince's tapes.

Inside the corner box I found the VHS cassettes labeled *A Day*. There were six. As I grabbed them out and put them in a smaller box near the door, I wished more than once my dad had left something like these for Mitz. She would have loved them. The photo album. It had been in one of these cartons too.

I went back to the boxes and started digging. The album had shifted near the bottom. Head down, I grabbed it out. When I looked up Lorraine, dressed in a purple sweater, shadowed the doorframe. I startled. She clutched a Hello Kitty flashlight in her hand. It didn't seem dark enough to need that. Perspiration beaded across her lip. It was seventy-five degrees outside. She must be boiling in that cardigan.

"Lorraine," I said, straightening. "Hope you didn't mind that I came here. I wanted to grab a few things for Stephanie since she's not well enough to come herself."

She smiled, but it didn't reach her eyes, which were narrowed. "No worries."

"You okay?"

She aimed the flashlight my direction. Before I realized there was no bulb, the sound of a pop followed by a rattle hit my ears as the prongs propelled at me like a barrage of bullets. My brain registered a moment too late. The electrodes pierced my T-shirt, burning as they embedded into my arms and chest. My body jerked. Lightning rushed through me like a raging river. I toppled, face planting into the floor. Every second intensified and my teeth chattered. I was one big charlie horse with my muscles convulsing, cramping. No control. I screamed for help. No sound came out before my world went black.

THIRTY-FIVE

I WOKE TO the sound of humming. Lorraine. She sounded as mad as Kathy Bates' character in *Misery.* Instinct forced my eyes open and my mind to send signals to bolt upright. To get away. My body had other ideas. Every muscle screamed like someone had crawled under my skin and was ripping them apart with a fork. The only thing I could move was my eyes. Not only were my limbs useless, but my wrists had been duct taped in front of me and my ankles bound together.

That cute pink flashlight she'd aimed at me was a Taser. The seared memory of burning pain made me cringe. It could also be the pulsating wounds from the electrodes that she yanked from my body since I didn't sense anything hanging off me. Whatever, the last seconds of the attack were the longest of my life. She might have even zapped me twice and I hit my head when I fell because it throbbed too. Something happened that made me black out.

I'd read somewhere the effects of a Taser could last up to thirty minutes. Longer if she'd zapped me twice. I seriously should take up lighter reading. I didn't know how long I'd been unconscious and couldn't depress my Fitbit to see the current time. Or move my head off the floor to even see.

My eyes fixed on the bathroom fan. Shifting my focus, the shower curtain hung to my left. To the right, a dingy wall. Lorraine had dragged me into Vince's bathroom. Drool wetted my cheek. I didn't want to think about whether I'd peed myself.

I heard footsteps. More humming.

She stood in the doorway. "Oh good, you're awake." Her lips curled up at the corners. Her meticulously done hair had begun to fall out of the bobby pins. She looked frazzled. I hoped she threw her back out getting me in here.

"What's going on, Lorraine? I'm a little confused." I forced myself to sound calm.

"You shouldn't be." She tilted her head. "You brought this on yourself by not leaving well enough alone. You had to keep asking questions. Keep coming back. You found the dirt. You riled up Jackson."

All along I'd thought it was Mickey. Then Olivia. How had I missed Lorraine? "Is that why you tried to beat him to death?"

She pursed her lips, disgusted. "He knows that I'm privy to everything that goes down in this town. After you'd gone to see him, he suspected me of doing something to Vince. Which wasn't the worst of it. The man was starting to get cold feet on the land deal and that couldn't happen. But no worries. Easy fix. Since he has no family, his will gives everything to the city that he loved."

If he pulled out of the deal while alive, the sale would be dead. But if Jackson was dead, the transaction would continue, with the city reaping the full benefit. I'd been right about that. I just believed Olivia was the beneficiary. "Perfect plan. Except you didn't kill him."

Her lips lifted into a full, distant smile as she pulled

on my hands to make sure the tape was secure. It was. "An air bubble in his IV should have done the trick."

The embolism. She must have slipped upstairs while Detective Kuni and I were talking. Unless she and Olivia were working together. "Well, you screwed that last one up."

Her eyes narrowed, clearly not having anticipated failure. "What are you talking about?"

"Sure, you caused him a backward slide, for a minute, but the doctors were on it."

She leaned over me again, spittle formed in the sides of her mouth. "You're trying to mess with me now, dear, and I won't have that."

Feeling started to return in my feet. "Don't believe me then."

She straightened and waved me off. "No bother. I'll go back and finish him when I'm through here."

She might have acted alone, but that didn't make Olivia any less guilty. "I don't understand why you'd do it. Are you one of the investors?"

"In the waterpark, no. In Riverview, absolutely. Half the buildings in this town are mine. The Tip Top Tavern. The bowling alley. Thirty homes. A quarter of the apartment complexes. If that land deal goes away, do you know what would happen?"

Nothing compared to what was going to happen if I could get upright. My bravado tried to bust through my fear. "No."

"Land values would plummet. Riverview would become a wasteland. Industry is already on its way out. It's the last chance for this town to survive. I will not let my years of hard work and smart investments crumble because some man wants me in jail or to change his mind on the deal."

"But the land is contaminated and I've turned over everything to the detective. He's going to figure it out. When he does, it's over anyway."

"You've led him down the trail of Olivia Chambers, who will take the fall. It's not like she's truly innocent. I'll finish Jackson. The deal will go on. I'll make sure of it."

I wasn't sure that was possible, but I had to keep crazy talking. "You knew what was on the videotape, didn't you?"

She grabbed a red container from behind the wall. "Hon, I know everything including Wheeler screwing the mayor's wife. I told Wheeler about the soil sample that Vince had taken. Me and Vince were close. Good friends. Vince was quick to tell me he was blackmailing Jackson, but then Jackson called his bluff. Vince was so desperate for money. That's when he called that damn reporter. He wanted to sell the story and let her bring Jackson down." She had a far-off look. "Which is why Vince had to die. I couldn't let him ruin everything."

"Did you try to reason with him?"

"His need to help his daughter before cancer got him trumped everything." She unscrewed the lid. "I went to the Tip Top to chat with him one last time, but he was leaving, so I followed. When he took the Gee Creek turn, I knew what he was up to. I passed him around that corner and nudged him over. The look of shock on his face when he realized it was me is right there." She pinched the air in front of her. "Really, I did him a favor. Cancer is a horrible way to die."

I hoped Vince haunted her every waking moment for the rest of her life. But you'd have to have a conscience for that. Instead, a look of accomplishment crossed her face. I focused on the red can. Gasoline. "But you said you lent him money because he was sick. You went looking for him at the Meadows."

More self-satisfaction oozed from her pores. "I'm very good at setting the stage. I'm the last person you'd expect. But you've caused me far more trouble than you're worth."

She poured the liquid onto the floor. The tang of gasoline hit my nose at the same time panic set in.

"Too bad the bomb failed, huh?"

"It didn't fail. You're alive because I wanted you that way," she said, although I seriously doubted that. "Regardless, you should have taken the hint to go away and sadly, you didn't." She set the can down and walked out of the room.

My hands were coming back. I worked them into fists. I froze as she returned with a cotton blanket and threw it on top of me. Cotton acted like a wick. If every muscle in my body could have, it would have shuddered.

She continued as if she hadn't stepped away. "Unfortunate for you, but burning this place down does serve two purposes. Besides putting you to rest, it destroys the pull-tabs Vince had collected. I'll give him that he was smarter than I thought."

"Chuck *was* screwing him on those games, wasn't he?" Along with every person that bought into them.

"Of course, and I kept it quiet as long as I got my cut. Vince didn't know that angle though, or he would have never trusted me." She seemed lost in thought. "He might have put the pieces together at some point. Had I not broken in here a few days ago, I would have never known about it either."

"You were the one that broke in?"

She laughed. "Misdirection is a wonderful thing. You showed up and called the police. It couldn't have been more perfect. Now insurance will help me rebuild."

This woman was shy a few cards in her deck, but she clearly had things figured out. My calves tingled. My leg muscles were coming back to life just not fast enough. "Look, I don't have to say anything. I just want to get home to my daughter."

She continued to pour gas on the floor nearest my feet. "Kids aren't worth their time. Mine left me long ago. Said I was unstable, if you can believe that." Her eyes became slits of bitterness and rage.

Yes, I wanted to scream. "That's terrible. My daughter is young though and she has an event tonight. Please."

She shook her head. "I wish I could believe you. Every time I thought you'd leave well enough alone, you didn't. In time, you would have unraveled it like Vince. The good thing is the pain will be brief. The body shuts down when it hits a certain threshold. The land transaction will go through, and things will go back to normal. Everything in its order."

Signs of her need for control had been all over her house in our first meeting. The precise line of the silverware on the buffet. Her removing the smudges immediately from the glass frog on the table. The memories of my own grandmother and comparing them clouded my ability to see Lorraine as a suspect. What else had I let my emotions blind me to?

My legs ached again, but I didn't want to reveal that I'd be back to full force in a few minutes. Full except for being bound. Tears filled my eyes. "Please don't. You're a mother, a grandmother..."

She raised a single crooked finger to her lips. “Shhh.” Then she cackled. The sound that erupted from her mouth made my skin crawl.

She doused the blanket with gasoline, the fumes tearing at my throat and nose. She leaned in close with that Taser again. This time I was ready. I got my arms bent to my chest like I was praying. Which I was. As she came at me, I lifted them up through the blanket. Batted her hands. She made it through, the prongs brushing my chest.

“I knew I couldn’t trust you.”

“You bitch,” I managed through clutched teeth. The ripples of labor through my midsection had been less excruciating, but thankfully she hadn’t held the Taser against me long to have me burst into flames or incapacitate me this time.

Lorraine scurried away like a cockroach and slammed the door. Fighting back had at least bought me time. The next sound was the door handle being messed with. Was she locking me in? Every ounce of me willed my body back to life. Get up.

A shuffle. Click of heels crossing the living room. The back door slamming. The smell of smoke. My chest hurt, but my arm muscles were recovering despite the latest attack. My brain worked on the rest. I rocked to get the blanket off, dragging it away from the door so the gasoline trail couldn’t find the flames and light me ablaze. But if the flames didn’t get me, the smoke would. This wasn’t how I’d thought I would die.

THIRTY-SIX

MITZ'S FACE OCCUPIED the crevices in my mind. I'd tried to be a good mother. I had done the best I could. But like my father had failed me, I had done the same.

He'd left me blind. He thought the less I knew, the more protected I'd be. By not disclosing the facts of his cases, his connections, and the things he'd done, he'd left me unprepared for the crazies of this world.

Tears started to fall. I squeezed my eyes closed until they stopped. There wasn't time for feeling sorry. Or to blame him for my mistakes. If I didn't want to be just a memory for Mitz, I had to find a way out of here. But all I could do was think of my own memories. Of how much I wished my dad had said to me. That he was proud. That he loved me. It was always unspoken. To hear the words.... Would they have changed who I was? Made me doubt people less?

There was so much I wished I'd said to him. That he had been my hero. That I wanted to be like him. Maybe he knew and like Jeff and Arlene had said from the beginning, he wanted to avoid that. That's why he'd said nothing at all.

Time. We ran out. It wasn't fair.

The tapes.

Stephanie. I'd come here for the tapes Vince had left her and the baby. She could have something I would never have, if they survived the fire—messages from her father. Words that she could carry forever. I wanted tapes. I wanted those memories. I wanted those words. If I couldn't have them, Stephanie and her baby should.

I rocked again. There was only one way to make sure those tapes survived and that was for me to get them to her. One of us shouldn't lose everything. With Brandon's lies and her father's murder, she'd already lost so much.

I had to stand—at least try. My arms were the strongest. Using my forearms against the rim of the tub, I wobbled to my knees. If I had any chance, my hands had to get undone first. In self-defense, I'd been taught a technique to break the tape around my wrists. Speed and velocity were necessary. Unsure if I could muster either, I got upright on my knees, lifted my wrists over my head and in one movement, brought them down to my waist, using what strength I had to bust them.

The tape didn't tear.

The smell of smoke started to permeate the room. Ignoring the sting of my skin and aches in my muscles from the mini knives Lorraine had yanked out of me, I inched off the bath rug I'd been laying on and shoved it under the door. I needed more time; I couldn't face the fire with my legs and hands bound.

With the use of the tub again, I pushed up on my forearms and got my feet underneath me and hopped over to the toilet and plopped down onto the lid. My breaths were fast and shallow at the effort. I had to slow it down or I was going to hyperventilate. I opened the vanity drawers. Vince's razor.

Angling the blade, I worked on my feet first. A few slices, and the tape ripped apart with some tension from my legs. But getting the right angle to undo my hands was nearly impossible. I stood again, my steadiness returning, and planted one foot against the tub and the other against the wall for leverage, raised my hands overhead, and whipped them down in one frantic motion. This time the tape busted with a satisfying snap.

The crackle and hiss of fire eating wood outside the door echoed in the small space. There was no time to unwrap the tape from my wrists. I reached for the knob. It turned, but the door didn't budge. Lorraine had secured it somehow so it wasn't going to open. I kept my hand too long on the metal and winced at the scalding hot. The flames must be right outside, the gasoline feeding them. The fire would be insatiable, hungry, wanting to devour. Quelling my panic, I turned the water full blast in the bathtub to douse the flames if it came to that.

As the water filled, I wetted a towel and wrapped it around my face before pushing my shoulder against the door with some of my weight to see how easy it would break. I bounced back. The door opened inward. Crashing against it wasn't going to get me out; the hinges were inside.

My throat dry, my heart racing, panic was threatening to take over. If I didn't get that door open, I'd be burned alive.

The drawers must have something I could use to get out. I yanked each one open, digging through, searching for anything that could help dislodge the pins. A metal-handled gum stimulator was all I could find. It would have to work. The medicine cabinet had Vince's meds, but the plastic containers would crumble. In the bottom cabinet, was a wood jewelry box. I'd use that as a hammer.

A few attempts had the bottom two pins popping out easy enough. The third wouldn't budge. I thought of Jeff having to tell Mitz how I died. I gripped the box harder. Giving up was not an option. I smashed wood against the metal. Slammed my finger. Screamed. Ignored the pain. Again. The box disintegrated in my hand. The gum gadget bent. The last desperate crash with a wooden wedge dislodged the pin.

I dropped to the floor on all fours and lifted the door enough to shift it out of the hinges. It dropped awkwardly and I stood. Using both hands, I pulled the door back on the unhinged side. The fire licked my fingers, singeing them. I jerked them inside. Flames danced on the floor. Returning to the tub, I snatched the shower curtain from the hooks. It would melt onto me if it wasn't wet enough. I submerged it into the water, creating a puddle in the middle and tossed water on the floor. On the door. Stepping into the bathwater, I dunked up to my neck.

Dripping wet, I was as ready as I'd ever be. Hands around the door, I heaved backwards with every ounce of my body weight and it wrenched open. The fire was waiting for me. Sizzling. Smacking its lips. Black smoke curling against the walls.

I took the drenched shower curtain and tossed it out. The fire hesitated, I leapt over the flames. I was out of that room, but not out of danger. I could barely make out the backroom, but I had to try. For Stephanie. For the tapes I wished my father had left for me.

The box of tapes was in the small box in the room where I'd left them. I crossed to the window and ripped open the blinds. No slider. Who didn't have a slider on their bedroom windows? The camcorder. I grabbed it and launched it with all I had against the glass. It sprung back at me. Plexiglass. I was in a freaking fun house.

Box in hand, I sprinted to the back door. Locked. Not

again. I couldn't stop panting. The towel around my face had dried with the heat. Smoke filling my lungs. Flames and black plumes climbing the walls and ceilings. Had to control my breathing. The terror of what would happen if I couldn't get out had me gulping the air too deep. Too much. Sharp coughs stabbed my lungs. Had to find something to help me get out before it was too late. Find a chair.

Everything was in flames. Setting the video box down, I darted into the hallway. Back into the dining area. Hard to breathe. I'd made it out of the bathroom only to die in the open flames. Can't leave Mitz.

I found a metal legged chair and drug it to the back door. Flung it. The bounce back nearly took my feet out from under me.

Then the smoke did. I fell to the ground, crumpling over the videos. My daughter's red curls filled my mind. Her smile. Her eyes. The last things I'd remember. I'm sorry…

The back door crashed like thunder piercing the night. Splinters flew. A black arm reaching for me. Grabbing hold. Dragging me. I gripped the box. Out. Fresh air rushing into my lungs. My eyes locked onto my rescuer as we hit the ground. Tyrone.

"What?" I managed. Gasping for oxygen. Coughs gripping me. My chest exploding as it expelled the black smoke and soot. "Lorraine. She's getting away."

Sirens in the distance.

"No, she's not." He got to his feet and lifted me like a child, cradling me in his arms.

"Box," I whispered.

He scooped it up.

"Why are you here? How are you here?" Tears stung my eyes. "Thank you."

"Mickey had me follow you. Thought you might get into trouble."

We rounded the house. Lorraine was sitting in the back of my car. Zip tied. Swaying side to side. Humming. "How'd that happen?"

"Saw her leaving the house and wondered where you'd gone. When I asked, she tried to come at me with some pink flashlight. Except I knew it was a Taser. Got the same one for my mom last Christmas."

I looked up into his face. "Seriously?"

He nodded and set me on the cool grass. "She hit me with it, but I swatted her like a fly."

I imagined the voltage didn't do much to three hundred pounds of ox.

"Then there was smoke. And here you are." The sirens drew closer. "That's my cue." Tyrone left me sitting and trotted back to his rust-colored Lincoln. It had been him that day. Had he seen me in the back of that patrol car? Had I misread his intent right then and he was keeping an eye on me ever since? Before he ducked inside he met my eye. "By the way, Mickey says no more favors."

"Actually, I'm going to need one more."

THIRTY-SEVEN

I MUST HAVE looked like hell when Detective Kuni, another police unit, and two Riverview fire trucks arrived at Vince's bonfire. I ignored Lorraine, or Madame Loon, as I referred to her now, in the back of Arlene's car and sat, knees drawn to my chest, on the curb.

Ready to give the rundown of what had happened, the detective didn't give me a chance. He wanted me in a hospital. "I'm calling an ambulance."

"I'll drive."

"You're not in any shape to do that."

"I'm not staying in this town another second." Our eyes met. "Please."

It might have been the tone of my voice. Or that he realized he wasn't going to win this conversation. Maybe he knew he owed me for never giving up on this case. "Go."

He took Lorraine into custody, and thirty minutes later, I was finding a back way into Mitz's school. Her program had started twenty minutes ago and I was afraid I'd already missed my daughter's performance. But I also couldn't let her see me in my current state. I'd gone in undetected and found a place in the shadows near the stage. Her teacher gave me a thumbs up once when she saw me. Thankfully she was too busy to come close and couldn't see the soot marks on my cheeks in the dark setting.

Mitz didn't know I was even there. Neither did Jeff or Arlene who I spied near the front row. Jeff must have picked her up from the hospital and came straight there. But it didn't matter. I saw Mitz shine on stage for her three minutes on a pogo stick before silently sneaking out the back door and to my car. The pain in my chest had intensified. I'd better take Detective Kuni's advice and get to the hospital.

When I walked into Legacy in Portland, they had the same reaction to me as Detective Kuni. My singed hair and blackened T-shirt gave me that science project gone terribly wrong vibe. They seemed concerned and I was glad I'd stayed hidden at the school.

I shot a text to Jeff saying I'd seen the performance but had to be seen at the hospital for a minor injury. Next, I sent a text to Kyle to please check on Floyd. After an hour in triage and emergency, I was tucked into Room 412 with oxygen flowing into my smoke-filled lungs, bandages on my Taser wounds, and ointment on my scorched fingers. Guess the injuries weren't quite so minor, but I didn't want anyone worrying about me. The meds they pumped through me were good. They put me in the room right next to where Arlene had checked out. Upside—her car was in the parking lot now. Score.

I must have drifted to sleep, because I opened my eyes to Arlene staring down at me and hadn't heard her come in.

"What have you done to yourself?" she asked, looking much better than the last time I'd seen her.

"It's a long story."

"Hmm. One I think you owe me."

I reached out my IV'd hand to her. "Would later be okay?"

It could have been the mist in my eyes or the raspy tone of my smoke-laden voice. She nodded. "Seems like

I'm getting to take care of you more as an adult than you ever let me as a child."

I wrinkled my nose. "I might have been wrong about that."

Her eyes brimmed and she cleared her throat. "I hope my car is at least intact."

There she was. "Yes. I owe you a new tire, but it's in the parking lot downstairs." She raised an eyebrow but didn't ask for more on that so I continued, "The keys are in the drawer there." I pointed, and she retrieved them. "Mitz was great."

"You saw her?"

I managed a nod. The desire to not leave Mitz had helped me get out of that bathroom alive. But alive wasn't so good if you never showed up for the people you loved. Even if Mitz hadn't known I was there, I did. Lorraine being abandoned by her own family could have pushed her over the edge. Although I wasn't sure it had been a far distance to go.

Arlene squeezed my arm. "Well, her and Jeff went for ice cream, but I wanted to make sure you were okay. I'll come get you when you're ready to come home."

The door opened again and Detective Kuni walked in. His face serious, but his eyes were filled with relief. "How's the patient?" When he saw Arlene standing at the dresser rummaging through my purse, he stopped. "I'm sorry. You have company."

Arlene looked up and met the detective's eyes. Flush crept up her neck into her cheeks and her face softened. The air had a bit of electricity in it. "I'm Arlene. Kelly's my daughter-in-law."

"Ex," I added.

She waved at me. "And who are you?" Her smile warmed. I hadn't ever seen her so—nice. Sweet.

"Detective Kuni, ma'am. You have quite a brave daughter-in-law," he said.

"Ex," I said.

"Really?" Arlene placed her hand over her chest, ignoring me.

Who was this woman?

"Absolutely." The detective pulled up a chair next to the bed and she came and sat on the edge next to me as he gave us the quick rundown that when he'd arrested Lorraine, she started to babble like a raging brook. She'd been transported to a mental facility for observation. "If it hadn't been for your bull-headedness, Lorraine might have gotten away with murder."

My cheeks felt warm. The compliment felt good, but I'd been duped. What was he talking about? "Yeah. And she almost added another one to her collection."

He put his hand on my arm. "But it was your tenacity. You never gave up. You could have stopped on this case many times, and you chose not to. You kept pushing, even though my hands were tied. No matter how it happened, you got to the bottom of it. Your father would be proud. I am."

A lump consumed my throat. My dad would have been proud. Despite everything, it went both ways. "When you put it that way, I guess you're right. But it was Stephanie. If she hadn't wanted to make things right with her dad, I would have never gone down the path." Thank God for family. I stared at Arlene. "How are you going to get her for Vince's murder though? She admitted that she ran him off the road to me, but is there evidence?"

"Something about the Traffic Division's report on

Vince's accident always bothered me. They indicated the tiniest strip of green paint on his side mirror and a slight dent. They kept dismissing it. They couldn't determine when it had been transferred on the car because of the severe damage done to the vehicle on the way down the embankment. It's also consistent with damage often done in parking lots. When we took Lorraine into custody, we took her very green Monte Carlo into custody as well. Guess what color is on her passenger side mirror."

"The color of Vince's car?"

He smiled. "Yep. As well as a dent that is consistent with a sideswipe. While it could be deemed circumstantial, I'll take my chances. When I throw that on her, along with yours and Jackson's attempted murder, assault, and arson...." He straightened in the chair. "Let's just say she isn't going to be strolling through any parks for quite some time, if ever."

The news had me settling back into the pillow.

"There's more. Jackson Wheeler gained consciousness an hour ago. He's singing like a bird on a sunny day. That waterpark deal is dead at this point. He's going to be busy cleaning up the watershed for quite some time."

I wanted to hear more details, but my eyes were heavy. "That's great."

Arlene scanned my face. "She needs to rest."

"Sorry," I said.

"No worries." He turned to Arlene. "Can I buy you a cup of coffee? We might have a few stories we could share about Ms. Pruett here."

Her face blushed. "I'd love to. But I have to join my son and granddaughter, who had a program tonight."

"Another time?"

"I would love that."

I barely heard my door close. What just happened there? I wasn't sure I wanted to know as sleep overtook me.

I DIDN'T REALIZE it was possible to sleep nearly 40 hours. Apparently, my lungs had taken in more smoke than recommended by the FDA. Plus I needed IV antibiotics to combat an infection from the electrodes ripped out of me.

Vague images of Kyle coming and going tickled my memory, as well as Arlene checking in again. I'd received a text from Detective Kuni that he'd arrested Olivia Chambers for collusion with Jackson Wheeler. Wheeler would be indicted for dumping on the toxic land. Lorraine had acted alone, but Wheeler was offering anything he could trying to bargain a few years off any sentence. I could see all about it on the news if I turned to Channel 8 when I was awake. Dora hadn't waited for her exclusive. She was on it.

Chuck didn't have Wheeler's advantage. The Washington Lottery was launching a full investigation into his activities and for the moment no more unsuspecting bowlers or bar goers would be taken for the cash.

I didn't gain full function until Sunday afternoon. Jeff had texted me video of Mitz's performance from the front view. Mitz was even more awesome. And I felt horrible. My dad had missed a million school events for me. Even though I had made it to see Mitz, she had no idea and that wasn't the kind of mom I wanted to be to my daughter. I wanted to make it up to her, but before I could restore all order in my life, I had to do a few things.

At some point during the weekend, Arlene had brought me fresh clothes. I showered, dressed in jeans and my Nike zip-up, and checked myself out. Stephanie needed my full report, which could include some good news depending on my first stop. The Uber driver dropped me at the Meadows and I had him wait. This wouldn't take long.

Mickey and Tyrone sat at a corner table in the Paddock Bar, Mickey perusing racing stats. Tyrone had one arm bent over his head. He eyed me as I approached. How did you say thank you to the man who'd saved your life? I just smiled and sat down, searching Mickey's face. "I owe you an apology. I suspected you of being involved in Riverview, of Vince's death, and I was wrong."

He removed his hat and ran his hand over his thinning gray hair. Without the hat, he looked several years older. "Accepted."

"Thank you for sending Tyrone."

He and Tyrone both nodded. Mickey glanced at his muscle, and Tyrone got up and left us sitting.

I scooted to the edge of the chair. Uncertain. "I need to ask you for one last favor."

Mickey's eyebrow raised.

"I know what my dad did for you. For your daughter. What I'm about to ask, will make us even."

"I'm listening."

I drew in a breath. "Brandon. His debt. It's been the root of a lot of pain and loss. I'd like it to not be the end of a marriage. I'd like you to forgive the debt."

He worked his jaw. "It doesn't work that way."

I nodded. "I'm aware it doesn't. Usually. But it's not every day that someone saves your daughter. And it's not every day that I am releasing you of your duty to protect me. Which you apparently felt you needed to do."

He flared his nostrils as he inhaled.

I pushed. "It's only thirty thousand."

His head rocked in a backward nod. "Quarter million."

My gaze narrowed at the inflated figure and he flinched.

"You realize all favors will be used up? I will no longer help you if I give this to you."

"I do."

"You would not use this for yourself? You would give this to the likes of Brandon?"

"I would."

The silence was thick between us as he contemplated. "Done." He slid his chair back and stood. He turned on me and walked away. For a moment, I hesitated. But my heart knew I'd done the right thing.

The Uber driver took me home. I didn't once look back.

EPILOGUE

THIS CASE HAD caused me not only to miss out on being front row at my daughter's event, but her weekend visit. So the next day, after spending the morning with Floyd, and securing a rental car, I drove to Vancouver to pick Mitz up from early release at school.

Having the morning to myself had given me plenty of time to contemplate a few things. Kyle's note was on my kitchen counter. I'd read "Love you," a few dozen times between laundry cycles. I did remember his lips on my forehead at the hospital, but we hadn't spoken other than texts since. He'd been sucked into work. Despite my case being over, his were not. There'd been a mix of peaceful turned violent protests going on in downtown Portland, and that had kept him doing double shifts. With me home, he at least had one less thing to worry about.

The distance was okay. Kyle had been there for me in the past months, and I believed he'd be in my future. Yet every time I thought of those words, a part of me panicked.

My father had loved my mother and that hadn't stopped him from betraying her. He'd ignored the ramifications of that choice, and simply chose to do nothing about it. Instead, he had chosen me as his focus.

Or had he? It could have had little to do with me and more to do with his inability to connect with someone else. He could be tough and cold. We had our moments. I had spent my entire life trying to get his approval. While he had been a hero to some, I struggled with resentment. Might be time to start that therapy Arlene always suggested.

I turned into the school round-about and Mitz, who recognized me despite a different car, burst out the front door and ran my way. Within seconds, she plopped into the passenger side, shoving her backpack down by her feet. Floyd was in the back, up on two legs, paws over the seat and nuzzling at Mitz's ear.

I signed, "Good day at school, Ladybug?"

"The best," Mitz said. "Where's Daddy?" I thought he would have told her I was picking her up.

"Home. Thought we could hang for a bit and then I'll take you there."

She nodded and proceeded to sign everything she'd been up to since the last time I'd seen her. Two hours later, a double scoop ice cream each, and feeling tired from the walk around Esther Short Park, I pulled up in front of Jeff's house.

"You come in." It wasn't a question.

An SUV with California plates was parked across the street. "Not this time." We were not one big happy family. I'd said all I needed to say to Linda.

"Please," Mitz signed, pouting.

Before I could respond, Jeff strode out his front door with a weak smile on his face. He swung open Mitz's car door. "You're back. You doing okay?" He directed the question at me.

I nodded. "Much better. Thanks."

Mitz got out and wrapped her arms around Jeff and he hugged her back. "Glad to hear that. Mom was worried about you."

The feeling had been mutual when I'd seen her in the hospital too. I wasn't sure how I felt about the new sharing is caring territory Arlene and I had entered. "Cool."

"By the way, who's Detective Kuni?" Jeff slammed the passenger door closed and threw Mitz's backpack over his shoulder.

"The cop on the case I finished. Why?"

"Sounds like he and my mom are going out for lunch this week."

I hadn't imagined that electricity in the air. "Wow, okay. Good for them." I liked Detective Kuni. I only hoped he could fend for himself.

"Can Mommy come in?" Mitz signed, her doe eyes gazing at Jeff, then at me.

Jeff glanced at me but addressed Mitz. "We have company right now, sweetie. Your little brother is waiting to meet you."

"Little brother?" She broke out into a huge smile.

The results had come back. It was official. My stomach oozed onto the street. The muscles in my face ached at forcing them into a smile. "How fun," I said to Mitz, but felt the heat rise that Jeff hadn't prepared Mitz for the meeting ahead of time.

"Yes. I'll explain in a second." He turned to me and leaned into the car. "I'd invite you in, but assume you don't want to see Linda. Again."

"We've worked out everything we're going to. Although tell her thanks. The tape worked. It answered a few unanswered questions but didn't make anything all right in the end."

"What's that mean? What tape?"

"She'll know what I'm talking about."

He nodded. "She showed up unannounced earlier today wanting me to meet Seth."

That at least explained his lack of communicating with Mitz about their arrival. I cleared my throat. "That's great for you, Jeff. Are you going to make a go of it with her?" I'm not sure where that question came from.

He tilted his head. "Does it matter?"

I shook my head. "No. It doesn't. I wish you both well." I meant it.

Saving me from any more on that subject Mitz darted over to my side of the car. I gave her a fierce hug and kissed her head through her curls. "See you Friday."

She squeezed me hard around my waist and skipped back over to Jeff. Jeff lifted his head at me as a *see ya* and wrapped his arm around Mitz as they headed back to his house.

I watched them disappear until the smack of the screen door broke my trance. I felt numb, and stupid for standing there. How quickly everything changed.

Floyd made his way to the passenger seat and I hit Interstate 5 to Stephanie's place. I glanced at the box of videos in the back. I'd brought my dad's VCR along figuring she only had a DVD player.

Inside Stephanie's house, I gave her the full report.

In the end, her father had tried to do the right thing. With his cancer about to take him, he stepped in to help his bumbling son-in-law to get out of debt. He'd stumbled on the conversation with Jackson and Olivia and thought blackmailing Wheeler to get the money he needed for Brandon was a great idea. Those choices cost him everything. It had cost Stephanie as well. I hesitated to add to it, but I had no other choice.

"Has Brandon come clean with you?"

She looked at her hands and then fiddled with the tie on her blouse. "Yes," she said quietly.

"I'm sorry about that. I do have some good news though. The loan he took is taken care of."

"How?" she asked, although the muscles in her shoulders immediately relaxed. Her face softened.

"I called in a favor."

She didn't ask what that favor was, and I didn't volunteer. We sat in an awkward silence before she said, "Thank you."

"Of course."

"I mean for everything. For finding the truth. Even if it wasn't what I'd hoped for."

"We can't be responsible for the things our fathers do. Or our husbands, or anyone else for that matter." As I said the words, I tried to believe them for myself, unsure if I sounded convincing.

"You're right. Brandon has agreed to get help for his addiction. He admits he has a problem."

I nodded. "That's great."

"I just wish..."

"I know." She wished her father hadn't gotten involved. The truth about Brandon and her father had shattered Stephanie's illusions. I thought of my dad. The truth had a way of doing that.

I handed her the box.

"What are these?"

"Videos. Your dad was doing a day in the life series for you and the baby. I think he was afraid to see you in the last months because he was in deep trying to help Brandon. He might have been afraid he wouldn't be able to keep it from you. But he knew he screwed up and wanted to leave something good behind."

The tears in her eyes had me swallowing a golf ball sized lump in my throat.

"Can we watch them together?" she asked.

My heart pinched, not wanting to, but Stephanie shouldn't have to watch them alone.

For the next couple of hours, we laughed at Vince's jokes. We cried at his sentiments. The tapes weren't filled with fancy things, or great explorations. Just Vince talking to Stephanie and her Little Pea, who would be coming into the world soon.

What a treasure. It was all I could think about as I watched. Lying in Vince's bathroom I had felt sad about wanting the same from my own dad. But I had at least had him with me for several years with Mitz. He was at her birth. Held her when she had her first bout of colic. Bounced her on his knee. Kissed her boo boos. Taken her to the park. He'd learned a few words to sign. Mostly, they had their own special language. I didn't need the tapes. Neither did Mitz.

It was nearly five when the last tape finished, and I wanted to go home. I'd texted Kyle earlier to let him know where I was, and to tell him if he wanted to stop by the house later that I would love to see him.

After hugging Stephanie, and a promise to help her figure out Vince's funeral in the next week, I stepped out into the evening to find Kyle leaning against his 4x4. He was out of uniform and dressed in blue jeans and a form fitting navy T-shirt.

I relaxed at the sight of him. "What brings you here, stranger?"

His arms were crossed over his very fine chest. "When you said you were watching videos with Stephanie, I thought you might need me."

I closed my eyes. More than I could express to him in that moment. "I wish there'd been a better outcome."

"Vince was dead before you even took the case. There was nothing you could do to change that. You did get to the bottom of why, and you brought his daughter peace. That's sometimes as good as it gets."

He might be right. It didn't help me feel much better.

"How about I get you out of here and we grab a bite to eat?" he said.

As wonderful as that sounded, I had envisioned myself climbing into my PJs and watching a good movie. "How about you follow me home and we can make some spaghetti and curl up on the couch."

"I'd follow you anywhere," he said.

I bit into my lower lip. "Let's go."

On the drive back to my place, I glanced in the rearview mirror a couple of times to find Kyle bobbing his head to music on his radio. I wasn't sure what my future held with him, or if it did. Did I love him? I didn't know what that meant exactly. For the moment, I'd take what he offered and try to offer some of my own. On the radio, I found the song he was keeping time to and tapped the steering wheel. Life was a dance. I had never been good at dancing with other people. But Kyle made me want to try.

* * * * *

ABOUT THE AUTHOR

Mary Keliikoa is a Pacific NW native and spent the first 18 years of her adult life working around lawyers. Combining her love of all things legal and books, she creates a twisting mystery where justice prevails. She is the author of the PI Kelly Pruett mystery series and has had short stories published in *Woman's World* and in the anthology: *Peace, Love, and Crime: Crime Fiction Inspired by Songs of the '60s.*

When not in Washington, you can find Mary on the beach in Hawaii where she and her husband recharge. But even under the palm trees and blazing sun she's plotting her next murder—novel that is.

For more information, please go to www.marykeliikoa.com.